"Time for bed," Thea murmured to Lucas

"Good idea." Donovan followed mother and child into the bedroom. "We could all use an early night."

Thea laid Lucas in his crib, patting him gently back to dreamland when he stirred. Turning around, she discovered Donovan sitting on her bed, removing his shoes and socks.

"W-what are you doing?" She stared as he pulled off his shirt, then stood up and stripped off his jeans and briefs.

"Getting ready for bed," he whispered. "I'm tired, too. After all, I'm still getting over the flu."

"But in here? And naked?" Thea started to feel feverish herself.

"I always sleep naked." He gave her an innocent look. "Have you forgotten already?"

"No, but you can't—"

"Hush, you'll wake the baby." Crawling under the covers, he grinned at her. "And don't try to put any moves on me. I'm a sick man, remember. Just stay on your own side of the bed!"

ABOUT THE AUTHOR

Like the heroine in *A Piece of Cake*,
Leigh Roberts is a lover of bakeries. "I had
great fun researching this book," she tells us.
Leigh confesses she also kept a plate of
goodies next to the computer as she worked.
"For inspiration," she quips. This delightful
author lives in California with her husband
and two children.

Books by Leigh Roberts

HARLEQUIN SUPERROMANCE
81–MOONLIGHT SPLENDOR

HARLEQUIN TEMPTATION
20–LOVE CIRCUITS
55–SIREN SONG
97–HEAD OVER HEELS
147–BIRDS OF A FEATHER
186–THE WISHING POOL

A Piece of Cake

LEIGH ROBERTS

Harlequin Books

TORONTO • NEW YORK • LONDON
AMSTERDAM • PARIS • SYDNEY • HAMBURG
STOCKHOLM • ATHENS • TOKYO • MILAN

Published February 1990

First printing December 1989

ISBN 0-373-70390-2

For Ruth Cohen,
a woman of great patience, enduring wisdom—
and good taste!

CHAPTER ONE

"BABY STUFF."

There was a squawking noise from the phone, and Thea Willits held it away from her ear briefly. "That's right," she said when the sound subsided. "I project the most growth in infant-related items—car seats, biodegradable disposable diapers, that sort of thing."

This time the client on the other end of the phone was silent. Thea propped her feet on the shiny mahogany of her desk and said sweetly, "Would you like me to transfer some of your holdings, or did you want to think about it?"

The client made a suggestion, and Thea shook her head as if he could see through the receiver. "Not software companies," she said decisively. "The bottom's fallen right out of them. High tech investments are getting more risky. Educational software, now, that's a possibility, but very speculative."

She made some notes on her lap-top, said a cheerful goodbye, and hung up the phone. There was just time before the markets closed in New York to add some shares to her client's portfolio, and she spent a few minutes with the data base used by Morton Shaeffler Cunningham, the investment-counselling firm she worked for.

Mission accomplished, she leaned back in the luxurious desk chair and stared out her window. True, it was a tiny window, with a view only a pigeon could love of the eighteenth floor of the next-door office building in San Francisco, but it was a window. Along with the fancy desk and chair and the little private bathroom, it made a statement about her importance in the firm.

"The rich got richer that time," she murmured, thinking about her client, whom she secretly designated Mr. Big, for both his girth and his account. Mr. Big had been dubious about her when she'd inherited his account during her first year with MSC. But over the past five years he'd become a believer. Thea had an instinct for what was going to soar in the stock market and what was going to plummet. Her clients had good reason to be satisfied.

That had always been a point of pride with Thea. She'd enjoyed the feeling of using that mysterious sense of hers to benefit others. Now she waited for the rush of well-being that flooded her after a job well done.

It didn't come.

She tried to imagine her client's children going to better schools, his house benefiting from a new roof. But she knew that to people like Mr. Big, investments were only counters in a game called More Money Now. As long as it helped their portfolios, they wouldn't care who the counselor was or what kind of investment she recommended.

Trying to regain her usual cheerful acceptance of the world, Thea opened the paper bag that hid in her desk drawer and pinched off another bite of croissant. It was a chocolate-almond croissant, and normally she could have eaten the whole thing before her ten-o'clock coffee break.

"I'm just out of sorts," she told herself, staring out the window once more. "Coming down with something." Her stomach didn't reject the bite of croissant, so she tried another. Delicious. The bakery down the street made the best pastries in San Francisco, just like the one on the corner made the best muffins, and the one by the bus stop produced excellent sourdough bread. Patting her hips, Thea put the rest of the croissant away. If she didn't stop sampling the wares of every bakery she passed, she would need a new wardrobe soon.

The door to her office opened and Guy Cunningham strolled in. "Thea, my dear."

He perched on the edge of her desk in an effort, she guessed, at casual fellowship. He was middle-aged and balding, and even in his shirtsleeves, formidably well-groomed.

Thea glanced down and brushed some crumbs off the crisp white blouse that looked so professional with her navy skirt and blazer. There was a tiny spot of tomato, too, left over from the sandwich she hadn't been able to finish at lunchtime. She hoped devoutly that Guy wouldn't see it.

"So," she said, moving some file folders. "What can I do for you?" A senior partner at Morton Shaeffler Cunningham never sought out the counselors spontaneously.

"I've just been speaking to Mr. Shaeffler," Guy told her. Thea blinked. This was momentous indeed. Mr. Shaeffler's office was the Inner Sanctum, rarely entered by anyone of such lowly rank as Thea. She'd seen Mr. Shaeffler seven times in her five years with the firm.

"How...how exciting," she said lamely, as Guy seemed to expect a reaction.

He frowned a little, crossing his arms over the well-tailored vest that minimized his paunch. "Mr. Shaeffler is very impressed with your record of success," he confided. "In fact, we all are." *We*, in this case, referred to the senior partners. There was no longer a Morton, and of the rest only Guy had rated inclusion in the name. The four other senior partners had at one time seemed interchangeable to Thea, though after all these years she now knew them, their wives and the names of the prestigious schools their children attended. Polite conversation was possible when she met them at the water cooler, but that was as far as it went.

"I'm gratified," she murmured, wondering where all this was leading. Perhaps there was a raise in it. She couldn't get too overwhelmed at the prospect. Thanks to her own expertise, money was never in short supply.

"I have been asked," Guy went on, "to offer you a junior partnership in the firm." He took her unresisting hand and pumped it up and down. "Congratulations, my dear."

Thea had the wild desire to giggle and had to choke it down fast. A junior partnership! A share in the profits instead of the commission she now enjoyed. Perhaps even a chance to influence company policy.

"A voting partnership?"

Guy was taken aback. "Not just at first," he said stiffly. "You must see that this is a radical step for us, Thea. We've never taken a woman into partnership before."

The unspoken message rang loudly—*a woman might not measure up to our standards.*

Thea sighed, and then summoned a bright smile. "This is a great honor, of course," she hedged.

"Of course," Guy agreed promptly—a little too promptly.

"I must think it over," Thea continued. "Look at all the, ah, options."

"If you must. I would have supposed—however, think it over by all means." He beamed down at her. "Perhaps you'd like to attend a little cocktail party my wife and I are giving tonight. Bring along your, uh, friend, if you like. We've enjoyed getting to know him at the office functions these past years. Larry—or is it Lionel? Isn't he with that big venture-capital firm?"

"It's Lucius. Lucius Donovan. And yes, he is at Gaskell Associates," Thea said, keeping her voice even.

"They're funding Omnidata, aren't they?" Guy chuckled jovially. "We rather wondered that you hadn't recommended their new offering. Do you know something we don't know?"

"I don't discuss business with Donovan," Thea said, sitting very straight at her desk. "In my opinion it would be a conflict of interest. That's why I don't recommend companies he's working with."

"Of course, of course." Guy got to his feet. "Very commendable of you, I'm sure."

"Thank you." Thea inclined her head.

"And about the cocktail party?"

"Sorry," Thea said politely. "We've got another engagement. Thank you for the invitation."

"Another time." Guy paused at the doorway. "Let me know if I can help you make your decision."

When he was gone, Thea stared in front of her at the little Mary Cassatt print that hung behind her client chair.

Partnership. She took a deep breath. It was a real advance in her career. But . . .

She leaned back in her chair and tried to analyze the reluctance she felt to enter the esteemed firm of Morton Shaeffler Cunningham.

She'd told herself it was just the stress of turning thirty. But work had lost its savor in the past few months. She had the uneasy feeling that helping the wealthy amass more wealth was contrary to the idealism she'd grown up with, the liberal sentiments with which she'd graduated from college.

Becoming a partner in the firm, and a partner with no voice in firm policies, was not the way to get back to those impulses—"do-gooder stuff," Donovan had called it when she'd tried discussing it with him once. "That's what you get for going to a liberal-arts college like Antioch," he'd teased.

She knew he liked the friends she'd left behind in the Midwest—they came to visit once in a while. But Donovan considered their interest in Central America and various other causes a little off-the-wall.

Certainly Thea had no desire to throw herself into working with refugees or writing six letters a day to her government representatives. But there had to be a middle ground, she thought now, watching a woman in the office building next door as she took care of a copy machine, bending to insert paper, straightening to fiddle with the controls, bending again like an acolyte at the shrine of technology. There had to be some way to feel connected with more than just the manipulation of money.

The manner in which Guy had so pointedly mentioned Donovan bothered her. As if in making her partner, MSC would have access to Donovan's wide knowledge of Silicon Valley action.

"Good grief," she muttered. "We're not even married."

She thought about Donovan, taking comfort in conjuring up his lean, hard body and long-nosed face. Those gray eyes could be forbidding in business, but she knew them as tender and affectionate. His attitude toward money was understandable, she supposed. When you'd spent the better part of your youth in foster homes, you were likely to see money as the only security there was.

He'd been suspicious of her when they first met—at a Morton Shaeffler Cunningham party, in fact, celebrating an investment tie-in with the venture-capital firm where Donovan worked. But the chemistry between them had been undeniable, and it wasn't long before they were seeing a lot of each other.

They'd been living together almost four years. The arrangement suited both of them, she supposed. They owned a condominium jointly, they spent their spare moments with each other—in every way as if they were married. "But without the inconvenience," Donovan had once said, and Thea agreed. When he threw his clothes on the floor, she didn't feel responsible for making him pick them up. When she let the coffee table drown in *Wall Street Journal*s, he didn't nag her to put them away.

It was a very comfortable and companionable relationship. If they were married, Thea told herself, she might not be able to accept the late nights Donovan's work demanded. He might not be able to deal with her early rising to catch the markets on the East Coast.

She'd always been a morning person, so that wasn't what bothered her about joining MSC. "Just what is the matter with you, girl?" She spoke to herself as she used the little bathroom that adjoined her office. She'd been needing to use it more and more often in the past few days. It was one more factor that had her worried about her health, that had led her to drop off a discreet container at her doctor's office that morning. She had a busy calendar for the next month. If she was sick, if some part of her body was not functioning at top level, it must be nipped in the bud.

Examining herself in the mirror, Thea was forced to note that she looked pale—or maybe it was just the fluorescent light. She fluffed her medium-brown bangs and peered earnestly at her medium-brown eyes, thinking that it was nice having her own bathroom, where she could talk to herself and no one would think she was nuts. "If you were a partner," she told her reflection, "you'd have a private shower, too." Her reflection was unimpressed.

Despite an uneasy stomach, she was hungry. Returning to her office, Thea reached into the paper bag for one more bite. She'd read somewhere that croissants weren't quite as bad for you as doughnuts, another treat she enjoyed. "It's okay," she told the croissant, finishing it off. "I didn't have much lunch."

Her intercom buzzer sounded. She squished the bag up and tossed it into the trash before answering, as if the telephone could broadcast her consumption of empty calories. "Your sweetie on line three," Jill, the receptionist, announced. "And you had a call from your doctor's office while Guy was in there with you. I told them you'd call back."

"Thanks, Jill." Thea punched down the button and let pleasure flood her as she heard Donovan's deep voice on the line.

"Hello, stranger."

"Stranger yourself." She leaned back in her chair. "You were working late again last night."

"It was the only way to get off at a reasonable hour tonight," he said. His voice went a husky notch lower. "Sorry for waking you at midnight, Sleeping Beauty."

"I'm not sorry." She lowered her own voice. "Wake me up anytime for that kind of action."

His chuckle sounded pleased. "When are we meeting Pam and Rob?"

"Six-thirty, at the Golden Palace on Clement." She doodled a picture of a baby carriage on her desk pad. "Aren't you coming home before we go? I'm keeping little Angela before dinner while Pam does some stuff."

"Too bad. I can barely get away in time to make it to the restaurant."

He didn't sound particularly sad to miss little Angela. "You mean," Thea teased, "you don't want to play pat-a-cake with a ten-month-old and watch her drool all over your suit?"

"You know how I feel about babies," Donovan said, laughing. "Out of sight, out of drool range."

"What about those kids on the softball team you coach? They were babies once."

"Hard to believe." Donovan sounded embarrassed, as he always did when she mentioned the inner-city softball team he spent time with. "At least I've never had to burp one of them."

"No, you just have to take away their handguns periodically."

"Easier than facing a diaper any day. 'Scuse me a minute." Donovan spoke to someone else, then back into the phone. "Listen, honey, I gotta go. See you at six-thirty."

Smiling, Thea hung up the phone. Her smile changed to a sigh. She used to feel the same way about children, before Donovan's best friend, Rob Galbraith, had become a proud father. Pam and Rob were different now, a mysterious difference that intrigued Thea. And there was something about the way Pam cuddled Angela when she nursed her that gave Thea a heretofore-unknown ache in her heart.

"That's what turning thirty will do for you," she said to herself, punching out the number for her doctor's office. "You get tired and crotchety and subject to strange fancies."

While the doctor's office put her on hold, Thea tried to think about being a junior partner in MSC. But her thoughts wandered away from that topic, preferring to picture Donovan in his shirtsleeves at work, meeting with businesses in need of venture capital, exuding a smooth, slick power. He wasn't like that at home, and she found the transformation fascinating.

Dr. Rhinfelt came on the line. "Sorry to keep you waiting, Thea."

"That's okay, Ginny. What's happening? Do I have to take an antibiotic or something?"

Ginny Rhinfelt didn't answer right away. "Thea," she said at last, "it's not a bladder infection."

"Well, that's good," Thea said tentatively.

"Right. That's good." Thea could hear papers being shuffled at the other end of the line. "There is, however, a reason for the symptoms you reported this morning."

"What reason?"

Another pause. "Have you missed a period lately?"

"Well, I don't have them so regularly anyway, you know...." Thea's voice died away. "What are you trying to tell me?" she whispered.

"You're pregnant."

THEA STARED down at the teakettle, looking at her distorted reflection in its stainless steel side. She'd taken sick leave to come home from work early. Jill had thought it was her doctor's advice, but Thea needed time to think about her dilemma.

That late-night loving, when Donovan got home after working long hours and found her already in bed. Sometimes she remembered to use protection before she went to bed. Sometimes he reached into his nightstand drawer.

Apparently one night, they'd done neither.

Thea tried to picture herself at Morton Shaeffler Cunningham in a nice dress-for-success maternity outfit. Only too clearly could she visualize the expression on Guy Cunningham's face—unless she were married. Guy would still disapprove of her getting pregnant. "That's what we get for taking a woman into partnership," he'd say. And if she wasn't married, he'd probably have a lot more to say.

It still seemed unreal that one phone call, one small action in a person's life, could change that life forever.

Carrying her tea, Thea went into the living room to put away things on low tables before Angela came exploring around. Then she lay down on the sofa and stared up at the ceiling, her hands going unconsciously to soothe her belly. There was a baby growing in there. A baby whose father wouldn't want it.

"Maybe he would," she whispered, watching shadows chase each other across the white walls. Thea knew when she told Donovan she was pregnant, he would do the right thing. They would get married. The baby would be born into a family.

But he would feel fenced in, coerced. He'd been married before and it had ended badly. And he really didn't like babies. The boy who'd grown up in foster homes had spent a lot of time forced to care for other people's babies.

Certainly children couldn't easily be pictured in this elegant room. Their condo was in a nice complex near the Embarcadero, with views of the Bay Bridge from the living room, and the Golden Gate Bridge from the bedroom. She and Donovan had spent many pleasant Saturdays finding the furnishings in out-of-the-way spots through the Bay Area.

The decor they'd ended up with was eclectic, clever and amusing, some pieces expected to appreciate in value. But it wasn't a family ambience.

She propped up her head, sipped her tea and wished she didn't feel so tired. If she had more pep, maybe she could think of a good way out of this mess. A way that let her keep the baby she'd already begun to love.

The doorbell rang. Pam was early. "I hoped you'd be here," she said, sweeping into the room like a small blond whirlwind. Angela was perched on her hip, looking apprehensive. "I wanted to stop and try on a dress they're holding for me at Magnin's. And Françoise is impossible if I'm late."

Thea held out her arms to Angela. "Come here, honey," she crooned. Angela decided to be contrary. She buried her face in Pam's neck and snuffled.

"She's just feeling a little shy, aren't you, darling?" Pam detached the plump arms from around her neck and handed over her child. "I know you get a kick out of Aunt Thea's house," she said, planting a kiss on Angela's round cheek. "Thanks, Thea. See you at dinner. All her things are in here. And I brought her car seat." She dumped an enormous mass of stuff on the floor and was gone.

When the door closed behind her mother, Angela stiffened her little back and began to wail. "Now, now," Thea said helplessly, trying to hold on to a child who'd suddenly begun to resemble a giant piece of cooked macaroni. No matter where she grasped her, Angela flopped away. Thea was afraid the baby would fall, so she sat on the floor. "No need to cry," she said in her most soothing voice. "Auntie Thea has you now. Auntie Thea gets to play with you and—" There was something very squishy about the nether portion of Angela's anatomy, Thea realized. "Is that a surprise for Auntie Thea? You should give these surprises to your mommy."

She pulled the diaper bag closer and, with her nose wrinkled up, began the messy process. "Good thing Uncle Lucius isn't here," she told Angela, who'd stopped howling to watch Thea with enormous blue eyes. "This kind of stuff makes him queasy."

That was the wrong thing to say. Angela didn't mind, but Thea herself suddenly felt queasy. She finished her task in double-quick time and sent the dirty diaper down the incinerator chute with relief. Washing her hands, she gulped peppermint tea. It helped—a little.

By the time she was ready to leave for the restaurant, she was frazzled. Angela had needed total attention to keep her happy. Thea felt overburdened with the car seat, diaper bag, baby and her own purse. Somehow she staggered into the elevator, where a neighbor took pity on her and helped her out into the garage.

Pam waited at the entrance to the Golden Palace, her hair shiny perfection, a big shopping bag proclaiming her success at I Magnin. Thea pulled up in the street. "Take your child," she hollered, cranking down the window. "I'll find a place to park."

It was ten minutes before she got back to the restaurant. Pam and Rob were holding down a table in the main dining room, and Thea joined them, sinking into her chair with relief. "Quick, give me some tea. It's a jungle out there."

Rob poured beer into a glass. "Want one of these instead?"

Thea shook her head. "Tea's fine." She accepted the small handleless cup Pam gave her and cradled it thankfully. San Francisco in February could be foggy and raw. "Donovan here yet?"

"The great Lucius Donovan has not arrived," Rob said solemnly. "I don't suppose this restaurant runs to champagne, does it?"

"With Chinese food?" Pam lifted one well-groomed eyebrow and rummaged in her purse for a plastic bag of the thick crusty toast Angela seemed to live for. Angela accepted a piece graciously, gnawed on it for a moment and threw it onto the floor.

"Litterbug." Donovan came up to the table, clapping Rob on the back and bending to kiss Thea. He pulled out the chair next to her and smiled at his friends. "She'll get a ticket if she's not careful."

Thea could detect a little edge in the remark, but Angela's fond parents simply smiled. "Shall we order?" she asked.

After the waiter had served wonton soup from a big tureen, Donovan raised his beer glass. "You are dining," he said impressively, "with the new vice president for development at that prestigious venture-capital firm, Gaskell Associates."

"It's about time!" Thea kissed him quickly and smiled her pleasure. Donovan, she thought, studying the man she loved, was cut out for success. Only the lock of hair that fell over one eyebrow marred his high-powered look.

Now he pushed the hair out of the way with an absent-minded gesture and turned to Thea, his smile flashing out to give warmth and light to his face. "Just one slight problem, darlin'," he said, laughing. "The job's in New York."

Thea didn't hear Pam's exclamation or Rob's eager query. She sat, frozen in shock, the teacup halfway to her mouth.

Donovan parried his friends' remarks, then turned to Thea. "Honey, are you all right? Didn't you hear?"

"I heard," Thea whispered. "You're going to New York."

He frowned and clasped her hand. "We'll talk later."

THEA STOOD at the bedroom window, watching the distant gleam of the Golden Gate Bridge and the city that rose steeply up from the bay in terraces of light. Donovan turned off the water in the bathroom and came up behind her.

"Tell me what's bothering you, Thea." He put his hands on her shoulders, but she didn't relax back against him.

"You said it at dinner so I wouldn't make a scene, didn't you?"

His hands fell away. "I don't know what you're talking about."

"You didn't want me to get upset about your going to New York, so you deliberately waited to tell me until Rob and Pam were there to act as buffers for you." She spoke as calmly as she could, masking the tension that roiled inside.

Donovan turned her to look into her face. "It's true that I wasn't sure how you'd take it," he admitted. "I know it's tough to relocate and all, but—"

"Are you asking me to come with you?" Her throat was tight. It was hard to get the words out.

He looked shocked. "Well, of course."

She took a deep breath. "Why?"

"Well—because." He turned away and began unbuttoning his shirt. "We're a couple. We belong together. I'm not too good at the words," he muttered. "But I love you, Thea. We love each other—I thought."

A trickle of warmth replaced some of the chill that pervaded her. "You love me," she said levelly. "And yet you just calmly expect me to drop everything and go with you to New York."

He pushed his hair back in agitation. "Damn it, Thea," he said, exasperated, "New York is Mecca for investment counselors. You spend half your time on the phone to New York. I thought you'd be thrilled."

"You're not the only one to get a good offer today," she said quietly. "I was asked to join Morton Shaeffler Cunningham as a junior partner."

He paused in the act of unbuckling his belt, staring across at her. "Congratulations," he said at last, hollowly. "That's quite a plum."

Thea nodded. "They've never offered a woman partnership before."

He swallowed. "Guess that makes it tough for you. I know career advancement is important, but—" He took a step toward her. "I want you to come with me, Thea. It never occurred to me that you wouldn't."

"Well," she said, her gaze straight on his. "Now that it occurs, does it change your mind? Would you stay here with me?"

He turned away, fiddling with the change that heaped his dresser. When he spoke, his voice sounded stifled. "I can't," he said finally. "This vice presidency—I've angled for it. I've fought for it. I want it." When he faced her again, she could see his strained expression. "It's just for a year or so, they said. Just to get the office started. Then we'd be back."

"New York." Thea clenched her fists, wondering if she could tell him, how she could tell him. "You're asking me to go to a city I hate, where I have no friends, and to give up a partnership, maybe not even find another job—it's hard to get anyone to hire you for one year."

"What are you saying—that you won't do it?" He had gotten control of his face now. She knew that expression— the focused look of someone who could find and exploit weakness. She'd never thought to see it turned on her.

"I could be persuaded to go," she said at last, slowly, trying to think through the horrible morass that surrounded her. "Under one condition."

"Well?" He stood, his shirt unbuttoned, a faint graze of beard on his face, and she thought he'd never looked so dangerous, even in his corporate-shark outfit.

"That we get married."

She dropped her bomb and waited, twisting her hands together until she made herself try to appear relaxed.

It was obviously a bomb, too. He looked at her, dazed and unbelieving. "Marriage!" Turning away, he paced over to the bureau. "So that's what this is all about."

"Whither thou goest," Thea told him, folding her arms around herself against a sudden chill, "is part of the marriage ceremony. Not part of the living-together ceremony."

Donovan turned to face her. "Listen," he said bluntly. "New York is not forever. Marriage is—or is supposed to be." He shrugged off his shirt and tossed it toward the hamper. It fell on the floor, and he stalked toward it purposefully, stuffing it into its proper place. "I've been married before and it wasn't forever," he said finally. "It was a nightmare. I thought we were in love, I bought the whole trip, and yet—" he put one hand over his face "—whatever we felt for each other, it wasn't enough. The way we fought—the way it ended—I don't see any reason to put myself through that again."

Thea started to protest, but he gestured her into silence. "Besides," he added, his voice infinitely weary, "I don't make enough to support a wife. I can't afford to get married."

"That's bull, and you know it." Thea ran a brush through her hair and put it down quickly when she saw how it trembled in her hand. "Maybe you didn't make enough for Cecily, but that was what—seven years ago? You're established now." This time she cut him off before he could speak. "Besides, I don't recall asking you to support me."

His jaw set stubbornly. "Marriage changes people. You might not think so now, but I know. I can't take the responsibility again."

With an effort, Thea kept her voice from quivering. "I'm me, whether we're married or not. Whether I work or don't. Not some abstract wife, not a clone of Cecily." She thought of what he'd told her about Cecily, about her self-centered behavior, her extravagance and her infidelities. "I don't want to be supported in some grand style. I just want an acknowledged tie between us." Sighing, Thea turned away. The fog was enfolding the bridge now, shrouding it in misty veils, creeping over the bay. "Forget it," she said, staring into the dim whiteness. "I'm not going to New York to sit by myself in the evenings in a totally unknown place while you wheel and deal. Not now."

His hands on her shoulders were less gentle as he whirled her around. "You won't come?"

"You can't really give me a good reason why I should," she whispered, staring at the sharp face she loved. But now her love for him was overshadowed by other knowledge. "You don't want commitments. You just want your bed warmed at night."

He shook her a little, his eyes snapping. "You're crazy," he yelled. "I want you with me. I need you with me. Can't you see that?"

"Then stay here." She held it out as a last test. "Or marry me. We can start a family—"

His face closed. "No way," he said with finality. "I don't think it's good to bring children into this mixed-up world. What kind of father would I make, coming from the background I have? And I'm sure not ready to be tied down like Rob is." He snorted. "Rob has to rush home from work every day or Pam gives him hell for not doing his share. He doesn't feel free to pull up stakes and move when something better comes along." Donovan shook his head. "This promotion is important to me." He took her hands, staring into her eyes feverishly. "I worked for it—worked damned hard. Now I'm getting the reward. I—I guess I can understand why you want to stay. You feel the same way."

"I feel the same," she said flatly. In that moment she knew her choices were narrower than she'd thought. Not between job, child or lover. Just between job and child. Not for her the I-can-have-it-all of luckier women. She was alone in this. It was her responsibility to make the right decision.

There was still time to tell him. But quickly she rejected that option, as well. No matter what his response, it wouldn't be what she needed to hear. She couldn't tell him, not after what he'd just said. Even if he offered, now, she wouldn't marry him. She loved him too much to tie him to her and watch him chafe at his bonds.

She loved him, but she wasn't responsible for his choices. Only her own.

"Don't try to decide now," he urged, watching her. "Let's sleep on it."

She didn't tell him that, though she might have been willing to leave the partnership behind for his sake, she couldn't do the same with their unborn child. "We'll sleep on it," she agreed instead, and let him lead her toward the bed. Tomorrow was soon enough to confront the future. His love for her now seemed to belong to the past, but she could still take comfort in it.

He stopped beside the bed and folded her against him. The feel of his bare chest had always been arousing to her. She let her hands roam the muscles that corded his back, and when his lips found hers, urgent and demanding, she melted against him as she always did. He untied the robe she wore, sliding it off her shoulders. His mouth moved to her neck and to her ear, whispering the dark, rough words that made her tremble.

Lowering her onto the bed, he ran his hands over the full curves of breast and hip. The haze of passion was already in his eyes, bringing a stab of heat to her. Then he paused to reach into the drawer of his bedside table.

She put her hand on his, gazing up at him, at the dark lock of hair that was the only thing he couldn't control, at his stubborn chin and firm lips, at the lean, muscular length of him, and felt she was memorizing him to keep forever. "You don't need that tonight," she managed shakily. "It's the wrong time."

He kissed her hand and put it gently away. "Just in case," he whispered, "I want to protect you, love."

He lowered his mouth to hers again, and the words spiraled away until she lost herself in the heat he called up, the love they shared so sweetly together and soon would share no more.

CHAPTER TWO

One year and two months later...

THE APRIL DAY was already unreasonably warm. Morning sun streamed down from the clerestory windows, and gentle puffs of hot, salty breeze ventured through the open door.

Thea angled the floor fan to bring cool air her way and went back to her struggle with the thirty-quart Hobart mixer. Somehow she'd gotten the dough hook in crooked, and when she turned it on the most awful racket issued from the massive piece of machinery.

Helen Macaphee came in from the store, frowning in concern. "What's happening back here? Is it chewing you up, Thea?"

Collapsing against a nearby cutting table, Thea admitted defeat. "This batch of dough is giving me nothing but trouble. I vote we throw it out now and start over."

Helen shook her head, setting the shiny black hair on her shoulders swinging. "No way, honey. Waste not, want not. Somewhere out there are twenty hungry people, thinking about a nice warm loaf of raisin-nut bread. It won't be ready when they get here if you don't get your act together."

"Right, chief," Thea said, saluting smartly. "Do you think you can help me out here, from your infinite experience?"

Helen strolled over to the Hobart and examined the problem. "You didn't goose the dough hook enough," she said kindly. "You have to grab it like so and really engage the little doodad here. See?"

"Clear as mud," Thea muttered. "Somehow *doodad* seems too nice a name for this thing."

Helen took a try of éclairs and backed through the swinging door. "Holler if you need more help," she called cheerfully.

This time when Thea turned on the huge mixer, it went to work in relative quiet, with only the sound equivalent to an airplane taking off. She watched the contents of the bowl carefully, adding ingredients in the precise formation that Helen had taught her. The dough began to cling to the hook, and as it kneaded itself she was free to let her thoughts drift for a few minutes.

The radio in the corner of the kitchen broadcast a brief market update, and Thea thought back over a year to her former position as almost-partner with Morton Shaeffler Cunningham. If she hadn't bolted for Santa Cruz the day after Donovan left for New York, if she hadn't been intrigued by a bakery with the apt name of Babycakes, she might still have been sitting in her office at Morton Shaeffler Cunningham.

Not the bigger office of a partner, though. Guy Cunningham had made that abundantly clear when she'd told him of her pregnancy. It was as if she'd confirmed all their hesitation in taking a woman into partnership. Men didn't go off and get pregnant at the drop of a hat. His chins had quivered a little in indignation at the thought of an unwed mother joining the ranks of partners.

Looking around the spacious white-painted workroom, she smiled contentedly. Being a woman and a mother didn't matter in this partnership. Investing in Babycakes was the smartest move she'd ever made. Her friends had scolded her for quitting Morton Shaeffler Cunningham, for putting her savings into a failing bakery in a little coastal town. But Thea felt needed here. She chuckled a little at her pun.

Needed for kneading—and more. After nearly a year, she still found it exciting, energizing. Her feet didn't even hurt so much anymore.

The only sore spot in her contentment was Donovan.

Thea tilted a jar of raisins into the mixer's giant bowl, her smile fading. "It was for his own good," she muttered. She'd had this argument so many times in her head. She'd let him go, she'd bought out his share of the condo, so there'd be no need for further communication between them. Hurt, angry, he had gone. She hadn't answered his letters, hadn't returned his phone calls. And when she'd relocated to Santa Cruz permanently, she had left no forwarding address and gotten an unlisted phone number.

Pam had said she was overreacting. Scowling now, Thea sprinkled in nuts, let the dough hook work a little longer and turned off the Hobart. Pam had decried the necessity of severing all ties. "Someday," Pam had said darkly, "you'll feel guilty about it, and then you'll be in real trouble."

That was the problem, all right. Thea reached into the giant bowl for the kneaded dough, flopping it in an ungainly armful onto the cutting table. She patted it into shape and began chopping pieces off, weighing them on the scale and shaping them into loaves for the pans that stood already greased in their attached rows of five.

She felt guilty. Each day that she tasted the pleasures of her new life, she wondered uneasily how she could be denying those pleasures to Donovan. He didn't want them, she told herself constantly. He'd made that clear.

But people could change. She certainly had.

Of course, if he'd really been affected by their breakup, she thought self-righteously, he would have hunted her down by now. She had more or less expected him when February rolled around, and with it the one-year anniversary of his departure for New York. She scowled, remembering the trip to Betty's Coiffures that had ended up burdening her with a bag of expensive hair-care products and a big hole in her checking account.

And Donovan hadn't shown up. And her hair had grown out of the careful trim into a casual mane of sun-streaked brown.

She shook it back, enjoying the sensual caress of long hair brushing her shoulders, comparing the faded jeans and sweatshirt she wore beneath her big white apron with the dress-for-success wardrobe of her previous life. From her point of view, there was no comparison.

Yes, she reflected, surveying the row of bread pans, life was good. She'd made new friends, was learning new skills, and most important, her life was richer by far than the bland, sterile existence she'd led in the city. No matter that the trappings of success—fancy car, fine surroundings— were absent from this life. She didn't miss them, that was sure.

If there was anything missing, it was nothing important, she told herself firmly. Donovan would just have to go back into that corner of her mind where she tried to keep him penned. Sooner or later, the space he occupied would shrink to nothing, and then she'd be totally content.

She pulled a long piece of plastic wrap off the industrial-sized roll and tenderly covered the bread pans. The loaves would rise, would be baked in the oven, would go home with delighted customers who'd probably be forced by the wonderful fragrance to break off a piece to eat in the car. It was infinitely more satisfying to produce such a product than to manipulate stocks and bonds for profit, although she still got a little market action.

She wondered how Donovan would react to her change of career and then shook her head at the way he'd once again invaded her thoughts. He certainly wasn't thinking about her.

"How do I know?" Thea heaved the empty mixer bowl up to the stainless-steel sink and began to scrub it out. "He could have tried to call every day for the last year, and I wouldn't know." After all, she had cut the ties. She had put the distance between them.

But Pam Galbraith knew where she was. If Donovan had really wanted to find her, he could have. Thea hadn't seen Pam for a while, but her friend would have let her know if Donovan wanted to get in touch. "Face it," she told herself. "He's long since forgotten you."

Helen came in with several empty trays.

"The muffins are all gone," she announced. "The next batch of bread won't be out for twenty minutes more, and Maria can handle the front for that long. Come upstairs and have some breakfast."

Thea looked at her watch. Her stomach growled, but she hesitated.

"Oh, come on," Helen said, noticing her troubled look. "You don't have to rush home. Isn't R.J. holding the fort?"

"True," Thea conceded, following Helen out the back door and up the wooden steps that led to the second-story apartment. "But I need to get home before much longer or she might stage a rebellion."

"R.J. worships the ground you walk on," Helen declared. "She'd never leave you in the lurch."

"I don't know about that." Thea pressed her arms against her chest in the protective gesture she'd learned the past few months. "There are certain things only I can do, you know."

"We'll just have the last two muffins and some juice," Helen said, breezing into her kitchen. The apartment was one big room with a tiny kitchen partitioned off and a bathroom to the left of the entrance. In contrast to the large-scale efficiency below, Helen's kitchen counters were piled high with juice extractors, fruit-drying trays, bamboo steamers, and boxes and bags of grains and herbs and powders. "Maybe a cup of herb tea."

"Don't you have anything with caffeine in it?" Thea removed a stack of health and fitness magazines from a scruffy rattan chair and sat down at the little table. It, too, was cluttered with pamphlets, jar upon jar of vitamins and several paper bags filled with what looked like lawn clippings.

"You shouldn't be drinking caffeine," Helen said, filling the teakettle from a rusty faucet above the chipped enamel sink. "It's absolute poison to your nervous system."

"All financial people drink caffeine," Thea said firmly. "It's the only way to jump start their brains." She picked up the nearest little bag and sniffed the contents. "Besides, I only drink a couple of cups of tea a day. It's hardly enough to turn me into Ms. Hyde."

"Ms. who?" Helen reached into a cupboard for two small glasses. When they'd first started working together, Helen had been petite and voluptuous and getting more so every day as she sampled her own wares to ease her heartache. She'd started describing herself as being on the near side of chubby.

But several months ago, turning thirty-nine and alarmed by a supermarket cholesterol test, she'd begun leading the world's healthiest life-style with the maniacal fervor that characterized all her activities. Admiring the clearness of her partner's dark brown eyes and her slimmer figure, Thea had to admit the changes had worked, but she mourned breakfasts of earlier times, with coddled eggs and homemade sausage.

"Dr. Jekyll's counterpart." Thea picked up another bag. "What is this stuff, some kind of feedlot reject?"

Helen plucked the bag away. "Raspberry leaf tea, just what you need. It's a tonic for women."

"Says who?" Thea grabbed for one of the muffins Helen had brought upstairs. "At least I know what's in this," she declared. She'd whipped them up at five-thirty that morning for the early muffin crowd.

"You make fun of my diet," Helen complained, bringing over the juice, "but I'm in better shape than I've ever been. I probably have the cardiovascular health of a ten-year-old."

"Better, I'm sure," Thea said placatingly. "Ten-year-olds are notorious for junk food."

"We should really make more of those low-fat, high-fiber muffins," Helen persisted, pouring water into the teapot. "They go like hotcakes. I'm telling you, everybody's into their bodies these days."

"Sounds perverted." Thea took an appreciative bite of apple-spice muffin. When she'd first started making them, they'd always come out with flat caps or had been sunken and doughy in the middle. Now they were invariably perfect, big and fluffy and well shaped.

"You know what I mean." Helen glanced pointedly at Thea's waistline. "You could stand to get into shape, too, you know."

"Spare me," Thea groaned. "I'll do it, I'll do it! Just as long as you don't want to replace the pastries with rusks and make the chocolate cake with oat bran."

"That's not a bad idea, the oat bran." Helen tossed off the contents of her juice glass and Thea took a big sip.

"What is this stuff?" She choked and glared at the glass. "It's not orange juice!"

"Carrot-papaya-turnip juice," Helen said airily. "Very high in zinc and beta-carotene."

Thea put down the glass and transferred her glare to Helen. "I think I hear R.J. calling."

Helen laughed and got up to rinse out the glass. "Relax," she said over her shoulder. "There's really no turnips in it. Here's some fresh-squeezed orange juice and a cup of Earl Grey. Will that do?"

Appeased, Thea took another bite of muffin. The sun streamed into the apartment, highlighting the pleasing disarray of stacks of books, rampant houseplants and shabby furniture. Helen had been living over her bakery during the seven years she'd been in business, and it had been the prospect of losing her home, as well as her bakery, that had had her in tears on a gloomy March day the previous year when Thea had walked in.

"It's lucky you didn't have to move," Thea remarked, taking a sip of tea. It was good, and the familiar aroma lifted some of the oppression her sense of guilt had conjured up earlier. "You've got more stuff in this room than would fit in that mobile home you were talking about."

Helen nodded, glancing around her home with approval. "I have you to thank," she said soberly, no longer teasing. "If you hadn't come along and saved my ass, I hate to think of what would have happened."

"You saved me, too, you know," Thea said quietly. "For the past year I've felt like I'm really alive, instead of just going through the motions."

"Terror will do that to you," Helen agreed amiably. "It hasn't been easy, Thea."

"No, of course not." Thea savored her orange juice and recalled the past year, filled with long hours, an immense investment of energy and most of her available cash. "But it is richly rewarding."

Helen raised her eyebrows. "I take it you don't mean financially," she said. "Or have you found something in the books that I haven't?"

"Oh, money." Thea waved it away. "Who cares about that stuff? We're scraping by, and that's what counts. If we were making any more we might have to pay income tax."

"Don't mention the T-word," Helen begged. "The thought of income tax reminds me of paperwork, and paperwork reminds me of Raymund, and the thought of *him* makes me want to throw something!" Her fingers tightened around her juice glass.

"No throwing!" Thea protested. "Please! Those broken windows are expensive to replace."

"Right." Helen smiled sheepishly. "You'd think I could remember that. But if I can't throw things, my troubles seem to upset my digestion." She mixed some of the powders from the table into a fresh glass of juice and drank it.

"Raymund did a real number on you, didn't he?" Thea regarded Helen sympathetically. "But you weren't the only one, you know. Betty from Betty's Coiffures was in yesterday just before closing time, and she was all down about some awful thing Raymund had done."

"He ran off a year ago," Helen said sourly. "What was she still moaning about?"

Thea dropped the subject. Even now it was painful for Helen to remember those days after her erstwhile accountant, Raymund Neves, had absconded, taking with him the contents of her business and private bank accounts and everything he could find that wasn't nailed down. The revelation soon following that Raymund had also gotten away with Betty's savings, as well as the funds of some other small businesses in the neighborhood, had just rubbed salt into the wound. It had been so bitter that, even though Thea was a stranger, Helen had poured it all out the fateful spring afternoon over a year ago.

Helen wasn't ready to drop it yet. After a moment, she smiled reluctantly. "Actually, now that I think of it, picturing Raymund with Betty is pretty funny. He was only a few inches taller than me, and Betty's such an Amazon—" She began to laugh. "The line that man had! Even now when I remember how I believed him, I feel like I should have had my head examined. But he was so convincing."

Thea was still hung up on the mental image Helen had conjured up. She'd seen a picture of Raymund before Helen had ripped it into tiny pieces and flushed it down the toilet. He had been rather slight, dapper and sleek. "You don't think they—no, I can't believe it. Betty must be fifteen or twenty years older than you are—at least fifteen years older than him!"

"You're not the only one Betty's confided in," Helen said, rinsing out her juice glass. "She came over several evenings right after he split, telling me what a great lover he was, and how lonely she was without him." Her mouth twisted. "I didn't need to hear that."

"You need to meet someone else," Thea offered. "Someone to take your mind off the creep."

"Men aren't worth the bother," Helen sniffed. "They just take, take, take! Well, you must know about that."

Thea fell silent. Not even to Helen would she talk about Donovan. Of the few people who knew the facts, most had not hesitated to tell her she was handling things all wrong. She didn't want to listen to Helen say it, too.

"Forget the men," Helen said briskly. "What we need to do is decide about the espresso machine."

"I thought we had decided." Thea pulled her attention back to business. "On the back wall, where it won't be so noisy to people sitting at the tables."

"How about a juice bar instead," Helen suggested. "Fresh-squeezed everything! So much healthier than all that caffeine."

Thea thought for a moment. "I don't know," she said, listening to her inner voice. "A juice bar starts to put us in restaurant territory. Espresso goes with baked goods, but carrot juice?" She pondered the idea. "Why don't we add to our cooler space, and expand the bottled juice we carry? Not so much cash outlay there."

"That's probably better," Helen conceded. "And it's your money, after all."

"Well, it was your bakery," Thea pointed out. "I don't want you to feel I'm usurping your power, Helen."

"I don't really feel like that." Helen smiled reluctantly. "It's just rather galling to have made such a mess of things that you have to bail me out, that's all."

"Hey, I was looking for a good investment." Thea jumped up, glancing at her watch. "As long as you don't regret it—"

"Listen," Helen said, squeezing Thea's hand. "If you hadn't bought into the bakery, it wouldn't be here now. I would have sold to pay my many creditors, and they would have torn it to pieces between them. If anyone should feel regret, it's you. I guess you could have been the investment queen of San Francisco if you hadn't put this millstone around your neck."

"Not really," Thea said. "Not after I made up my mind to add mommy to my job description." She pushed her chair up to the table. "Let's feel mutually gratified by our wonderful business deal and leave it at that." Picking up her cup, she carried it to the sink. "I'll be back around eleven to work on the books and help out if you need me. Okay?"

Helen made a dismissing motion with her hand. "Take your time. Take a nap, if you like. Roxie's coming in at ten, and Maria's staying till two."

"I'll be here," Thea promised. "See you." She ran down the stairs and climbed into the car she'd bought when she'd moved, an ancient, shiny Volvo. She'd been up since five that morning, and a short nap did sound attractive. If she got the chance. There were duties waiting for her at home—wonderful duties. She nearly ran a stop sign getting to them.

DONOVAN STRETCHED long legs in front of him and smiled at Pam Galbraith, forcing himself to seem relaxed. "It has been a long time," he agreed. "Over a year, in fact."

"I guess men just aren't good correspondents," Pam said, shaking her blond curls. Her movement was echoed by the little girl on her lap. The two of them made quite a picture on the blue sofa. Glancing around at the comfortable furniture, the luxurious rug, Donovan had to admit that Pam was very clever at decorating. The room was perfect, with nothing out of place. It set his teeth on edge.

Pam had been surprised at his visit and somehow taken aback. Donovan supposed that just dropping in on people was kind of boorish. But he hadn't wanted to lose any time. "You didn't even write back after I sent you those pictures of Angela's first birthday party," Pam said, sounding faintly aggrieved.

"I'm not much on letter writing," Donovan admitted. He didn't mention that pictures of Angela were not high on his list of important documents. "And New York was very hectic. I—kind of lost touch there with a lot of people." He cleared his throat, hoping to get to the point of his visit without too much preamble. "Thea, for instance. What's she doing these days?"

"She hasn't told *you*?" Pam regarded him shrewdly. "She's left San Francisco, you know."

"I gathered, when my letters came back 'address unknown' from the condo, that she might have relocated." He tried to keep the peevishness out of his voice. "Don't see why she couldn't come to New York with me, if she was going to move anyway."

"Oh, I don't blame her," Pam said airily. "Since you didn't want to get married—"

"She told you that?" He struggled upright in the too-soft sofa, glaring.

"I asked," Pam said.

"Oh." He let the sofa engulf him again.

She peered at him. "Did you think she'd be waiting for you?"

"I hoped so. I thought that was the agreement," he muttered, inserting a finger between the too-tight collar of his shirt and his neck. "We agreed to give each other space for a year. She was the one who insisted on cutting off all communication." A spurt of anger filled him. "Damn it, a man isn't offered a vice presidency every day! I had to take it! What did she expect, that I'd hang around here forever because she didn't want me to go?"

"So how is the job?" Pam unerringly probed another sore point. "Do you enjoy being a veep?"

Donovan counted ten. "I've been very busy," he said, attempting a smile that wouldn't reveal his clenched teeth. "I don't have time to think about whether I'm happy or not."

"Well, what brings you back to San Francisco, anyway?" Pam soothed Angela with a cuddle and set the child down. "Why don't you see if your bear needs company for his nap," she suggested. Angela scooted off down the hall.

Donovan ran a hand through his hair, pushing it off his forehead with an automatic gesture. He didn't notice that it fell right back again a moment later. "I'm on vacation for a couple of weeks."

Pam opened her eyes wide, resembling little Angela. "Vacation," she said wistfully. "That's nice. We never seem to get out of town anymore. Where are you going?"

"I'm going here." Donovan got a grip on his exasperation. "I mean, this is where I'm vacationing."

Pam looked dubious. "For two weeks. Uh, did you want to stay with us?"

"No, of course not," Donovan said with another strained smile. His manners weren't the best in the world, but he'd never invite himself to stay—not with Pam and Rob, anyway. He was hoping to do just that with Thea, though. "I'm going to be around the area—maybe go to Yosemite, get down to Santa Cruz."

Pam flinched a little, and he wondered at it. "You probably won't have time for that," she gabbled. "Why don't you go up the coast—maybe to Oregon or somewhere?"

He frowned down at his clasped hands. "No need," he said gloomily. "They want me to open a new office in Bellevue, Washington. I'll have plenty of time for the north Pacific coast."

"Bellevue," Pam said. "How—how nice. I thought you were supposed to be coming back here after a year or so."

"They changed their minds." Donovan realized that he was referring to the firm that employed him in a highly paid position as "they." But since he'd been told about Bellevue, an us-against-them attitude had been growing in his mind. Bob Metlock had acted as if Bellevue was practically San Francisco. And no place was San Francisco unless Thea was there.

He almost blurted this out to Pam, it was on his mind so much. Almost told her how lonely he'd been in New York, how in spite of constant work, he felt on the verge of screwing up all the time. He never felt comfortable for a moment, or at least that's how it seemed. This vacation was necessary—he would have taken it even if they hadn't offered him a couple of weeks to scout around Bellevue, to see how nice it was. He took the time, but he changed the tickets. He didn't care about Bellevue, though it was undoubtedly a fine place. He just wanted to see Thea.

"So where are you staying?" Pam was curious.

He'd expected that, but looking at her he thought he saw apprehension of some kind. Shrugging, he tried his most charming smile. "I thought I'd see if Thea could put me up, if she's still in the area. We—I'd like to talk to her."

"She won't like the idea of Bellevue at all," Pam murmured, shaking her head.

"What's that?" Donovan leaned forward. "So you still keep in touch?" His voice was sharp, and Pam stared at him in surprise. "Sorry," he mumbled, smoothing back his hair. "I'm getting testy in my old age." His smile came out crooked. "Put it down to mid-life crisis."

"Don't you have to be older for that?" Pam didn't appear to have her mind on the conversation. She was frowning in thought.

"I am older," he said, more to himself than to her. "About a hundred years." New York had really piled it on.

"You're thirty-five, exactly three months older than Rob. He's told me often how you held that over his head when you were in the army together."

Donovan relaxed into a real smile. "How long is he going to be out of town, anyway? I want to see the old son of a gun."

"He'll be back Friday." Pam looked as if she couldn't wait.

Donovan went back to the attack. "What's Thea up to these days?" He thought of that stuffy investment firm she worked for. "Did MSC send her off to a branch office?"

"Hmm? No, she doesn't work for them anymore."

Donovan sat bolt upright. "Doesn't work—wait a minute! She turned me down to take that partnership they offered. Or didn't they offer one?"

"They rescinded the offer, she said." Pam was staring at him now, speculation in her gaze.

"Oh, poor Thea." Donovan felt a little dazed. The woman he loved had taken this body blow, and he hadn't been around to console her. "That must have really hurt. And she was one of the best counselors they had! What reason did they give her?"

"I don't recall," Pam said. Donovan could tell she was lying.

He dropped all pretense. "Where is Thea?" His voice was quietly insistent. "Why don't you want to tell me?"

Pam hesitated. "She said you two had severed all ties, Lucius." He winced at her use of his first name, but she didn't notice. "I'm not sure she wants to hear from you after all this time."

He closed his eyes briefly. "I'm not going to make any demands on her. I just want to talk."

She didn't answer for a moment, and little Angela came bounding back into the room.

"Unka Lush-us," Angela shouted, evidently electing him to family status. "Unka Lush-us."

This time Pam noticed his wince, but didn't realize it stemmed from his dislike of his given name. "You still have that problem with children, I see," she said rather frostily. "Are you afraid of them, or what?"

"I'm not afraid of children," he said, startled. "I just—they just...well, I'm not afraid of them, anyway." He tried to smile at Angela, who promptly burst into tears.

Pam hugged her daughter and restrained a laugh. "This reminds me of that night we went out to dinner with you and Thea, just before you left." The laugh came bubbling out, and Angela stopped crying to gaze at her mother.

"I remember that night, too." He had been full of his promotion, but it hadn't stopped him from noticing the way the bread had mixed with drool on Angela's chin and streaked the front of her ruffly little dress. Right in the middle of dinner a horrible smell had come from her. Before Pam had taken her away, Donovan had had time to remember all the things that smell triggered for him—a tired, whiny baby thrust into his twelve-year-old arms by a frowsy foster mother, with the command to take the brat out of there for a while and give her some peace!

Now he tried to dismiss the memories. After all, nothing could be further from perfect little Angela than the grimy, crying babies of his memory. Somehow every foster home—and there had been several of them before he'd managed to graduate early from high school—had had a little kid attached to it, a kid that became his responsibility for part of each day. He'd known how to change a diaper since the age of nine—and hated the duty, even when he'd come, reluctantly, to like the baby involved. And even that liking would be turned against him sooner or later when he was uprooted once more and sent to start all over again in some other place, with some other family.

"You had the same look on your face then," Pam mentioned, giving Angela a kiss. The little girl scrambled down and headed for the hall. "A sort of where's-the-skunk look." Her laugh was rueful. "Angela's only been to Burger King since then."

Donovan thought of little faces smeared with ketchup and barely repressed a shudder. But he said gallantly, "She seems very precocious for her age."

"She is." Pam beamed and launched into a tale of Angela's astonishing cleverness. Donovan ceased to listen. Instead he replayed the scene with Thea that evening, after they'd come back from the dinner of disaster, as she'd referred to it.

They'd made such sweet love that night. It had never occurred to him that the next day she'd calmly offer to buy him out of the condo. She wasn't going with him. She thought it would be better if they made a clean break. And though she listened to his protests and arguments, she hadn't changed her mind.

"... and she pointed right at it and said, 'teddy bear goes nighty night' as clear as can be," Pam finished up proudly.

"Amazing," Donovan murmured, jolted back to the present by the expectant silence that followed Pam's anecdote. "Tell me, Pam, is Thea married now? Is that why you don't want to tell me where she is?"

"She's not married, as far as I know," Pam said cautiously. "To tell you the truth, I haven't seen her for a while. We're both pretty busy with our—" She stopped abruptly, as if she'd been on the point of indiscretion.

Donovan leaned forward eagerly. "Busy? Doing what? Is she counseling for some other firm?"

"She doesn't do that work at all now," Pam said after a moment's thoughtful pause. "You really are out of the picture, aren't you?"

Donovan turned away, uncomfortable in that direct, searching gaze. "Not by choice," he muttered. "I just don't understand it. Why did she shut me out like that? What did I do?" He buried his head in his hands. "I'll marry her, if that's what she wants. I'll do whatever it takes."

Pam sat up alertly. "Really?"

He stared at her. "Of course. Just tell me how to find Thea, and you won't be able to see my smoke."

Pam twisted her hands and glanced longingly at the phone. Donovan didn't notice. He was getting his little notebook out of his jacket pocket. He held the pencil over a blank sheet of paper, gazing at Pam with what he hoped was fervent appeal.

Evidently it worked. "I promised Thea I wouldn't hand out her address or anything," Pam said in a rush. "But I can give you a hint."

"A hint?" Disappointment rose in him. "A hint is all I'm going to get?"

She nodded vigorously. "Remember where you guys used to spend a lot of weekends?"

He wrinkled his forehead. "We went all over the place, as I recall," he said finally. "Mendocino? The gold country?"

"You just mentioned visiting there on your vacation," Pam prompted anxiously.

"Can't be Yosemite—Thea's no park ranger. Santa Cruz?"

Pam leaned forward. "And remember Thea's favorite thing to do when she cruises a town?"

Groaning, he held his head in his hands. "I feel like I'm on *This Is Your Life*. Thea has so many interests—antiques, the Big Dipper at the Boardwalk, dancing at the Coconut Grove, bakeries—"

"That's it!" Pam sprang up, shrieking excitedly. "You got it!"

He seized her hands and hugged her spontaneously. "Bakeries! Thea has something to do with a bakery in Santa Cruz."

"I didn't tell you," Pam said, smiling. "You guessed."

"Damned straight." Donovan pushed the hair off his forehead in distraction. "There are only about a million bakeries in Santa Cruz."

"You can't miss it," Pam assured him. "It's right down by the B—" She clapped a hand over her mouth.

"The Boardwalk," he guessed. "Thanks, Pam. Thanks a lot!"

"Listen," Pam said, looking a little nervous. "Just let Thea think you kind of stumbled in, okay? I mean, you don't have to—"

"Fink on you?" He grinned. "Don't worry. I plan to keep her too busy to have time to question me."

Pam smiled—a strange smile, as he recalled later. "You do that, Lucius."

He was going to find Thea. He was going to wipe out the memory of that last morning, when she'd told him she wouldn't go to New York, when she'd stood there, arms folded protectively over her chest, and listened to him cajole and order her to go, saying anything he could think of. At last he'd told her he'd marry her, if that's what she wanted.

She'd just stared at him. "I want you to *want* to marry me," she said finally in a soft voice. "I want that more than I want to be married to you."

At the time he'd accused her of not making sense, but he'd known all along what she meant. "I'll be back," he'd said at last, desperately. "I'll be back in a year or so. I'll come for you then."

She hadn't replied. And here it was, a year, two months, and three days after he'd left. He was back. He only had two weeks, but he could do a lot in that time. He'd find her. He'd persuade her that they belonged together. She had run, but she couldn't hide.

"Unka Lush-us." Little Angela ran back into the room. She came right up to him, and Pam's cough recalled Donovan to his surroundings enough so he could kneel down.

Angela piped, "Unka Lush-us pitcher."

He winced at the name. "Don-o-van," he told Angela. She stared at him blankly, holding out a piece of paper drowning in finger paint—red, black and yellow finger paint. Gingerly he took it between a thumb and forefinger. "Uh, thanks, Angela."

"What a lovely picture," Pam cooed. "Uncle Lucius will treasure it always."

"Sure," Donovan said. He straightened, feeling foolish with the picture dangling from his fingers. "Listen, thanks for the hints. I'll drive on down this morning."

Pam stood, too, lifting Angela to ride on her hip. "Will you be coming back up to the city later? Rob will want to see you. Maybe you and Thea could come for dinner some evening."

"We'll try," Donovan temporized. As much as he wanted to see Rob again, he wanted to be with Thea more. If she still rejected him, if she didn't want to get back together—if another man had stepped in to take what he'd left behind—

Donovan's lips tightened momentarily before he told himself to relax. He would simply drive to Santa Cruz, find Thea and make her see that they belonged together. No big deal.

"Hug Unka Lush-us," Angela announced. She extended her arms and reluctantly he went closer. At the last minute she launched herself at him, plastering the finger painting between them. He felt its wet gooeyness through his shirt.

"Oh, dear," Pam said, her lips twitching. "Angela darling, you made a mess of Uncle Lucius's shirt."

"It's all right," Donovan said, peeling the picture away from his shirt and looking at the result with dismay. "You can paint me another one sometime."

Refusing all of Pam's offers to wash his shirt, he left, relieved to shut the door on Angela's sniffles. He'd have to change before he could leave for Santa Cruz, but he didn't want to do it anywhere near a child.

He got into the rental car with caution, trying to keep the stain on his shirt from spreading farther. The corner gas station provided a place to change, and he took off his suit and tie with a sense of relief. He'd been a chump to get dressed for business this morning, as if scouting start-up companies instead of the love of his life. He put on jeans and a sweatshirt, filled up the car with gas and set off down Highway 1 for Santa Cruz.

It was a long drive, over two hours, and he had plenty of time to think about the choices he'd made a year ago. Now that he was back in California, New York seemed like a dream, a bad dream. True, he'd really churned up the capital for his firm, sniffed out the good start-up companies, managed to pick mostly winners, cut the inevitable losses quickly. But he'd been working constantly. Even leisure time was filled with meeting the right people, being in the right places, making contacts and talking business all the time.

He missed Thea. After the heady first few months, after he'd tired of being the workaholic wunderkind of Gaskell Associates, he'd missed her more and more. In the middle of the night he woke aching for her, for her warmth and softness in his bed.

He'd tried to keep in touch, despite her suggestion that they make a clean break. But his letters had vanished into the void, his calls had been met by a disconnect message.

The need for her had grown like a nagging heartache he couldn't quite get rid of. When Bob Metlock had told him at work that he had been chosen to find new challenges in Bellevue, he'd raised enough stink to get this vacation. Bellevue was closer to San Francisco, but not close enough.

He drove through the suburban sprawl around Pacifica and stole glances at the magnificent waves that thundered and broke around the headland where the Montara lighthouse perched. South of Half Moon Bay, the hills swept down to the ocean, wild and beautiful. He rolled down his window to let in the brisk, salty air and the cries of the gulls. Compared to this, the Atlantic coast looked like the edge of a pond.

It was good to be back in California again. It was unbelievably fine to be on his way to Thea.

CHAPTER THREE

THE MESSAGE LIGHT blinking on her answering machine sent a shiver of uneasiness gliding through Thea's spine. She rarely got telephone messages. The people currently in her life were right around her, as close as the path to the big house outside her cottage door, or the bakery she'd just left. There were often messages on the computer network that kept her tied in to the financial world. But on her telephone?

She rewound the tape, and Pam's voice came into the living room. "Thea, why aren't you there? I hate answering machines!" Angela wailed in the background, and Pam sounded even more harassed. "I thought I should tell you—but then, there really isn't any need, is there? You can—" Angela became more imperative. "Just a minute, honey. Mommy's talking—" More wailing. "Oh, this isn't working. You call me, okay?" Click. Beep.

Frowning, Thea punched out Pam's San Francisco number. No answer. Her uneasiness grew.

She tossed her bag onto the sofa and tiptoed into the bedroom. R.J. sat up in the comfortable chair, her mouth slightly open in sleep. Next to the chair was a crib, whose small occupant was also sleeping.

Leaning over the crib, Thea watched her son's back rise and fall evenly. His head was turned sideways, his sweetly curved mouth just open. Long lashes shaded rounded, rosy cheeks. He wore only a T-shirt and a diaper, and his little rump stuck up in the air.

She longed to pick him up, but he would wake soon enough and relieve the fullness that grew in her breasts. Silently she left the room.

The kitchen of her small cottage was immaculate, the way R.J. always left it. She drank a glass of milk and glanced into the washer on the back porch. It was full of clean diapers. While she thought about Pam's message, she emptied the dryer, transferred wet laundry into it and took the basket of dry clothes into the living room to fold.

It had been at least a couple of months since she'd spoken to Pam. They'd both vowed to get together soon. Would Pam have been so hassled about making a lunch date?

Possibly. Thea put it from her mind and concentrated on moving as quietly as possible. It was convenient having a washer and dryer in her cottage, but since the big house in front had no laundry facilities, people tended to drift through the garden to her place, clutching a garment or some socks that simply had to be washed right away.

Here, for instance, was one of Marlon's shirts. She tossed it over a chair and spent a moment admiring the bright purple and red hibiscus blossoms it flaunted. Marlon's collection of Hawaiian and bowling shirts was much envied by his circle of surfer friends.

And this rigid undergarment in an improbable rosy pink, with much lace trim, must be Miss Sophie's. Miss Sophie Belden's family had owned the big house since it had been built at the turn of the century by her father, a prosperous banker, for his blushing young bride. Miss Sophie hadn't come along for twenty years, their third and last daughter. The house had a lot in common with Miss Sophie's foundation—both faded and worn, but somehow incurably optimistic.

R.J. had thrown in some thick wool socks, the kind she wore with her sturdy denim coveralls and tool belt. She did odd jobs at the big house in return for her little attic room. And she'd proved invaluable to Thea in the past few months. At first it had been helping to remodel the cottage, with R.J. insisting on a more modest wage than Thea was willing to pay. And then, after Lucas was born, R.J. had moved into the position of child-minder—a nanny with a tool belt. The salary she received was welcome, Thea knew, but R.J. did far more than any salary could repay. If R.J. wanted to fill the washer with socks and coveralls, it was fine with Thea.

And the same went for Faith's gauzy cotton skirt. Faith Harper was the midwife who'd assisted at Lucas's birth. She was also the reason Thea had found this cozy little cottage tucked away in Miss Sophie's back garden. Miss Sophie had allowed the free clinic where Faith worked to occupy her unused parlor once, when they were out of a home temporarily. Faith had ended up renting one of the upstairs bedrooms, an arrangement which Miss Sophie had once confided, "led me to realize I couldn't let Papa's house stand here so empty."

When Thea had shown up at the clinic, needing prenatal care and a place to stay, Faith had suggested Miss Sophie. The gardener's cottage was in disrepair, but Thea had undertaken to put it into shape in return for a nominal rent for the first year, and other legal considerations Miss Sophie had insisted on. It was a bargain that had pleased everyone. Now, glancing around at the beamed ceilings, the random-plank floors, the casement windows open to catch the breeze, Thea couldn't believe her luck. Full of silent congratulations, she went back to her laundry.

There were suspicious pink streaks on the white crib sheets. Thea rummaged through the basket and pulled out a pair of gaudy red braces. Mr. Castigliano's, no doubt. Thea glanced in dismay from the shrunken suspenders to the streaky sheets. R.J. did not believe in pampering the laundry. You washed it, you dried it, you wore whatever came out.

Thea looked at the suspenders disgustedly. Mr. Castigliano was new at the big house, renting one of the vacant rooms on the second floor. Thea and R.J. had tried to persuade Miss Sophie to rent to a woman, but with her usual fluffy logic, she pointed out that no woman had asked to rent the room, and Mr. Castigliano had.

Thea put the suspenders on top of Marlon's shirt and went to hang the crib sheets on the line in her little backyard, where the red streaks might bleach out.

Mr. Castigliano found her there. "Hello, missy," he shouted jovially. Shouting appeared to be his main form of communication. "Seen any sign of my braces?"

"Come inside," Thea said reluctantly. "The baby's sleeping, so we need to be quiet."

"Mustn't wake the baby." His whisper was nearly as loud as normal conversation.

Thea led the way into the living room and handed him the suspenders. "They ran," she said briefly, "all over my white things. And the dryer shrank them."

"Gracious me." Mr. Castigliano accepted the braces and looked from them to Thea. "How did that happen?"

"I don't know," Thea snapped, hands on hips. "This isn't a laundry service, Mr. Castigliano. If you're going to toss something into my washer, you have to be prepared to take the consequences." She held up the last crib sheet. "Look what happened to my wash!"

Mr. Castigliano was abashed. "Sorry, missy," he said, controlling a quirk of his mouth when he looked at the pink stains. "At least it's a right pretty color."

Thea surveyed the damage and had to laugh. "It is that," she agreed. "I guess all those detergent commercials got to me for a minute there."

Mr. Castigliano nodded solemnly. "Use White-O-Rama to remove the most stubborn stains from your laundry," he said.

Thea found herself liking him. His snowy hair and grandfatherly twinkle projected a benevolent image, but he could be brash and outspoken, befitting a man who'd worked on the Boardwalk, the amusement park that graced Santa Cruz's beach. He wouldn't say how old he was, but he'd been more than a few years past retirement when arthritis finally forced him to quit.

When his laugh boomed out it was contagious, irresistible. Thea laughed, too, helplessly, but held a finger to her lips. "Napping going on," she reminded.

There was a rustling noise behind her. "I'm up," R.J. said, yawning as she came into the room. "Didn't mean to go to sleep like that."

"No problem," Thea told her. "Why don't you make yourself some tea while I take the rest of these things up to the big house?"

R.J. regarded the extraneous laundry. "I told people to take their clothes elsewhere. Guess no one listened."

"I believe Miss Belden said something about having a washer put in at the big house," Mr. Castigliano said.

R.J. and Thea exchanged looks. "There's not much likelihood of that," R.J. said bluntly. "The plumbing in there is as old as the hills, and there's no proper wiring. We looked into it when Thea moved in and wanted a washer. It was far easier to upgrade the wiring and plumbing out here than up there."

"Oh, well," Mr. Castigliano said, bright eyed. "If that's all it is perhaps I can be of help. I have a good deal of

plumbing experience, what with working on the maintenance crew at the Boardwalk for the past thirty years.''

R.J. looked skeptical. She'd been under enough sinks at
the big house to consign its plumbing to perdition.

''Let me take those things up, missy,'' Mr. Castigliano
urged. Thea was tempted, but Miss Sophie, the soul of
faded gentility, would probably faint if she was to receive
her unmentionables from Mr. Catigliano's manly hands.

''I'll walk with you,'' she said instead.

The path leading from her cottage to the back door of the
big house was crowded with feathery redwood branches, big
trusses of blooming rhododendrons and rampant climbing
roses, their fragrant blossoms filling the air.

Mr. Castigliano discoursed on plumbing all the way to the
house, and Thea had to admit he sounded knowledgeable,
despite a tendency toward florid phrasing.

He held the door open gallantly, flourishing his braces
before he began to climb the back stairs toward his room.
''Thanks again, missy,'' he boomed. ''And don't worry.
We'll have our own washer set up pretty soon!''

When Thea got to Miss Sophie's door, it was already
open. Sophia Belden stood there, watching Mr. Castigliano
with an anxious frown. ''I'm afraid you and Rosalie Jane
were right,'' she whispered, ushering Thea into her room.
''Mr. Castigliano is certainly very noisy, isn't he?''

''Perhaps he has a hearing problem,'' Thea suggested,
handing over Miss Sophie's corset. ''I'm afraid this got put
in the dryer, and it probably should have been hung on the
line.''

''That's all right.'' Miss Sophie blushed and hustled the
garment into her bedroom. She occupied the biggest part of
the old house—the former living room, dining room and
kitchen. The dining room was her bedroom now, and it and
the living room were crowded with a house-sized accumu-

lation of furniture. Lately, however, the clutter had been lessening.

Thea glanced around, concerned. "What happened to the rosewood cabinet, Miss Sophie?"

The older lady fluttered her hands in the air. "Oh, I sent it out for some repairs," she said airily.

Thea knew what that meant. "I hope you got at least a couple of hundred for it."

"Don't worry." Miss Sophie's glance was shrewd. "I took your advice and asked two different dealers in." She shook her head. "It was hard getting them out again with just the cabinet. Can you believe they tried to buy my bed right out from under me?"

"Your bed is wonderful," Thea assured her. "Don't let them have it."

Miss Sophie's triumphant smile vanished. "Not until I have to," she said gloomily. "A plumber came to see about putting in the washer—I don't want to inconvenience you, Theadora."

Thea felt guilty. "Nonsense," she said briskly. "You're welcome to borrow my washer any time."

Miss Sophie shook her head with gentle dignity. "I couldn't do that," she said. "And somehow, my old wringer machine gets harder and harder to use. Anyway, the plumber was quite disheartening about the cost to fix my pipes."

Thea could imagine. "Mr. Castigliano seems to be an expert plumber," she offered. "Let him take a look."

Miss Sophie brightened. "What an excellent idea. And I could take it off his rent, you know, and not be beholden." She smiled gallantly at Thea. "One more room to rent, and I know some nice person is going to show up wanting it soon. Then my income will be more settled."

Thea bestowed an impulsive hug on her landlady. "I know how hard it is for you to see strangers living in your home," she said gently.

Miss Sophie shook her head with a faint smile. "Actually, my dear," she confided, "I find I enjoy it immensely. All those years after my sister died, I just rattled around alone in here." She leaned forward. "If Faith hadn't wanted to rent a room, and then you in the cottage, I might have gotten a little strange!"

"Never," Thea murmured, smothering a smile. Miss Sophie was already a little strange, but in the nicest possible way. Though she couldn't be more than seventy, she was like a throwback to the mores of her turn-of-the-century parents.

"And I have you to thank for the funds to put a kitchen in across the way. It is pleasant to have my own kitchen to myself. I don't think," she added confidentially, "that I would enjoy sharing a kitchen with Marlon, dear boy though he is."

"No, indeed," Thea agreed. It was only through R.J.'s heroic efforts that the communal kitchen was kept in anything approaching order. Marlon Jackson was like the Charles Schulz cartoon character, shedding disorder wherever he went. "Speaking of your investment fund, Miss Sophie, I think it'll have dividends enough to buy your washer and dryer, maybe even pay for some of the plumbing."

Miss Sophie's faded cheeks turned pink. "That's wonderful," she said, clasping her hands. "You truly are a magician, Theadora. To think that little dab of money from the claw-foot table has grown so much!" She pressed Thea's arm gratefully. "Just keep—how do you say it?—rolling it over, dear. I have something else in mind for the washer."

Her gaze drifted to the magnificent walnut-inlaid side-board that covered one wall near the door.

"You don't need to sell your treasures, Miss Sophie."

"I want to, my dear." Miss Sophie turned her clear gaze on Thea. "When you get to be my age, it's time to let go of material possessions. I believe Papa would say the same, if he knew that the furniture he chose so carefully was sup-porting me in my old age."

Thea kissed the soft, wrinkled cheek. "You're the youngest old lady I know," she said impudently. "See you later."

Across the hall was the former parlor and study. When Miss Sophie had rented the gardener's cottage out back to Thea over a year ago, she'd been desperate for income, her own small annuity seeming smaller every year. Thea had invested a nest egg for her, choosing stable yet growth-oriented stock that would supplement Miss Sophie's in-come so that she wouldn't have to keep selling her assets—the wonderful furniture her parents had commissioned from some fine cabinetmakers in the area. And Thea had plugged a small portion of the money into a wildly speculative start-up, just in case.

It had turned out better than she could have hoped. The start-up went straight up, split two-for-one and was ac-quired by a larger company for money and shares. There was enough profit on one small transaction to adapt the ground floor of the house so that Miss Sophie could pro-vide kitchen privileges to lodgers without having to share her own kitchen.

Now the former parlor was an informal sitting room, with a sturdy, comfortable sofa and chairs, and a TV set. The study had been transformed into a kitchen-dining area; nothing fancy, but very functional.

Thea glanced into the kitchen. The counters were wiped clean and the dishes stacked neatly in the drainer. Marlon must not have come down yet.

Climbing the stairs, she ran her hand along the curving mahogany rail and thought about Miss Sophie selling her furniture.

Thea could understand that feeling of being controlled by possessions. When she'd decided to move to Santa Cruz after Donovan had left, she'd been faced with a condominium full of them. She had most of them still, put into storage, and each month when she paid the bill she berated herself for not selling the stuff, partly to avoid the memories thinking about it evoked. That walnut commode they'd found in a junk store in Port Costa. The redwood-and-glass coffee table they'd commissioned a Mendocino craftsman to make.

Her cottage was small and Lucas's paraphernalia took up a good bit of room, so she was spared the daily association with some of the ghosts of her past life. But if she sold the things, it would help to put her firmly in the future, ceasing to nourish that last little hope that Donovan would return to her.

It was a good idea to clear away the past every so often, she thought, stopping in front of Marlon's door. If only it would serve to permanently cure her of yearning after that man.

She knocked briskly at Marlon's door. There was no answer, and after another knock she walked over to the big arched window at the end of the hall that overlooked the street. Marlon's transportation was easy to spot, and it was nowhere in sight.

"He must have been up early this morning," Thea muttered, stalking back to his room. She threw open the door. Anyone unfamiliar with Marlon Jackson's housekeeping methods might have assumed a burglary had taken place. Thea knew better. She disregarded the tornado-stricken bed, the jumble of sunburn creams and lotions that cluttered the dresser, the wildly patterned shorts and shirts that were strewn over the floor. Stepping over a heap of rubbery wet suits, she went to the closet, found a hanger and put the hibiscus-print shirt onto it. There was nothing else hanging in the closet, although the floor was knee-deep in shoes, swim fins, sandals and assorted scuba gear.

Thea closed Marlon's door behind her and walked toward the back stairs. Mr. Castigliano's door was closed, too, but Faith's was open. Thea looked in.

Faith was sorting pictures at the desk in one corner. In the middle of her room was a enormous bed, set low to the floor, where women in the early stages of labor were sometimes found.

"Getting your album in order?" Thea strolled into the room. Faith glanced up with a welcoming smile. She was a tiny weather-beaten woman of indeterminate age, with long, straight gray-black hair and the liveliest eyes Thea had ever seen. They positively snapped in her small, pointed face.

"Where's my baby?" Faith accepted the skirt Thea held out. "Thanks for letting me monopolize your washer. Lucas napping?"

"He's down with R.J. I've got to go feed him in a minute." Thea looked at some of the pictures. Faith specialized in home births, and her pictures showed babies arriving in fancy bedrooms and in trailers.

"I've got a picture of Lucas's birth in here somewhere," Faith said, searching through the pile of photos. "Here you go."

Thea stared at the picture. There she was, propped up in bed. And there, whizzing into the world, was young Lucas D. Willits. Tears came to her eyes; she blinked them away.

"Can I get a copy of this?" She cleared her throat. "I didn't even know anyone was taking pictures."

"R.J. took it. I thought she'd given you a copy." Faith made a note on a piece of paper. "She's photographed a few births for me. She seems to have a real knack for it."

Thea looked at a few more pictures, then said goodbye. Faith replied absently; her attention was already back on the album she was putting together.

Thea hurried down the stairs and along the path to her cottage, forgetting the uneasiness Pam's strange message had aroused. The tightness in her breasts told her that somewhere nearby was a baby in need of lunch. And when you were the meal ticket, it behooved you to be in the right place at the right time. She would lie down with Lucas while he nursed, and get a rest herself. Soon it would be time to go back to the bakery and work on the books, making sure her new life stayed financially sound.

HELEN MACAPHEE WENT into the kitchen for a tray of brownies, glancing around to see if Thea had returned. It was nearly noon, but there was no sign of her partner.

Shrugging, she slid the tray of brownies out of the rack and carried it into the store. She had learned over the course of the past year or so that Thea was to be relied on. She'd arrive soon. Maybe she'd bring Lucas with her.

Going back again for a tray of croissants, Helen looked over at the playpen that had been set up by the desk, where Thea spent a lot of time. As usual, Lucas's toys were lined up neatly against one side of the mesh wall, with a couple of blankets draped over the other side. It was so domestic and cozy looking that it made Helen smile.

But it was more evidence of the change that had happened in fourteen months. And Helen was no friend to change.

She shrugged her shoulders and rolled her head to get rid of the stiffness that plagued her occasionally these days. In six months she would be forty. Not that it bothered her. Oh, no, forty was fine with her. Life began then. And hers seemed to be taking a turn for the better in the past year.

Though she thought she didn't look forty, Helen could not deny that the years since the divorce had not been easy. At first, after Sean's betrayal, she had been dazed with the pain. The divorce, the settlement, had all passed without her really being aware of it. A year later she'd woken to the fact that she was thirty-three, with no husband to provide for her future, as she'd been unconsciously assuming. Her part-time job as a baker's assistant barely paid the rent. And she wasn't getting younger.

Buying Babycakes had been fortuitous—it had been the first small business she looked at that she could afford. She'd had the luck or sense to get a ten-year lease on the funky building—the rate had seemed steep then, but all around her, businesses were paying five times as much now. She'd put everything into building her clientele, giving a good product for a great price, coming up with new and creative breads and pastries.

Those had been good years in retrospect, though at the time she hadn't realized it. The work had been unending; it had been her life, allowing no time for thoughts of Sean, of his unfaithfulness and his sudden, annihilating request for a divorce, so he could marry the other woman she hadn't even suspected.

She had been, she realized now, content, after a fashion. And then Raymund Neves had come along. She snorted to herself. "I fell into his hand like a ripe apple, that's for sure."

"Pardon?" Maria looked up at her from arranging what was left of the raisin bread.

"Nothing." Helen slid the tray of croissants into the display case. She had been lonely, vulnerable. Raymund had been a lot of help at first, when she'd hired him to do the accounts and prepare her quarterly tax statements. They'd gotten—close.

"Stupidity," Helen muttered, checking the cakes in the refrigerated display case. She must have been lonelier than she knew, to let Raymund get under her defenses like that.

Raymund had persuaded her to invest in a computer—to make her life easier, he'd said. The only thing it made easier was his access to her funds.

"Never again," she vowed under her breath. No man would ever get close enough to take her for a ride again. It hurt to feel she was no more perceptive than Betty, the hairdresser. She had let Raymund insinuate himself into her life, let him sweet-talk her into bed. And the next thing she knew, she was cleaned out.

Forcing a smile past the bitterness that accompanied memories of her foolishness, Helen waited on customers. She ignored the yawning void behind her where the remodeling crew had torn out partitions and pried off the old plywood paneling. The bakery had closed for a week to get the new ovens and the thirty-quart mixer installed. Soon they would need to close again to finish up the front of the store. It would take a couple of weeks of frantic work, but the contractor was clearing his calendar for them, thanks to generous bribes of his favorite almond croissants.

When the work was done, there would be new display cases trimmed with polished oak, the espresso bar, ceiling fans and neatly plastered walls to set off her collection of old bentwood chairs and oak tables.

It would look very nice, Helen admitted. Was she a total dog in the manger because it galled her that someone else's capital was providing the new look? Babycakes would be a fine, upscale bakery, granted, but certainly not the funky storefront she'd bought with a shoestring and in which she'd invested her creative energies.

"I'll take another croissant for the office," the woman at the register said. Helen bagged the pastry and made change, accepting the woman's compliments with a smile. Thea had been like that, she mused, watching the woman walk away. She'd worn a neat business suit and nibbled pastries in an office, secure in the knowledge that a paycheck would roll around every so often.

Now she worked at a crowded desk where everything was often dusty with flour, where a baby crowed from the playpen.

There was a lull in the customers, and Helen allowed herself to think about things from Thea's perspective. Helen had spent the first couple of months of their association secretly resenting her new partner. Thea had amassed enough money to put the bakery back on its feet, to buy the new equipment and pay for remodeling the front, not to mention paying off the creditors who'd been yapping at Helen's heels. It had seemed unfair that after so much hard work, Helen should have so little to show for it and have to hand a half interest in that little to an interloper. A woman, moreover, who was eight years younger than herself and infinitely more successful.

She didn't feel that way about Thea anymore. Helen assured herself of this while she put a birthday cake in a box. Thea wasn't overbearing with her suggestions. Everything she'd done, in fact, had worked out fine. She'd done a cost analysis on all the baked goods and revised the price list accordingly. And the old customers had cheerfully paid more—sometimes a lot more.

Maria called down the counter. "Helen, we need more almond crescents." Nodding absently, Helen went into the workroom to get them.

She took a moment for a drink of water, staring at the bank of new ovens Thea had suggested and paid for. She'd been more than generous, Helen admitted. That was the real problem. Helen felt like an employee in her own business. True, she was in charge of baking operations, but her expertise was all she had to put into the partnership—that and the lease on the building. Thea had really done everything else.

When she went back out with the almond crescents, there was a man standing by the cash register. He was tall, with dark hair slashing across his forehead and a taut, focused look about him.

Maria came to take the tray of cookies. "He's asking some questions," she said, nodding toward the man. "I told him you're the one to talk to."

Helen approached the man, who held a plate with a big hunk of the lemon-poppy-seed cake on it. "You wanted some information?"

The man cleared his throat and glanced around. "You're the owner here?"

"Yes," Helen said, then added, "part owner, actually."

"Is...is the other part here?" He craned his neck to look past her into the kitchen.

There was something about him that made Helen wary. "Why do you want to know?" she asked pointedly.

"Is it Thea Willits?" The knuckles of his hand whitened noticeably as he clutched his fork. "I heard she was involved with a bakery down here."

"Do you know Thea?" Helen was surprised. Though a couple with a youngster occasionally came in on weekends, they were the only people Thea had introduced from her previous life. Thinking of Lucas, whose father was never mentioned, Helen scrutinized the man in front of her carefully.

She could see no real resemblance to Thea's baby, except for the gray-blue eyes, and many babies had those.

The man seemed to force himself to relax. "I did. Been out of town for a while."

Helen looked him up and down. He appeared civilized. "She may be in soon. Why don't you find a table, read the paper or something? Give it a while."

The man's jaw clenched, but he accepted what she said. "At least this is the right place." He glanced around the room. "I almost didn't recognize it. You're having some work done."

"You've been here before?" Helen poured a cup of coffee and handed it to him. "On the house," she said when he reached for his wallet.

"We used—" The man stopped and corrected himself. "I used to come to Santa Cruz pretty often. We always stopped in here for your carrot-herb bread before going back to the city."

Helen noticed his slip back to "we" and wondered if the other person was Thea. Was this the man she would never talk about? There must have been one, Helen figured, at least at some point. After all, it took two to produce the occupant of the playpen.

There were other customers to take care of, so she let the man find a table, stealing surreptitious glances at him while she worked the cash register.

He was good-looking, she thought grudgingly. But there was something about him—some hardness of purpose—that made her wonder if she should have sent him on his way. As ambivalent as she was about having Thea as a partner, the alternative was much worse. If this man had the emotional clout to take Thea away, what would become of Baby-cakes?

Her speculations were interrupted. Another man approached the cash register with neither plate nor cup in hand. He looked around at the work in progress with a stony expression. Years of running a business made alarms go off in Helen's head, rousing her hackles.

"You Helen Macaphee?" He eyed her across the counter, like some kind of specimen in a bottle, Helen thought.

"Yep." She returned the look with interest. "And yes, we do have permission from the board of health to stay open during this phase of building. We'll be closing down soon to finish it off."

"I'm not from the health department." He eyed her appraisingly. "You're a feisty little thing, aren't you?"

"I don't care if you're from the president. State your business and leave out the personal remarks." Hands on hips, Helen glared at him. She had always been sensitive about her lack of height.

"Sorry, sorry." He held up his hands in mock horror. "I didn't mean to make a crack. It just slipped out." When he smiled, dimples creased his cheeks, doing interesting things to the sandy freckles that spattered his face. He was in his late thirties, she judged, medium height, with a lean, rangy body. His hair had been probably carrot red when he was young, but was toned down now with a liberal dose of gray.

Helen blinked, wondering why she was paying so much attention to a man whose smile didn't really reach his eyes. Nice eyes, she noted, the clear bright blue of noonday sky.

"It's not the president I'm from," the man added. "Not directly, anyway. Name's Lasswell. From the IRS."

She stared at him.

"Internal Revenue Service," he said helpfully.

"I know what IRS means."

"Do you?" The smile left his face. He set an attaché case on the counter and opened it. "We were wondering, at the office, if you did. We've been sending you all these notices." He held up a sheaf of papers and fanned them out in front of her. "And you never responded. Not once."

Helen fastened her stunned gaze to the papers. Even from where she stood, she could tell that they weren't about anything good.

She cleared her throat. "I—we never got them."

"Is that it?" The affable smile was back in place, the one that brought no real warmth to his face. He leaned against the counter and glanced around. "Looks like you've been putting a lot of money into your place lately."

Helen frowned. "What is this about, anyway? What were the notices for?"

A little line appeared between thick red eyebrows. "Tax delinquency, Ms. Macaphee." He looked around again. "Is there somewhere we can go to talk? Or did you want to let everyone in on this?"

Helen glanced quickly around. A couple of people, long-time customers who often spent a morning over coffee and Danish, were looking at the counter. So was the man who waited for Thea.

"Come back here," she said abruptly. "Maria, could you cover the counter for me?"

"Sure," Maria replied, staring speculatively at Lasswell.

In the back room, Helen led the way to the desk. There were only two chairs in the room, one at the desk and another straight chair in front of it. Lasswell took the desk chair before she could. She'd be damned if she'd sit in the straight chair, like a criminal in front of a judge. She perched on the edge of the desk, gaining a small advantage in height, and folded her arms across her chest. "What's all this about, anyway? I paid my taxes every year."

Lasswell shook his head. "Over a year ago," he said, opening his attaché case again, "you missed three quarterly filings of forms 940 and 941, together with payment of employees' withholding and social security."

"Over a year ago?" Helen was glad she was sitting down. "Three payments?"

"In July, October and January," Lasswell enumerated. "It takes us a while to catch up to this kind of delinquency. We began sending notices this January. We've sent four notices, each clearly delineating the amount of withholding and social security you're in arrears, the amount of penalty and the interest, which incidentally is accruing every day." He shrugged, smiling that easy smile. "So far, no response. So I decided to visit in person."

"And you—you're an IRS agent?" Helen stared at him, grasping dazedly for facts. Her mind was telling her that it couldn't be true, it was a dream. Penalties, interest—she barely heard his answer.

"Revenue officer, at the Santa Cruz field office."

"It's impossible." Helen returned her gaze to his. Though he was careful to give nothing away, she sensed his disbelief. "I saw the forms. I signed them, for heaven's sake."

"Nevertheless, the forms and payment did not reach the IRS."

There was a note of implacability in Lasswell's voice, masking the near-lilt of his words. "You're Irish," she blurted out.

"My mother is." The lilt was back. "Ms. Macaphee, do you have an attorney, someone to advise you?"

Helen wasn't listening. The back door had opened and Thea stood there, Lucas on her hip. She stared from Helen to the stranger seated at her desk.

"Thea," Helen gasped, springing to her feet. Thea had a handle on money matters. She would get to the bottom of it. Helen had never felt really competent with forms or paperwork.

Thea put down the enormous bag of Lucas's requirements for the afternoon and came forward.

"This is Mr. Lasswell from the IRS," Helen said numbly. "He wants to know why I didn't file my forms 940 and 941."

"But you have," Thea said. "I have the copies right here."

"The IRS has been writing letters to me," Helen moaned. "Can I see those letters?"

Silently Lasswell handed them to her. Clutching Lucas, Thea squatted in front of the filing cabinet while Helen leaned against the wall and scanned the letters feverishly.

"Here you are," Thea said, handing Lasswell a file. "Quarterly payments for the last five years."

Lasswell glanced through the file. "I see you have copies of the forms for the quarters in question," he said to Helen, who paid no attention. "But no receipts."

"The canceled checks," Thea pointed out, shifting Lucas to her shoulder.

Lasswell shook his head, examining one check. "These checks don't have the IRS deposit stamp on them," he insisted. "They look like dummies to me. Doctored to provide a receipt."

"Listen to this!" Helen interrupted. "...'seize your property, wages or other assets—'" She looked up in horror. "They're going to take my bakery away!"

"Of course they won't," Thea said stoutly. "This is some kind of misunderstanding, Helen. Mr. Lasswell will find that you sent the payments." She plucked one of the notices from Helen's nerveless fingers and perused it, frowning. "It's no wonder she didn't get it," Thea pointed out to the man seated at her desk. "It wasn't mailed to the bakery. What address is this?"

Helen stared at the typed words. "I don't know," she said, mystified. "How could they make a mistake like that? How could they send it to the wrong address?"

"If a mistake was made," the IRS man said smoothly, "perhaps it was yours, Ms. Macaphee. Or yours, Ms.—?"

"I'm Thea Willits, Helen's partner in the bakery." Thea offered a polite handshake to the man. "Since I take care of the books, perhaps you should be talking to me."

"Perhaps I should." Lasswell abandoned Helen for Thea. He smiled easily on Lucas, who gurgled back, but his eyes were cold on Thea. "How long have you been keeping the books here?"

"Since last May. You'll see I sent in the payment coupon on time." Thea leaned forward and found the right paper.

Lasswell turned back to Helen. "Who was your book-keeper before then?"

Helen straightened and stared at Thea, who stared back. Their mouths shaped the name at the same instant. "Raymund."

"Thea?"

The voice came from the door into the front. Thea's head turned, and Helen remembered. "Oh, yeah, there's some guy waiting to see you, Thea."

Thea wasn't listening. In the doorway stood the man who had asked after her. He stared at her now, in an intense, hungry way.

"Donovan." Thea's eyes locked on the man. He strode around the Hobart toward her, oblivious to the baby that perched on her arm.

"Thea—" He reached for her, giving her a gentle hug, a kiss on the cheek, though Helen could see he wanted to make it the lips. "Why, what's this?"

Thea pulled away from him. "This is my baby," she said, nervous laughter belying the tears that sparkled in her eyes.

There was complete silence for a moment. Helen glanced at Lasswell, who watched the scene with bright-eyed interest, leaning back in the desk chair as if the whole thing were a performance put on for his benefit. And maybe he thought just that.

She stepped forward. "Why don't you two go upstairs and talk," she said, looking at Thea's strained face and the stranger's thunderstruck incredulity. "I'll handle this for now."

Thea allowed herself to be pushed out the door, and the man called Donovan followed her in an ominous way. "Will you be all right?" Helen searched her partner's face.

"Fine," Thea said hollowly. "I knew it was coming."

Helen looked anxiously at the man's furious face. "He won't hit you or anything, will he?"

Donovan heard and sent her a fulminating look. "Don't be ridiculous."

"Violence isn't his bag," Thea assured her with a ghost of a smile. "I'll be back soon."

Helen turned back to the desk, squared her shoulders and sat down in the vacant chair. She looked Lasswell in the eye, hating the faint smile she could detect beneath his official demeanor.

"Now," she said, leaning forward, "I'm going to tell you about my erstwhile bookkeeper, Mr. Raymund Neves. And by the way, I already know I should have checked his references more carefully, so don't bother to point it out."

Lasswell steepled his fingers and watched her from beneath impossibly long golden-red eyelashes. "I wouldn't dare," he said softly. "Tell on."

CHAPTER FOUR

LUCAS WAS INTRIGUED by the beams of colored light that filtered through a stained-glass ornament in Helen's living room window. He clapped his hands—a new accomplishment—and crowed, trying to imprison the rainbow that washed over his face.

Thea pulled a chair over so she could sit down near the reflections, Lucas on her lap. She wished that Donovan would sit down, too, but he was already pacing from the living room into the kitchen, looking around with eyes too angry to see more than the superficial layer of clutter.

She cleared her throat. "So how have you been?" she asked inanely.

He stopped by the table covered with bags of herbs and shot her a look compounded of bafflement and wounded pride. "I've been fine," he said tightly. "Isn't that what I'm supposed to say? Fine, thanks. And yourself?"

Thea tried a weak smile. "I've been fine, also. I've been—busy." She gestured helplessly around. "Everything's changed, Donovan."

"I can see that." He picked up one of the bags from those that crowded the kitchen table and opened it. "Good Lord," he muttered, sniffing, "is this legal? What is this stuff, anyway? What does that woman do with it? Looks like witches' brew or something."

"Probably pennyroyal or raspberry leaf," Thea said, brushing off the topic of Helen's health-food kick. "Donovan—I hope you can understand. About Lucas."

He swung around, fixing her with the full force of his sharp gray eyes. "Who's Lucas?" He glanced down at the baby, his face turning immobile. "This?"

"There's no other man in my life," Thea said steadily. "Nor has there been. Just him." She took a breath. "And you."

"You're saying he's my son," Donovan said tonelessly. "Don't bother. I knew it as soon as I saw him. You were pregnant, that night I told you about New York." The tight set of his jaw quivered just a little. "It seems you forgot to mention it."

"I'm sorry." In all the years they had known each other, Thea had never seen this kind of emotion on Donovan's face. She had always known about his ambition, his drive. And from the beginning he could reveal to her, if to few others, the tenderness and softness hidden in his nature. But never before had she seen his pain.

"No, I didn't tell you," she whispered. "I couldn't."

He passed a hand over his face. "Did you think for one instant that I would have left if I'd known?"

"Of course not!" She half rose to go to him and then thought better of it. "I knew you would marry me if I told you. And then we would have both gone to New York, and nothing would have been right."

"And you think it's right now?" He crossed the floor until he stood in front of her chair, not touching Lucas, who turned his head from one person to another like an infant spectator at a sporting event.

This spectator, though, didn't know the rules. The vibrating tension in Donovan's voice got through to his son.

Lucas began to look worried. Thea hugged him closer, grateful for his solid warmth on her lap.

"Donovan," she began, keeping her voice even to avoid alarming Lucas more, "you wanted and needed to take the New York promotion. I wanted and needed to make a change in my life. But going to New York wouldn't have been good for me." She could see the hurt and anger surfacing in him. "I'll bet you've been working long hours, right?"

"Yes," he said reluctantly. "But if you had been with me—"

"You still would have worked long hours, but you would have felt guilty for not spending more time with your pregnant, jobless, friendless wife," she said, trying not to sound defensive.

"So you moved down here, where you could be pregnant, friendless, jobless and totally alone." The corporate shark was appearing now, getting the upper hand in the argument. Thea had rarely seen this side of him, since in their life together she'd played the conciliator, jollying Donovan out of his go-for-the-throat tactics during any disagreements.

But she was damned if she'd take that role now. "If you want me to apologize," she said coldly, "you're out of line. I did what I had to do. As a result, I'm part owner of a business, I have made good friends, and I have my son." Her arms tightened fractionally on Lucas. "I've been happy this past year."

He turned away, but she could see she'd hurt him. "Donovan," she cried. "I'm sorry. But it's the truth. I missed you like crazy, I resented that you weren't here, I—felt guilty for not telling you. But I was happy. I have a good life here."

"I can see that you have," he said, his defenses well in place now. "Your business is being audited by the IRS, your new partner is evidently a crook or a fool, you're wasting your talent for investment, and you're changing diapers all day and night. A truly enviable life!"

She held on to her temper. "How was yours in New York? Fascinating business, delightful social whirl, nightclubs into the wee hours, the excitement of Wall Street?"

He took a deep breath, and his shoulders slumped. "I worked forty-eight hours a day," he admitted. "I missed you so much." He dropped to his knees beside the chair, bringing up one hand to brush her hair back behind her ear. "Why did you cut me off, Thea? I almost quit several times so I could come and find out what happened to you. Only Rob letting me know you were okay stopped me."

She flinched away from his hand. The touch of those strong fingers sent suppressed longings reeling through her. Lucas shifted uneasily on her lap.

"It seemed best," she said, trying to hide her breathlessness. "I—I really didn't know if you would come back."

"If I had known about—Lucas," Donovan said, glancing at him, "I would have been back like a shot." His hand moved from Thea's face to stroke briefly, wonderingly, along the soft skin of Lucas's cheek. The baby stared gravely at him.

"I know." Thea watched this encounter with a mixture of emotions so strong they almost choked her. She cleared her throat. "I didn't want you to come back because of Lucas. Or even in spite of him."

"I didn't come to stay." Donovan got to his feet, turning away. He spoke over his shoulder. "Or rather, to stay for just a few days." He rubbed the back of his neck. "I'm on vacation."

The words slammed into her brain. He hadn't come to stay. She'd been supposing that he was back, that he would be there, that after they got past his hurt and anger, they could be together again.

"Of course," she said stupidly. "Vacation. California is a good place for a vacation."

"Damn it, Thea," Donovan began, turning to glare at her.

But it was too much for Lucas. Twisting in Thea's arms, he began to cry.

"Now, now, sweetie," Thea murmured, cradling him against her shoulder. "It's all right. It's okay."

Donovan watched Thea and repressed the impulse to flee. She was the same woman he'd lived with, the woman he'd valued and loved and missed like crazy the past year.

But there was a totally different woman there, too. The one who comforted a baby in the most natural way, who had calmly discarded everything about their life together and achieved happiness anyway.

Resentment burned within him. He had missed her so much, had been lonely and unhappy, and she had been having the time of her life. And beneath the resentment was worry. What could he offer her now to tempt her to join her fate to his once more? She had completed her life without reference to him.

The baby in her arms still made noises that he found unpleasant, demanding cries accompanied by full-scale fist sucking. Turning slightly away from him, Thea lifted her shirt and put his son to her breast.

His son. Donovan tasted the words while he watched the two of them. Thea looked different than she had over a year ago. Her hair was longer, sun streaked and brushing her shoulders. There were faint shadows under her eyes that spoke of interrupted sleep and heavier responsibilities. He knew from touching her a moment ago that her skin was as smooth and silky as ever—almost as soft as the baby's. The feel of her made desire rush through him, nearly overpowering him.

Lucas made a greedy slurping noise that connected to and somehow caused a small sharp pain near Donovan's heart. He wasn't surprised that the baby liked suckling at Thea's breast. This time he identified the pain as jealousy. He was jealous of a baby—his baby. It was shaming.

"So you're vacationing." Thea had turned her attention to him now. Donovan dropped into a chair across from her, wishing he could have had another cup of coffee to sharpen his wits for this confrontation. He needed to win it, to come out the other side with this woman and his former happiness intact. But the baby was a total unknown, throwing the whole equation off. "Planning to get in a little sailboarding, maybe some wine-tasting?"

He shook his head irritably. Damn it, she knew him better than that. "I'm not taking a vacation," he snapped. "I'm here to see you. I took off from work and flew out here to talk to you."

She shook her head in wonder. "And they let you take off just like that? They didn't even tell you to scout a few good start-ups while you were here?"

"As a matter of fact," he began, and then unwillingly smiled. "You're too sharp for your own good," he growled. "They did mention it, but I turned them down. I can't get too concerned about cash flows and paybacks when I need to talk to you."

She turned her head away a little, and he could see her trying to hide a smile. "That's nice, I guess," she said carefully. "What did you want to talk about?"

"About us, what else?" He scowled briefly at Lucas. "I didn't expect this little spanner in the works."

As if he understood, Lucas stopped his slurping for a moment and rolled one eye at Donovan. The gentleness that had been growing in Thea's big brown eyes frosted over.

"Don't blame Lucas," she warned. "He had no control over any of it."

"I don't blame anyone." Donovan couldn't sit down for all the nervous adrenaline that poured through his system. "All of us did what we had to do." He paced through the room again, wishing desperately for a cup of coffee. "You say you've been happy this past year." He stopped in the kitchen archway to look at the picture of mother and child. Lucas was on the other side now, his greedy sucking modulating into soft, contented sighs. It was enough for him to be held in Thea's arms, nourished from her body. Donovan envied him.

"I have been happy," Thea said, her voice so low he had to go closer to hear it. "But I admit that when I thought of you, which was often—" she gave him a fleeting smile "—I missed you. I wanted you. And I felt bad for not telling you about Lucas. But I didn't want you to be here from a sense of duty. I still don't want that. You needn't feel obliged. Lucas and I can get along quite well."

Donovan tried to deal with the jumble of emotions her brave words brought him. "You have so far," he said at last, slowly. "Tell me, Thea. Was it an accident? Or did you mean to get pregnant?"

The red color washed up her cheeks as his words sank in. "It was unintentional," she said, flinging up her chin in the gesture he knew so well. "After all, we shared the responsibility for birth control—or at least that was my belief."

"True." He lowered his head. "But once you knew— why? Why did you choose him over me?"

The words were out before he'd even framed them in his mind.

Thea stared at him. "Is that how you see it?"

"No." He rubbed his forehead. "Maybe underneath. I don't want to see it that way. It just—came out." He tried a smile. "Maybe I'm in shock."

Lucas seemed to be finished. Thoughtfully Thea pulled down her shirt and held the baby on her lap, patting his back. "Actually, I can understand that. But it wasn't a choice between you and the baby—not really." She shook her head. "Once I knew I was pregnant," she said simply, "it was clear to me that I wanted a baby. *The* baby. Lucas, as it turned out." She looked squarely at him, her face serious. "I knew it was something we didn't agree on. That's why I didn't tell you, try to convince you. I thought—I still think—that it was simpler, cleaner, to let you go your way while I went mine. If you came back, we could decide where to go from here."

He uttered a short laugh. "You make it sound very simple."

"It is simple, on one level." Lucas burped loudly, and Thea gave him a little squeeze. "What did you come back for?"

"For you." He wanted to be forceful, to demand the return of her affections, but bravado deserted him. "I love you, Thea. I've loved you all this time. I want to be with you again."

Her mouth twisted into the travesty of a smile and she looked away. "Oh, Donovan." She rubbed her chin against the downy hair on Lucas's head. "I don't know what to tell you. I loved you so long, but I've put that love away. I don't know if it can come back again or not."

"I see." Thea had always rushed to comfort and soothe in the past, when he had felt hurt or angry. It was all too obvious she didn't intend to soothe him this time around. "Is there any use in my sticking around?"

It was Thea's turn to laugh. Distracted, she ran her hand through her hair and looked around at the untidy apartment. "You certainly chose your time to come visiting. Things might be complicated until we get this tax mess straightened out." She gazed at him, and he could see the old Thea in her look of appeal. "What do you want to do, Donovan? What do you want from me?"

Even as stricken as he was by the fear that things were over between them, he could still be ravished by the sight of her dimple. He wanted her so badly—much too badly to let her know, for fear of driving her further away. "Take me home," he replied at last. "Even if you're going to throw me back into the jungle, at least give me a decent meal first." He tried a smile, cajoling, low-key. "I promise, no heavy scenes if you don't want them. I'll even look over the books for you, if you'd like some financial advice."

The phone rang, interrupting Thea's reply. She hoisted Lucas to her hip and answered with one eye on Donovan, as if he was a mirage that might fade if she turned her back.

Helen was on the line, sounding harassed. "Thea? Everything okay up there?"

"Dandy," Thea said, trying to sound calm. "How about down there?"

"Things are not so fine." There was a note of false cheer in Helen's voice, almost disguising the panic Thea could detect. "The revenuer wants to go over the books with you."

"That's all I need," Thea muttered. Donovan, she could see, was studying Lucas, his gray eyes appraising. Was she fooling herself to think she could detect warmth in that flinty gaze?

"I have to get back to work right now," she said abruptly, hanging up the phone. "But of course I'll give you dinner. Do you have a place to stay?"

"Not yet," he murmured, still gazing at his son. Thea felt vague flutters of alarm. She wanted Donovan to accept Lucas, didn't she? Unconsciously her arms tightened around her precious burden.

"Well, you can sleep on the sofa bed if you like," she offered, feeling a strange mixture of reluctance and anticipation. "The nights can be rather unrestful, though."

"Can they?" His voice was a husky murmur, and his eyes found hers, a light burning in them that was instantly familiar.

"Lucas wakes up a lot," she said hurriedly. "Sometimes. Sometimes he sleeps through the night." *I'm babbling,* she thought, trying to stop the words tumbling out of her mouth. It was no use. "Did you plan to stay long? How—what—"

Donovan came toward her. He put his hands on her arms, Lucas imprisoned between the two of them. "It all depends," he said quietly. "We have to talk, Thea."

"Yes. Yes, we do." She twisted nervously away from him. "But right now I have to talk to someone else. That IRS man is waiting downstairs." She turned back to him, trying to make him understand. "At dinnertime, all right? We'll talk then."

"Fine."

He followed her to the door, down the outside steps. The breeze had freshened since morning; there were clouds piled on the sea's horizon. Closer to shore, long curls of wave frothed and broke against the sand.

Behind her, Donovan drew in deep breaths. "This air is wonderful, compared to New York," he murmured.

"I can imagine," Thea said over her shoulder. "When I moved, I felt my whole body unclench, just going from San Francisco to here."

She was at the back door of the bakery and would have gone inside if he hadn't stopped her with a hand on her arm.

"Look here," he said, turning her to face him. "I don't know where you live, and I don't want to sit around here waiting for you to finish with the IRS guy."

"Of course not," Thea agreed fervently. If she could be so muddled by him when they were alone, she couldn't imagine being able to speak coherently to a third person. "I'll draw you a map of where I live, and you can meet me there around five. I know you can find a lot to entertain you in Santa Cruz."

"Right." He watched her as she sketched on the back of the bank deposit slip that was the only piece of paper she found in the big bag slung over her shoulder. Feeling his gaze, her fingers shook slightly when she drew in the long driveway that went behind the big house to end near her cottage. "I thought I might visit a record store or two, see what's different along the Pacific Garden Mall. I'll get some lunch and meet you around five, then."

"Okay." She watched him walk away, climb into a shiny rental car and drive off. Taking a deep breath, she squared her shoulders and went through the door.

"I THINK THAT'S THE BULK of it, Ms. Willits." Patrick Lasswell stacked the last sheaf of documents into his briefcase and suppressed the urge to rub his head. He wasn't sure exactly when the headache had started, but soon after he'd begun to realize that this would be no clear-cut case of someone trying to shortchange the government.

The woman across from him flipped through the contents of the file folder. "If I run across anything more," she said, smiling warily at him, "I'll photocopy it for you. And could you let me have those things back as soon as you've copied them? I dislike incomplete files."

"These certainly appear very complete," Patrick admitted grudgingly. It wasn't that he wanted this pleasant lady and her baby to get into trouble. The baby had sat patiently in a playpen, carefully chewing on some weird-looking plastic blocks before sticking them together almost by accident. A couple of times he'd demanded attention, and Thea Willits had given it to him. On the whole, it had been less of a strain than Patrick had anticipated.

No, it wasn't this one that raised his hackles. It was the other woman.

Helen Macaphee came in just then, studiously not looking at the corner of the room where he sat with her partner. She lifted a tray of some kind of goodies out of a big rack and went off with it into the front of the bakery. She'd done this every so often during the hours he'd spent with her partner, and each time it had upset his concentration.

It must be her antagonism, he told himself. It fairly poured off her. Obviously she had no use for nosy men who came prying into her business, raking up past mistakes and giving her a hard time.

And as for himself, he had no time for small, dark, well-rounded women who were blunt to the point of rudeness, who didn't even try to make use of any womanly charm they might possess—who regarded him as nothing more than a nuisance in their lives. Watching Helen disappear through the swinging door, Patrick tried to remind himself of that, of the reasons why he had never allowed himself to get close to a woman.

Oh, he knew about women—any man with six sisters got some basic insights into the female mind. But he'd never understood them, never. His sisters, now—one minute they'd be discussing the world situation like rational adults, and the next minute they'd be getting het up about shoes.

Shoes! As if there was more to a shoe than finding one that fit you and went with every suit.

Six sisters and two brothers, and him the oldest. It was no wonder, really, that when his classmates in high school were learning biology firsthand in the back seats of their parents' cars, he'd been flipping burgers at the Tasty Freeze. He'd had a few close encounters with the female sex, but what they'd mostly taught him was that women needed things—presents, attention, someone to take them to a social function and look good doing it.

All through college he'd been too poor to compete with the guys who didn't have to work after classes and on the weekends. And his family had claims on him. His father spent six days a week down at the power company, trying to earn the extra dollars his brood needed. His mother, frail after Moira's birth, struggled valiantly with the housework and sewing for such a big family. Patrick's leftover energies went to them. He was a second father to the younger ones, and after he'd graduated from college, his salary had gone to help those behind him in their studies.

Now his parents, retired, were nearly alone in their little ranch house on the south end of Santa Cruz. Moira was the last one, and she was leaving in the fall to do a residency in pediatrics at Stanford. And the others were chipping in to help, now that they were established in life. His family didn't need him so much anymore. Patrick was just starting to realize that he'd concentrated on them exclusively when he hadn't been acting the bureaucrat for his job. His parents seemed to be enjoying their partially empty nest. But he was finding it harder and harder to watch the children go and realize he had nothing to put in their place.

Thea Willits said something, and he summoned himself out of his thoughts. "I'm sorry, I wasn't listening," he confessed, smiling the easy smile that had brought the girls to him in school—before they realized that he couldn't show them a good enough time.

"How long will it take you to get to the bottom of this?" Thea had picked up her baby again, and he sat cuddled on her lap. For a moment Patrick envied that unthinking security.

"Hard to say," he answered. "It really proceeds much as an investigation would. We need to talk to people, get confirmation of your stories, check the records, find out about the address we were given when this trouble started. We've had a rash of misfilings lately, so it may take a while. I assure you, we'll move with all the speed we can muster."

"And does interest accrue on the penalty while you investigate?" Thea pushed at the topmost of the notifications he had presented them with.

"Depends on the result of the investigation." He snapped his briefcase shut and stood up. "If we find you committed an oversight, with no intention to defraud, the penalty is lifted, and you owe only the amount underpaid and interest on it from the time of underpayment."

"But we've tried to tell you that no one here gave you that address," Thea cried, and the baby in her lap twisted around to stare at her curiously. "Isn't that obvious? As soon as I began doing the paperwork, that address was no longer used. Surely you can see—"

Patrick held up his hand. "I know. If we find that this—" he consulted his notebook, then put it back into his jacket pocket "—Raymund Neves has committed fraudulent actions, we'll file criminal charges against him. In that case, you would no longer have to pay the penalty or the amount underpaid."

"Thank God," Thea murmured.

"I must warn you, Ms. Willits, that very seldom are taxpayers released of their obligation to make good on underpaid taxes. You had better turn your energies to finding the money. My advice would be to pay now, or at least start paying. Your money would be refunded in the unlikely event that criminal charges were filed." He cleared his throat, disliking the bureaucratese that came out of his mouth, but forced by long association with the government to speak it. "We do have payment plans, and under some circumstances you could pay off the amount in increments. It all depends."

"I see." Thea stood up, too, and after a moment's hesitation held out her hand. "I'm confident you'll get to the bottom of it all, Mr. Lasswell."

He smiled at her, taking her hand for a brief second. "Call me Patrick," he said, and wondered at his impulsive request. "We'll be working together for a good while, I believe."

"Patrick, then." She shook his hand briskly and would have led him to the back door.

"I'll go out the front, if it's all the same to you," he told her.

"Of course." He could see the faint line of puzzlement between her eyes as she watched him go through the swinging door. But he found himself craving another word with that partner of hers.

Helen Macaphee was waiting on a customer, but after she'd put the slice of carrot cake on a doily-lined plate and taken the customer's money, she turned reluctantly to him where he stood beside the cash register. "Yes?"

"I want a piece of that chocolate cake to go," he said, surprising himself for the second time that day.

He'd expected the hostility in her gaze, but when she handed him the box and he gave her a couple of dollars, it changed to surprise. She lifted her eyes to him, and he could see that they were not black, as he'd supposed, but a dark, velvety brown, with long lashes. He knew from looking at her files that she was thirty-nine, but her smooth olive skin held only a few laugh lines at the corners of her eyes.

Pulling his gaze away with difficulty, he shoved the money into her hand. "What did you think," he said, trying for lightness, "that I'd take the cake without paying? That would be tantamount to your offering a bribe, I'm afraid. We civil servants have to watch out for those things."

She snatched the money out of his hand and punched the cash register viciously. "I'll bet you do," she muttered, putting a few coins on the counter.

He picked it up and made a show of counting it. "This is all I get back? Mighty pricey cake you sell here, lady."

"That it is," Helen snapped. "And the price will go up a great deal if we have to pay some outrageous tax bill all over again."

His eyes narrowed and he picked up the cake box. "I'll be seeing you," he said, staring into her eyes, trying to force from her some recognition that she deserved what was coming to her, that she carried the guilty secret he'd come to expect from those he investigated.

She stared back, fearless, defiant. "If you must," she said with dignity, and turned to the next customer.

With that he had to be content.

CHAPTER FIVE

DONOVAN PARKED his rental car at the curb of the address Thea had given him and got out, staring at the house in front of him.

It was a big old place, shabby and run-down. Repairs had been made in the floorboards of the wide front porch that were conspicuously new. Faded paint clung to the window-sills, except where it had been scraped off. The gingerbread trim that dripped from every cornice and railing gave the old house a jaunty, faintly disreputable air.

It was not the kind of setting he would have envisioned for Thea.

The front door burst open and a surfboard came out. Instinctively Donovan stepped back before he realized that a young man was carrying the board as easily as if it weighed nothing.

Seeing Donovan on the sidewalk, the young man gave him a wide smile. "Hey, man," he said, breezing past. "You look like you could use some directions. What's the skinny?"

Donovan cleared his throat, watching the kid, who couldn't be more than twenty, hoist the board into an ancient Volkswagen truck. "I'm looking for Thea's place. Thea Willits," he said finally.

The kid turned around, staring at him with interest. Donovan returned the look. He saw long, sun-bleached hair, friendly blue eyes and white teeth in a square-jawed face, and a tanned, muscular body easily assessed in faded knee-length jams and unbuttoned shirt. The shirt had voluptuous hula dancers all over its background of garishly erupting volcanos.

He didn't know what the kid thought of him, but a trace of wariness crept into those blue eyes. "You a friend of Thea's, or what?"

"An old friend." He could see speculation in the other's gaze. "I've already spoken to her at the bakery," he added. "She told me to meet her here."

"She's not around right now." The kid thrust out a hand to Donovan. "I'm Marlon Jackson."

"Just call me Donovan." The kid—Marlon—had a pretty good grip. Donovan was glad to reclaim his hand. "You live here?"

Marlon grinned. "Yeah. Great place. Miss Sophie is a sweetie pie, and the rent's reasonable."

"Miss Sophie?"

Marlon was already turning away. "Go on around," he said over his shoulder, gesturing vaguely toward the house. "Thea will be back pretty soon, I guess. R.J. could tell you. I gotta split. It's breaking really smooth at Steamers Lane this afternoon."

Donovan watched as Marlon roared away. Shaking his head, he started down the driveway. Although the pavement was cracked, someone had planted a flower border beside it; vivid poppies and sweet peas waved in the breeze, somewhat disguising the peeling paint along the sides of the house. "This place looks like Dracula's vacation home," he muttered. The driveway ended at a dilapidated carriage house.

"Yoo-hoo!" A quavery voice hailed him from the back porch, where an old lady stood fluttering her handkerchief. "Oh, sir—"

Maybe this woman knew where Thea was to be found. He walked along a narrow sidewalk to the screened-in back porch. The lady, he found, was not really so old. Her hair was snowy white, but her soft skin, though wrinkled, seemed fresh and pink. She wore old-fashioned steel-rimmed spectacles. "Yes, ma'am," he said politely.

"It's in here," she said, beckoning him up to the porch. "The pipes and things. You are the man from the utility company, aren't you? Come for the inspection?"

She peered anxiously at him, and he was seized with the unfamiliar sensation of wanting to reassure her, smooth things over.

He cleared his throat. "Not exactly, ma'am."

"I'm Miss Sophie Belden," she said, inclining her head to him. "You're not from the utilities? We're expecting someone about the pipes."

"That's right," boomed another voice. Donovan looked over Miss Sophie's head to see an elderly man standing in the doorway. He moved beside Miss Sophie. "These days you gotta have permission before you can even spit in your own yard. Begging your pardon, Miss Sophie, ma'am."

"Oh, Mr. Castigliano." Miss Sophie turned from one man to the other. "So kind of you, but—you see, I don't really think—"

"I'm not doing any inspection," Donovan said, hoping to clarify a muddy situation. "I'm a friend of Thea's. She told me to meet her at her place."

"Oh." Miss Sophie invested one word with a world of meaning. There was that speculation again. Everyone who met him, Donovan could see, would be wondering if he was Lucas's father or not. He must be the only person in Santa Cruz to know for sure—and, of course, Thea.

"Mighty fine girl, Thea." Mr. Castigliano rubbed his chin, causing the creases on his face to fall into a different order, and eyed Donovan. "You've known her a while?"

"A while, yes." Donovan refused to be drawn. "Does she live in your house, too, Miss Belden?"

"Oh, call me Sophie, everyone does. And Theadora lives here, in a manner of speaking."

Mr. Castigliano chimed in. "She did a fine job with that cottage, from what I can see. I wish I'd been around then to give her a hand with the plumbing. Nothing I like better than getting my hands on a nice plumbing problem."

Miss Sophie smiled weakly. "Mr. Castigliano wants to help me with my plumbing. It seems I'm not up to code anywhere, except the cottage, of course. Theadora saw to that."

"Cottage?" Donovan turned and surveyed the back-yard. There was a smooth circle of lawn, bordered by more flowers and shrubs, with a sandstone path leading through some bushes. He could just glimpse low white walls behind the greenery.

"The old gardener's cottage." Miss Sophie beamed. "At first I didn't want to rent it to her, it was so run-down. But Theadora insisted on putting it into shape for me. She said she fell in love with it, and indeed it is very picturesque, especially now that the roof doesn't leak anymore, and the bathroom—well, it's very nice."

"She fixed it up." Donovan found himself comparing the shabby turn-of-the-century ambience around him with the sleek condominium he and Thea had owned in San Francisco. The two pictures were totally incongruous, having nothing in common with each other. He felt as though he'd fallen down some rabbit hole of his dear love's digging.

"She didn't do it herself—in her delicate situation," Miss Sophie assured him, a faint blush coloring her wrinkled cheeks. "Rosalie Jane did quite a bit of it, and they had some people in for the complicated things—wiring and plumbing and foundation work."

"If I'da been living here," Mr. Castigliano put in, shaking his head, "I'd have been glad to oblige. Thirty-five years I've been a maintenance man—engineer, they call them now. Thirty over at the Boardwalk. There isn't much I don't know about pipes and plumbing."

Miss Sophie threw her grizzled boarder a look compounded of doubt and delight. "Mr. Castigliano is going to help me install the new washing machine," she confided to a bewildered Donovan. "Then we won't be taking such advantage of poor Theadora. A baby makes a lot of laundry, you know."

"I can imagine." Donovan didn't feel he could handle any more artless revelations from Thea's aged landlady. "Maybe I can wait for Thea at her place."

Miss Sophie seemed doubtful. "Rosalie Jane isn't there right now, and I'm sure it's locked." Her face brightened. "There's a glider behind the cottage, by the clothesline. You can wait there. If I see Theadora, I'll tell her you're here." She looked hopefully at him. "What name shall I give?"

"Donovan." She waited, expectant. He found he couldn't disappoint her. Resigned, he added, "Lucius Donovan."

"Certainly, Mr. Lucas. Lucius. I mean, Mr. Donovan." Miss Sophie gave him her hand. "I'll tell Theadora."

Donovan headed down the path, conscious that the two oldsters were watching him go. It was a relief to disappear into the foliage, away from the curious, inquiring eyes.

Thea's cottage was, he had to admit, picturesque in appearance. It was a low building, with board-and-batten walls, wide-silled windows and a new wood-shingled roof. Rambler roses cascaded over the arched trellis at the front door. The walls were white, the window frames and shutters green, gleaming with fresh paint.

He followed the path around to the back of the house, where a small brick patio was edged with blooming flowerpots. Behind a high hedge were the faint sounds of street noise. Otherwise all he could hear were bird song and wind, rustling the leaves on the rhododendrons and redwoods.

An old metal glider caught the late-afternoon sun. He sat down on it, suddenly aware of his thirst and wondering if he should try the back door.

Thirsty or not, he wouldn't do it. The cottage seemed inviolate, Thea's home and refuge. Unless she asked him into it, he could not enter.

Donovan leaned back, trying to shake off such fanciful thoughts. But jet lag began to catch up with him. By New York time it was nearly eight in the evening, and he had barely slept on his red-eye flight to San Francisco. Something about the silence and the fresh ocean-tinged breeze brought a rushing relaxation that made his body sink more heavily into the cushioned seat of the glider. The tension of his work had escalated over the past year, so gradually he'd hardly noticed it happening. Now its grip on him flagged, and he felt himself falling into the soft black clutch of sleep.

Thea found him there. She was forewarned by Miss Sophie, who had leaned out the back door as she hauled Lucas out of the car to yoo-hoo the information that a very handsome young man had shown up and was waiting at the cottage.

Not finding Donovan in front, Thea had carried in the diaper bag and her heavy briefcase full of financial records she meant to go over that evening. Lucas needed changing, but before she took him into the bedroom, she had gone through the kitchen to the back door and discovered Donovan sleeping in the glider.

Studying him, she found herself wanting to brush away
the lock of hair that fell over his forehead, to smooth out the
furrows in his brow. The year had not been kind to him;
there was the first, faint silvering of the hair at his temples.
His face was leaner, infinitely more tired. Her heart turned
over.

Lucas stirred on her hip and put up one small hand to pat
her face. She pressed a kiss on his chubby fist, still watching Donovan. The reluctant father, she mused. A good title
for one of the Regency romances Betty, the hairdresser,
read. But in real life, parenthood was a tricky proposition.
She had been managing, barely, to juggle child, business and
sanity. What would happen if she added lover?

Crowing, Lucas demanded more kisses. At the sound of
his baby laughter, Donovan's eyes opened, and straight-
away the image of vulnerability fled. No momentary haze
of sleep softened his crystal-sharp gaze. He found her and
pinned her with one look. This was no Prince Charming, no
imaginary hero. This was a man who was used to getting
what he wanted out of people.

It remained only to find out what he wanted from her.

"You were early," Thea said at last, when it became clear
that Donovan didn't mean to speak first.

"Yes." He moved, stretching. "You have a very comfortable glider."

She looked dubiously at the metal structure. Even with
cushions, it was not the place she would have chosen for a
nap. "The back door was unlocked," she told him. "You
could have gone in."

"It didn't feel right." His smile was crooked. "We're not
roommates anymore."

"No." Desperately she wished for something she could
say to him. Had it been only a year ago that they had been
able to talk of anything under the sun? Conversation had

never been stilted between them before. "Won't you, uh, come in now?"

"Of course." He stood, waiting for her to carry Lucas into the house, and followed.

In the kitchen, she felt his eyes on her as she filled the kettle and put it on the stove. "Coffee?"

"Do you have tea?" She looked at him, surprised, and again the crooked smile touched his lips. "I'm trying not to drink much coffee anymore. It began to do weird things to me."

"Health things, you mean?" She rummaged in the cupboard and brought down an assortment of tea bags and two mugs. "Nerves?"

"Some," he admitted, wandering over to the counter where she stood to sort through the bags. His move brought him close to Lucas, and she had to restrain herself from snatching the baby away. Who did she want to save—Donovan from the horror of associating with a dreaded baby, or the baby from his own father?

"Insomnia," Donovan said, and she realized that she'd asked him a question. "I couldn't sleep after a while, so I cut way down on coffee. It helped." His eyes found hers. "But not much."

"Donovan—" She wanted to bring this awkward conversation to a sudden end, before deeper issues could be touched on, before anyone's heart was wounded or broken. But he ignored her whispered plea, and she understood that the time for evasions was past.

"It was you I needed, not less caffeine," he said, moving one step closer. "I wanted your body in bed next to me. I was cold without you."

"You always were," she murmured, remembering nights when he had held her tightly, claiming she was the only thing that could warm him. "Maybe a nice flannel nightshirt—"

His laugh was unwilling. "Not just physically cold." She shut her eyes, trying to avoid the intensity of his gaze. "Something inside me was frozen, waiting for your touch. I think they call it a heart."

"This isn't fair, Donovan." She backed away, turning off the whistling kettle. "I can't handle this."

"Shall I do it?" Calmly he picked up the kettle and poured water into the cups. "You don't want to be messing with hot things, not with a baby in your arms."

It was totally perverse of her brain to read hidden messages into everything he said. He carried the mugs over to the table and looked around. "Nice little place you've got here."

"I like it." The corny clichés made her want to gag, but she seemed unable to do more than mouth platitudes or bleat protests.

He waited for her to sit down and then he sat, too, stirring his tea bag around. The sharp scent of lemon wafted into the air. "Your landlady said you put a lot of money into it."

Thea was surprised into laughing. "Miss Sophie never said such a thing," she declared. "Just mentioning that the rent is due is difficult for her let alone discussing anything so distressing as how much it cost me—" Abruptly she stopped.

"And how much did it cost?" There was a smoothness to Donovan's voice, a sharpness in his eye, that told her this was, for some reason, a touchy subject.

"Not that much," she said evasively. "It was mostly cosmetic stuff."

"Like fixing the roof and putting in new plumbing and wiring," he said, nodding. "That kind of cosmetic work doesn't come cheap."

"Why do you care?" She wanted to take a sip of tea to soothe the tightness in her throat, but her hands, she knew, would tremble. And that would give Donovan an edge. "What does it matter what I spent, or how I'm living? I didn't go into debt. I paid my bills on time. What's it to you?"

At last he glanced away, and she felt a small, hollow victory. "I wish it could be something to me," he muttered. "I just wondered if you'd spent your half of the condo proceeds here."

"And speaking of that," she said, glad to be able to change the subject, "why didn't you cash that check I sent you? You really screwed up my bookkeeping."

"I couldn't cash it," he said blandly, pulling out his wallet, "after I'd torn it into little pieces." He took a folded envelope out of the wallet, opened it and emptied the contents onto her kitchen table. "You can have it back."

Thea stared at the heap of scraps, feeling hysterical giggles well up inside her. With an effort, she choked them back. "That made a lot of trouble for me when I closed my San Francisco account," she said as sternly as she could manage.

"If you had stayed where you should have, it wouldn't have been a problem." There was an undercurrent of anger in his voice again, but he managed to get it under control. "Did you spend that money fixing up this place?"

"No." It suddenly occurred to her that he might expect her to fork over the very tidy sum that was his share of the profits on that sale. "I put it into a trust fund for Lucas."

He was silent, and she rushed to add, "I could scrape together what I owe you if you can wait for a while." She still had a few securities left, but most of her ready cash was tied up in Babycakes, and what she had available wouldn't even pay a third of the IRS's demands, let alone Donovan's share of the condo sale.

She came out of her reverie to find him scowling at her. "I don't want the money," he snapped. "I wouldn't have torn up the check if I'd been that mercenary."

"It's a year later," she pointed out. "Your feelings might have changed."

"Not that much." His gaze softened. "You did the right thing to provide for our child."

Something in his voice sent shivers through her. The way he said "our child," with an odd note of—almost of yearning. This was not the Donovan she'd expected, the one who believed fervently in negative population growth.

Lucas squirmed in her lap, and a sensation of dampness met the hand she applied to his bottom. "Excuse me," she told Donovan, not sorry to have a few minutes away from the charged atmosphere at the table. "I need to change him."

She carried the baby through the low-ceilinged living room and into the bedroom, laying him on the changing table and smiling down into his blue-gray eyes. "You're sopping wet!" she told him softly.

He laughed up at her as if it was the most delightful news he'd ever heard.

"Yes, you are!"

"So," Donovan's voice came from behind her, "if you didn't use the money from the condo sale, how did you pay for all the work?"

She stiffened for a moment, then went on folding a clean diaper. "Money is really no problem for me, Donovan. My investments have done well."

He came up to stand beside her, absently handing her the diaper pins. "I don't call it much of an investment," he said flatly, "to spend your money fixing up someone else's real estate. Did you sell stock?"

She nodded mutely, accepting the pins and then pulling a clean pair of plastic pants over Lucas's diaper.

"All of it?" His voice was implacable. She was glad he couldn't see her face.

"I don't know that it's any of your business," she began.

"Thea, please. We know each other too well for you to lie to me. When I went to New York, we each had a tidy portfolio, as you know. Mine has done quite well the past year, though without you to advise me I've hesitated to add to it. How's yours done?"

"Fine," she said lamely.

He let out an impatient breath. "Please," he said tightly, "do me the honor of telling me the truth. I need to know, Thea."

"Well, it would have done fine," she said, forcing out the reluctant words. "I mean, the others have..."

"What others?"

The fat was in the fire, she thought dismally. And then she wondered why she should feel ashamed of what she'd done. Gathering up her clean, dry baby, she turned to face Donovan.

"I'm doing portfolios for people at the big house who have money to invest. And I still have some shares and certificates of deposit, so you can see I haven't beggared myself."

He had his eyes fixed on Lucas, and when Donovan held out his arms in silent demand, she surprised herself by handing the baby over. Donovan held him a little awkwardly, looking down into the dimpled, gurgling face of his son, with his own features rigidly held. Lucas stared up at him and reached one hand toward the dark stubble that was so different from any face he knew.

Thea watched them, her hands unconsciously clenched. When she noticed that, she tried to relax, wondering what she was so nervous about. That Donovan would dislike his son—or that he wouldn't?

Lucas began to squirm, and Donovan took a few paces through the bedroom before stopping in front of her again. "At MSC," he said levelly, hoisting the baby onto his shoulder, "you were very well paid for putting together stock portfolios. Is that the case with Miss Belden and her gang?"

"No," Thea said, keeping her chin high. "I do it for free, because I care about them—because . . ." Sighing, she tried to decide how to tell him. "Miss Sophie is on a limited income. Her investments don't really amount to much, not now, but as the years go by she'll find herself well hedged against inflation. And a couple of things have done spectacularly well for her, enough to help her keep the house going."

"Washing machines," Donovan muttered.

"Exactly." Thea deposited the wet diaper in the diaper pail and straightened up the changing table. "Marlon had a little money and wanted to increase it. He's been very interested in the process of investment. And Helen—"

"You're even doing work for Helen?"

Thea had tuned out the sarcasm in his voice. "Helen has never really had security," she murmured, almost to herself. "I wanted to build some equity for her, a cushion to fall back on. Now—"

"Now you'll be lucky if she agrees to cash it in to pay off the IRS, instead of making you pay the whole thing." She turned away to hide her face, heading for the bathroom to wash her hands, but he followed her, alerted by something he'd seen in her expression. "What is it, Thea? What's the problem?"

"Nothing," she said, trying to brazen it out. "Really, everything will be fine, Donovan."

"Tell me about it." He stood with his shoulder propped against the bathroom door, and he didn't move even when she'd finished drying her hands.

Lucas gnawed his knuckles, and Thea felt her breasts begin to tingle at that sign of hunger. Or was it a different kind of hunger in herself, triggered by Donovan's presence? She didn't want to sort it out.

"There's nothing to tell." She tried to push past him, but he didn't move. "Helen will cash in her chips, I know. But so will I."

"You mean you'll sell up? Everything?"

This time when she approached the door, he stepped aside. "I'll have to, to pay the IRS," she said, walking over to the bedroom window that looked out on the backyard. "I put up the capital to remodel and reequip the bakery, Donovan. And it wasn't really cheap to get the cottage worked over, although I have a deal with Miss Sophie—"

Donovan sighed in exasperation. "Good Lord, have your wits gone begging? You used to be pretty sharp about money, as I recall. Now you're throwing away equity by fixing up someone else's real estate, and buying into a crooked bakery. I'm beginning to think the smartest thing you did was setting up the trust fund for Lucas—and that's granting that having a baby in the first place was such a good idea!"

They stared at each other, both aghast. Dazed, Thea looked around at the bedroom. It was still the cozy place she'd put together with such care, diamond-paned windows shining, oak ceiling beams highlighting creamy plaster, rose-splattered curtains billowing in a fresh, scented breeze. But a dark mist seemed to lie over everything. She stalked over to Donovan, and Lucas held out his arms to her, making urgent noises. Reluctantly Donovan relinquished him, following her into the living room. She dropped in the mission oak rocker and offered Lucas her breast.

"I'm sorry, Thea." Donovan sat on the sofa across from her. "I don't blame you for having the baby."

"Big of you," Thea snapped, holding Lucas tighter. "Maybe I don't worry about doing the smart thing anymore. It's much more rewarding to do the right thing."

"And that's what you've been doing?"

Donovan sounded goaded to the limit. Thea had to harden her heart. Part of her wanted so much to go to him, smooth his hair, soothe him into seeing her side. The other part, the part that said he could understand or else to hell with him, won. "That's how it looks from my corner," she said.

"Leaving me in the dark about my son, selling all your assets to make bad business decisions, cutting yourself off from everything you've ever known—that's all right?"

"You're twisting things to make your own point of view look better," Thea said stonily. "That's not the way I see it."

He didn't move, but somehow he seemed to recede further into the couch. "Tell me how you see it."

She cuddled the warm weight of her contented baby. "I chose to go my way instead of going yours. That's all."

His eyes closed briefly. "So why am I here? You don't seem to need or want me."

"That's not true!" Thea gazed at him, stricken. "Donovan, you just waltz in here and expect everything to be the same! It can't be."

"And is that my fault?"

"It isn't anyone's fault. It's the way it is."

He heard the finality in her voice. "Thea—"

She was looking down at Lucas. "Shh," she said softly. "He's sleeping. I'll put him down."

She carried the baby into the bedroom, arranging him in his crib, tucking the light blanket around him with a lingering pat. Somehow having Donovan around pulled her emotions into so many different shapes that only Lucas and her bond with him seemed constant.

"Sleep well, sweetie," she whispered, bending to place a feathery kiss on his soft cheek. He stirred briefly, and she patted him back into sleep, humming under her breath.

Donovan watched her from the door, where he'd followed. She was so remote now, this Thea who looked and sounded like his love, but who had given her love to a baby. His baby.

He couldn't make it real, somehow. Here he was, with the woman he'd been longing for, and all he felt was the sensation of being an interloper.

Her low singing was in his ears when he returned to the living room. Seeing a yellow legal pad on the coffee table in front of the fireplace, he scrawled, "I need some time to think. Rain check on the dinner. Love, Donovan."

He let himself quietly out of the house, striding back up the driveway to his rental car. The airport in San Jose was the closest place to get a flight back to New York. He would have to turn in the other half of his ticket and wait for a while, he knew.

For the past few days, he'd given in to instinct, following the need for Thea that had grown intolerable. Finding her had been instinct; leaving like this was, too.

But now he would put instinct aside. He had a lot to think about. It seemed that he'd been doing all his thinking on the job lately, and none at all to get his personal life into shape.

Now he would have the long flight back to the home that was no home to get some perspective on the situation.

"By the time I get back there," he vowed, heading the little compact toward the highway that would take him over the mountains to San Jose, "I'll have figured out what to do."

He just hoped it would be that simple.

CHAPTER SIX

THE PIECE of yellow legal paper crinkled angrily in Thea's jeans pocket when she pulled up a chair to Helen's table the next morning. She didn't know why she was carrying it around, since being reminded of the debacle with Donovan made her wonder which hurt more—her heart or her pride.

Helen was too preoccupied to notice Thea fingering the note. She moved around in her tiny kitchen, listlessly fixing tea and putting pastries on a plate. "The oat-bran muffins were very good this morning," she mentioned, setting the plate on the table.

Thea shook her head. "It's a wonder they were, with my mind in so many other places."

Helen sat down, too, and dunked the bamboo strainer up and down in her cup of hot water. "Are we up the well-known creek?"

"Not at all," Thea said stoutly. She crossed her fingers under the table, though. "We'll get all this mess sorted out and come through in fine shape, you'll see."

"It's great you can say that with a straight face." Helen helped herself to a croissant and broke it into little pieces. "The way I feel right now, I just want to put about a pound of butter on this thing and then go to bed for a couple of weeks."

Thea forced herself to put her personal misery out of her mind. "Helen," she said, leaning forward to look into her partner's face, "I'm depending on you. Whatever happens, the bakery has to keep going. If we slip on quality control, or your fabulous desserts lose their following, we really are sunk. Don't let me down."

Helen sat up in her chair. "I won't," she said after a moment. "And I'm glad you have faith that we can climb out of this." She sighed. "But I spent a good while last night reading all those letters I never got from the IRS. It's scary, what they're saying."

"Patrick Lasswell seemed very competent to me," Thea said. "I'm sure he can get to the bottom of it all."

"Yeah, at bureaucrat speed," Helen said gloomily. "They move slower than banana slugs in a drought. And if he decides we are liable for the fines and stuff after all, then we've racked up even more interest." She fiddled with some croissant crumbs. "The letters all said the same thing at the end. Pay us now, and we won't sock you for any more interest. And we'll give the money back if it turns out you don't owe it." She fixed troubled eyes on Thea. "Can we pay it?"

Thea took a deep breath. "We have some money left in our contingency fund—that's what we were going to use to finish the remodeling. And I can sell the rest of my personal holdings."

"Me, too," Helen said anxiously.

"You, too." Thea picked up a pen and looked around for some paper. There was nothing else available, so she pulled the note from Donovan out of her pocket and began to scribble on it. After a moment she shook her head. "We'd still be short by fifteen thou."

"Dollars?" Helen's voice was almost a wail. "Those bloodsucking, money-grubbing—"

"Good morning, ladies." Patrick Lasswell stood in the doorway, smiling amiably, but the smile didn't quite reach his blue eyes. "They told me downstairs where you were."

He strolled into the room, his sharp gaze taking in everything.

"We'll be done in a minute, Mr. Lasswell," Helen said icily, "if you'd care to wait in the kitchen."

"I'd prefer to wait up here, if you don't mind," he told her, sniffing the fragrant air. "Are those croissants I smell?"

Helen, Thea could see, was too choked with outrage to answer. So she tried to reply politely. "Yes, they are, Patrick. Would you like one?"

"Sure, I wouldn't turn one down," he admitted. "This place brings out the hunger in me."

Thea gave him a croissant on a napkin, deciding that he didn't really need or rate a plate. "We do our best to make you hungry," she said demurely. "We were up at five, baking these, along with other stuff. We're ready for a break, so we came up for breakfast."

Patrick's eyes summed up the shabby living room, the crowded table and tiny kitchen. "This apartment is included in your lease, isn't it? You could make some extra income renting it out."

Helen found her voice. "I do rent it out! That is, I live here myself! I've lived here for the past six years, and I don't intend to try to find another place now. And I don't see what business it is of yours, anyway!"

Thea waited apprehensively for Patrick to take offense at Helen's hostile words. But he smiled benignly and settled into the unoccupied chair at the table. "Just trying to help you out of the hole you ladies have dug for yourselves," he said around bites of the raspberry croissant. "These are great." The last mouthful vanished. "Are there any more?"

"Yes," Helen hissed. "Downstairs, in the display cases. They cost a dollar each. Maybe more for you. After all, we need all the money we can get!"

"Helen!" Thea protested. She knew from the past few months' experience that a bakery that greased the bureaucrats with the stock in trade did business a lot easier than other businesses with less potential for making offerings to the god of paperwork. "The croissants are on the counter, Patrick. Help yourself."

Patrick went over to the counter and took one of the chocolate croissants. He put it on the table, reached into his pocket and pulled out a couple of dollar bills.

"Here you go, Ms. Macaphee." He placed the money in front of Helen and sat back down. "Let it never be said that Patrick Lasswell is a freeloader."

Helen seemed unappeased. "I'll go ring it up," she said, jumping to her feet. "And we have cakes to ice, Thea."

"I'll be there in a minute." Thea waited for the apartment door to slam and then gazed calmly at Patrick. "We are very busy this morning. How can I help you?"

For one brief moment, real amusement shone in his eyes. "I feel like the proverbial cat among the pigeons," he remarked. "Ms. Macaphee is mightily put out at me, I can see."

"Helen's very protective of her bakery," Thea told him. "She's been struggling with it for years, just barely surviving from one year to the next. Now, when she sees the possibility of real growth and success, this happens."

Patrick's gaze hardened. "It didn't just happen," he said quietly. "I'm here because the government was defrauded. Success can't be built on fraud."

"Helen didn't do it." Thea kept her agitation out of her voice. "She isn't great with paperwork, but she's painfully honest. When you find Raymund Neves, you'll find your missing tax money."

Patrick nodded politely. "Meanwhile, I'd like to potter around with the files, if you'll allow me to do so."

"Do I have a choice?" Thea kept the words light, but Patrick could tell she meant it.

"Not really, no. If you have nothing to hide, you have nothing to worry about."

Thea took her cup to the sink and rinsed it out. "That sounds reassuring," she retorted, "but I know how you government types operate. You may not find what you're really looking for, but any little oversights or untidinesses that turn up will have you nibbling us to death for months."

"You sound like you've had past experience with the IRS," Patrick murmured, bringing his cup over to the sink.

"Some," Thea admitted. "I did investment counseling before I bought into Babycakes. Clients complained that twenty dollars of unreported interest income could result in lengthy correspondence with the IRS."

"So you're lucky that your peccadilloes are so extensive as to require the personal attention of a revenue agent," Patrick said, placing his cup neatly in the drainer. "I'll get right to the heart of the matter, I promise you."

Thea believed him. Leading the way down the rickety back steps, she wondered if it was better to have the personal attention of the IRS or simply to get letter after letter pointing out all sorts of picky details and demanding payment.

She unlocked her desk and filing cabinet for Patrick and joined Helen at the front of the kitchen. The early rush was over, both in the store, where people on their way to work had stopped for croissants and muffins, and in the kitchen, where those croissants and muffins had been baked, along with breads, cookies, tarts, pastries and an assortment of cakes. Helen had finished putting loaves of bread into the baskets that would be arranged at the front counter and was starting in on the cakes.

"Six birthdays," she told Thea, glancing back once at Patrick's crop of unruly red hair and then pointedly ignoring him. "Two anniversaries, and a sorry-you're-going."

"I'll ice if you'll decorate," Thea said hopefully. "My roses still aren't up to par."

Helen agreed, and they got busy. Thea spread thick fudge icing over the chocolate cakes, pale cream-cheese icing on the carrot cakes and sour-cream icing on the spice cakes. Helen began turning out garlands of flowers, surrounding them with piped leaves and vines and the message specified by the customers. As each one was finished, Thea took it to the capacious new cooler, trimmed in oak, that had just been installed in the store. She stocked the refrigerated display case, putting in éclairs, grenache-filled meringues, napoleons, and one each of the trademark cakes that Helen baked so beautifully.

"I need a generic birthday or two," Thea said, going back into the kitchen. "We're sure to get a couple of those last-minute shoppers who've forgotten someone's birthday."

"Fine," Helen said, her tongue slightly visible between her teeth as she finished inscribing a chocolate cake. "I'll do you a couple of carrot cakes and one chocolate fudge."

"That should work." Thea glanced at her desk. Patrick was still there, his head bent industriously over the desk.

Helen followed her gaze, and her mouth turned down. "Busybody," she hissed.

Thea shrugged. "If it wasn't him, it would be someone else. You want this resolved, don't you?"

"As far as I'm concerned," Helen said stubbornly. "I paid the damned taxes once, and there's an end to it."

Patrick had good ears. He shoved some papers into his briefcase and came toward them. "I couldn't help overhearing you," he said, his pleasant smile almost masking the edge in his voice. "Unfortunately, payment doesn't count unless the government receives it. You claim to have taken care of your taxes, but as far as I can see, only your boyfriend got paid.''

Helen stared at him for a moment as the implications sank in. Thea watched her partner's face turn white with fury and grabbed as many of the heavy items off the baker's table as she could hold. ''Now, Helen,'' she said hastily, ''we can't afford to replace any broken—Helen, not the cake stand, please!''

Patrick hadn't moved. He stood stock-still, his expression unreadable as the wild light slowly faded from Helen's eyes, to be replaced by cold, implacable hatred. She uncurled her fingers from the base of the glass cake stand. ''This man,'' she said, still staring at Patrick, ''must never speak to me again. If he has to come around, you'll have to handle it.''

She swung on her heel and marched away, five feet two inches of ramrod-straight outrage.

For a moment after she'd disappeared into the store, there was silence. Then Patrick Lasswell drew a deep breath.

''She really gets riled, doesn't she?'' He gazed after Helen with something close to admiration. ''Macaphee is a Scots name, but it's the Irish temper she's got.''

''You're lucky,'' Thea said, dumping the potential weaponry back onto the table. ''The time the UPS truck ran into her car, she nearly brained the driver with a popover pan.''

''Such a little thing,'' Patrick said, contemplative. ''Would you be thinking, now, that she means what she says?''

''Oh, yes.'' Thea folded her arms across her chest. ''She never wants to set eyes on you again. It would be best if I arranged to come to your office when you need information.''

"That would never do, would it?" Patrick shook his head, the suspicion of a smile forming on his mouth. "For it's the chocolate cake that brings me here, as much as the need to work on your mess of taxes."

"Suit yourself." Shrugging, Thea finished spreading icing on one of the chocolate cakes. "On your head be it. Literally."

Patrick watched the smooth fudgy frosting ripple out of the bag to form a decorative rim around the cake's edge. "It was uncalled for," he acknowledged handsomely, "to make that crack about her boyfriend. Very shabby of me, but what's a man or two to most women?"

Thea scowled at him. "I don't know who you've been hanging around with, but it certainly sounds like the wrong kind of people. Helen doesn't have boyfriends. She's been unfortunate enough to fall in love twice in her life, and the man was a complete heel each time."

"You sound a little bitter yourself," Patrick suggested, reaching out to rescue a fallen blob of icing. He sucked it off his finger and sighed. "Heavenly. How can such a prickly little thing make such sweet delights?"

Thea bit back a sharp retort. She had the feeling that the IRS man wasn't paying that much attention to her. He watched the swinging door as though hoping that Helen would come back through it. "If she does come back and you're still hanging around," Thea said after a minute, "I won't bother to save you again."

"The two of you certainly have no good wishes for a poor male," he said plaintively. "Just what have the men done to you?"

Thea slid her finished cake, still on its cardboard circle, into the large rack that dominated one corner of the kitchen. "It's not what men do," she said, feeling that scrap of legal paper crackle in her pocket. "It's that we're fools enough to invite it. We believe what they say, we let our emotions get involved and then, whammo! The old dropkick into the trash can." She looked squarely at Patrick. "One half of the population shouldn't treat the other half that way."

"And do you think the shoe is on your foot entirely?" His smile was mocking. "Believe it or not, there have been a few women who've done the same or worse to men."

Thea studied him. "I take it you know whereof you speak."

Patrick's smile faded. "Purely academic as far as I'm concerned. I've had the good sense to stay away from love." He picked up his briefcase again. "But if you think I'm going to let that pint-sized spitfire order me around, you've got another think coming."

Thea watched, awestricken, as he walked through into the store. She thought about hiding back by her desk, pretending total ignorance, but the opportunity to see the confrontation of a lifetime was too much.

Standing to one side of the door, so as to be out of the way of any flying objects, she peered into the store.

Helen was waiting on a customer, but from the rigidity of her shoulders it was obvious she knew Patrick stood just behind her. The customer, sensing the hostile vibrations, didn't linger; she picked up her boxed piece of cake and hightailed it out of the bakery. Only Maria, the counter helper, was left.

Helen turned slowly to face her adversary, the cake knife still in her hand. He eyed it warily. "Maybe you didn't understand what I said."

"I understood all right." Patrick maintained his smile, though it wasn't easy with her glaring so stonily at him. "You tossed down the gauntlet to me. I'm picking it up."

She took a deep breath, and he noticed that not even the baggy white pants and apron of the professional baker could disguise the voluptuous outlines of her figure. He kept the observation to himself, though. It was shooting off his big mouth that had gotten him into this trouble.

"Look, Mr. Taxman. You do your job and let me do mine. Don't get in my way. I'm warning you."

"Threats, is it?" He wanted to ask if she planned to use the cake knife on him, but forced himself to tamp down the imp of mischief that bubbled to life when he faced this woman. The sight of her did strange things to him. He couldn't even imagine why he was behaving like this, instead of the staid, proper manner in which he normally conducted the government's business.

"Is there a law against being badgered by the Feds?" Narrow-eyed, Helen examined him like something she'd find growing on an old loaf of bread. "Because if there isn't, there should be."

"I don't mean to badger you." He stared down at her, watching the anger flicker in her eyes. "I want to apologize."

That took Helen off guard, but she didn't suspend her glare. "Okay. Do it."

"Huh?"

"Apologize." She put the cake knife down next to the half circle of chocolate cake and crossed her arms over her breasts. "I'm waiting."

Patrick held on to his own all-too-Irish temper. After all, he'd gotten himself into this. "I regret making remarks and assumptions about your personal life, Ms. Macaphee. They were unwarranted."

She maintained her rigid stance, but some of the anger died out of her eyes. "Accepted," she said at last. "Now, if you don't mind, I've got a business to run."

There were any number of retorts he could have made, but all of them would have violated the spirit of the words he'd just forced out.

"Well, in the name of your business," he drawled, "I'll take a piece of that cake to go." He dug a couple of dollars out of his pocket and laid them on the counter.

Grudgingly Helen cut off a slab of the cake and stuck it into a little pink box. She'd given him a slightly bigger piece than last time, he noticed. That looked hopeful. Ringing up the sale, she put his change on the counter.

"No cracks about the cost?" she asked sarcastically when he picked up the change.

"I figure I'm just doing my bit to help you out of your difficulties," he said, correctly figuring that a bland smile would get her more worked up than a show of anger at her gibes. With that in mind, he dropped the change into the tip jar on the counter.

"You're asking for it," she muttered under her breath. He picked up his briefcase and walked toward the door.

"Oh, by the way," he said, turning. "I'll be back tomorrow to go over all the papers with you again. Looks to me like there's some problems with your returns from a couple of years ago, too."

One second after the door swung shut behind him, the remains of the chocolate cake spattered against it.

"At least it wasn't something breakable," Thea said philosophically, helping Helen scrape the sticky chocolate mess off the glass door.

"I'm going to write it fifty times on a tablet." Helen's face was gloomy. "I will not throw things. I will not throw things."

"Could be dangerous," Thea agreed. "You might hurt someone sometime."

"I wish I had hurt him," Helen muttered. "Oh, not really," she added, glimpsing Thea's expression. "But he was so irritating."

"I doubt if anyone's ever thrown a cake at him before," Thea said gravely. "He may change his style after this."

They looked at each other and burst into hysterical laughter. "The expression on his face!" Thea said, grabbing Helen's arm. "Like he couldn't decide whether he was glad to have escaped or sorry so much cake got wasted!"

"The way he strode off with his little pink box," Helen howled. "I thought for a minute he was coming in to toss it back at me."

"He might have." Thea stopped laughing. "It's not nice to mess with the IRS, honey. You'll have to stop harassing him."

"Me harass him?" Helen sprayed window cleaner on the plate glass and eliminated the last traces of chocolate. "It's the other way around, I believe."

"Men just live to cause trouble, that's for sure," Thea muttered. The piece of yellow paper was still in her pocket. She resolved to throw it away as soon as she got home.

"Oh, yeah, I almost forgot," Helen said, eyeing her curiously. "How did it go with the guy who came looking for you yesterday? What's his name?"

"Donovan," Thea said, gathering up the debris and polishing the floor one last time. "And it didn't go. He went."

"He's gone already?" Helen followed her back to the kitchen, swinging the bottle of window cleaner by its spray trigger. "Looked to me like he'd gone to a lot of trouble to track you down."

"He did." Thea compressed her lips. The urge to unburden herself to someone was very strong, but she didn't want to heap her own troubles on Helen, who had a plate full of them already.

"So, just out of curiosity, is he Lucas's father or what?" Helen seemed ready to add Thea's troubles to hers. "You don't have to tell me, if you don't want to."

"He is," Thea said, capitulating with a sigh. "He just didn't know it."

"I see." Helen nodded, stowing the cleaning supplies in their closet. "Pretty big shock to find that out."

"It must have been." Thea was mainly talking to herself. "If I'd let him know all along, or at least told him a few months before the birth—well, it couldn't have made much difference." She wandered over to the desk to pick up her handbag. "He has this hotshot job, you see. And it's in New York."

Helen pursed her lips, considering. "He looked to me," she said after a minute, "like the kind of guy who gets what he wants."

"He is." Thea found her car keys. "That's why he came back. But now I think he's decided that he doesn't want me and Lucas, after all."

She couldn't talk anymore, feeling her throat full of self-pitying tears. Helen nodded.

"Listen, don't worry about coming in this afternoon. Roxie's coming in, and Maria's here. We'll do fine without you."

"Not much I can do on the books anyway," Thea said forlornly. "Not with Patrick taking them away."

"Go play with your baby," Helen commanded. "Forget about all creepy men. I'm going to!"

Thea summoned a smile and left.

Driving to her cottage, she faced the thought that she had managed to avoid since the previous evening, when anger at Donovan had kept thoughts at bay. It looked as if she would be a single parent forever.

Now that she looked squarely at it, she realized that she had always believed, deep inside, that someday Donovan would return, that they would form a nuclear family together. Someday had come—and gone. The nuclear family was proven to be no more than a dream.

She was filled with the sense of aloneness that had been alleviated after she met Donovan, after they had become lovers and roommates. Now her orphan state bore her down again, as it had in her late teens, after her mother had died. Her father had died when she was small, so long ago she remembered only delighted baritone laughter and the sensation of flying as he tossed her high and caught her again securely.

Her parents, Thea knew, had been deeply in love. After her father's death, her mother had lavished tenderness on her little girl, but unspoken between them was the knowledge that the enchantment of life was over for Dora Willits. As Thea grew older, more confident and capable, her mother had seemed to fade, gradually, until by her freshman year in college, Thea was unsurprised when her mother's final decline made her an orphan before she was twenty.

She had not been able to wish her mother back into the world, unless Dora could have been accompanied by the man she loved so wholly. But now she felt the need of a mother's comfort for herself. "Mother," Thea said aloud, parking in front of the dilapidated garage, "would understand. Mother would know how I feel."

But she was a mother now, the source of comfort, not the receiver. When she walked into the cottage, it was to find Lucas twisting in R.J.'s arms, his face screwed up in defiance of the bottle she tried to give him.

"Thank goodness," R.J. said, relinquishing the baby. "He's decided he's not taking a bottle today, thank you."

"I can handle it," Thea said, sinking into the nearest chair and unbuttoning her shirt. "I've been bursting for a while now."

Lucas was too upset to nurse right away, but after she calmed him he latched on, and Thea almost groaned with relief when his greedy sucking diminished the heaviness in her breasts.

R.J. lingered, watching Lucas with approval. "That's what he needed," she said finally, in her gruff voice. "Mommy's got what it takes."

"You've got everything else," Thea replied, smiling gratefully at her. "I couldn't manage without you, R.J."

"I figured you wouldn't need me once that man moved in," R.J. said, clearing her throat.

"What man?"

"The slick guy who came to see you last night. Miss Sophie was real taken with him."

"She must have exchanged two words with him," Thea muttered. "Miss Sophie is too nice to be discriminating."

"I saw him when he left," R.J. volunteered. "Looked like you put a flea in his ear."

Thea switched Lucas to the other side. He barely paused in his intake. "I might have," she said. "But he left before I got the chance."

"So he's not sticking around?" R.J. sounded relieved. "I've kind of gotten to like the baby."

"You adore him and you know it," Thea said, summoning a smile. "Whereas Donovan—" She took a moment to collect her thoughts. "Donovan knew nothing about Lucas. He—he isn't real keen on children, especially babies."

"Humph." R.J. picked up the diaper she'd been using as a burp protector and arranged it on Thea's shoulder. "I used to feel that way, I suppose. But a baby like little Luke here—he's something special. Anyone would be keen about him."

"Maybe anyone that had seen him born, as you did, and looked after him from birth," Thea said softly. "I think I made a big mistake."

R.J. cleared her throat. "You've done the best you knew how, right from the start." She held up a hand as Thea began to speak. "You didn't tell me the circumstances, and I don't need to know. But anyone, being around you, would know that you did what you thought was right."

"Thank you, R.J." Thea blinked hard. That was the second time today she'd come close to tears. The tear ducts must be connected to the milk ducts somehow, and both were flowing freely.

"I'd better get along," R.J. said, with one last peep at Lucas, who was beginning to slow down in the intensity of his eating. "Miss Sophie's poorly, up at the big house, and Faith is down with some bug, too. That Mr. Castigliano is the only one that doesn't seem to have it."

"And you."

"Me? I never get sick." R.J. picked up the tool belt she'd left by the front door. "I'll be back this afternoon."

"No need." Lucas was done, and Thea held him against her shoulder, patting his back to get the burp up. "I'm not going in this afternoon. You have the rest of the day off."

R.J. snorted. "Not likely. If you don't need me, I'll get to those broken sash cords in the sitting room."

She stumped off down the path, and Thea sat for a moment after Lucas burped, feeling him grow heavier in her arms as he drowsed off. Carrying him to the crib, she smiled mistily when she covered him with a light blanket. This, at least, was right. She hadn't make a mistake in having her baby.

Wandering back into the living room, she stood by the diamond-paned window and stared out at the rhododendron blooms that lined the path. If she let herself view the situation from Donovan's corner, it was a bit much to expect him to walk in and embrace the family that had come as a complete surprise to him. She didn't really blame him for backing off.

But she did blame him for leaving the damned note. Why hadn't he stayed for dinner, talked it out? Just bolting like that was not in character for a man as dogged and persistent as Donovan.

She pulled out the piece of yellow paper and read the words once more, taking in the slashing black script, the economy of expression. Then she crouched by the fireplace, scraped a match along the brick and set it to a corner of the paper. Flame blossomed, crept blackly toward her thumb and finger, until at last she dropped the paper onto the grate and watched the last of his signature writhe and disintegrate into ash.

Standing, she dusted her hands together. "That's that," she said, her voice sounding loud in the quiet house. She had hoped to feel lighter, less burdened with expectation. But the physical destruction of the evidence had not succeeded in blotting it from her mind.

When the phone rang she answered it eagerly, hoping for something to distract her.

Helen was on the line. "Thea," she began. "I don't suppose you need to come in just because the straw has finally arrived that breaks the camel's back."

There was an ominous gaiety in Helen's voice. "Take a deep breath," Thea advised. "Tell me what the problem is."

"Nothing much," Helen said, giggling wildly. "The mail just came."

"Not more from the IRS, surely?"

"Oh, no, nothing like that." Thea could hear Helen's gulp. "It's from Bradford, Bradford, McKittrick and Slope, you know—"

"The real estate guys that handle the lease. What is it?"
Thea tried to keep the impatience from her voice.

"They want to break the lease." Helen spoke calmly, the
calm of the doomed. "They've had an offer for the building, and they want to sell it. They have lawyers and everything. They want us out."

CHAPTER SEVEN

DONOVAN FELT SATISFIED when he looked around at his denuded apartment. It didn't take long to pack if you'd never really settled into a place. He'd spent so little time there over the past year that most of the dishes he'd brought with him were still crated up. They could be shipped directly back to California without causing a bit of trouble.

There was a knock on the door, and he went to let in the two moving men. The one with "Frank" embroidered on his pocket was heavyset and gloomy; the one whose pocket said "Bill" was thin and gloomy. But their faces brightened at the sight of his living room, where crates of books were stacked neatly in the middle of the room. "Looks like ya got a good start here," said Frank. "This furniture go?"

"The furniture came with the apartment," Donovan told him, sparing a disinterested glance at the puffy gray couch, the sleek gray chairs, the gray laminated bookshelves. "You won't have to bother with it. My stuff is in the boxes."

"Need more boxes?" Bill spoke, his words slow and lugubrious.

"No," Donovan said. "I saved the ones from my last move. Everything's packed except the bedroom."

They followed him into the bedroom—queen-size bed with a gray tufted headboard—and stared with awe into his closet.

Bill spoke first. "You the only guy living here?"

"Yeah, it's all mine," Donovan said defensively. The closet was—well, full.

He had thirty-six shirts, forty-eight ties, twelve pairs of pants, six suits and eight sport jackets. The drawers in the pale blond oak dresser were filled with underwear. "I don't like to do laundry too often," he said lamely, and then wondered why he was making excuses to a couple of moving men. Spending long days in business clothes meant he had to be able to rotate them through the dry cleaners. More than anything else, that wardrobe symbolized his job for him.

And now he wasn't going to need it for a while. He had a leave of absence from his job, some time to think about where his life was headed, some time to persuade Thea to let him go her way. It might be a long time before he would put on a vice president's Italian-tailored suit. He had a distinct feeling, in fact, that he wasn't going to be a vice president much longer.

So how to decide what to do with all these clothes? Pack most of them into his BMW? It would be tough. Ship them to Thea's house, instead of into storage with the rest of his things? Presumptuous and perhaps unnecessary. He didn't expect to be wheeling and dealing in Santa Cruz. He didn't even know if it was possible there. And if hot deals were cut there, they were probably accomplished in raiment more like the surfer boy's hula-dancer shirt than the expensive Egyptian broadcloth he normally wore.

"You planning to get all of this into that wardrobe box?" Frank scratched the stubble on his chin, assessing the situation.

Donovan made up his mind. "Most of it, yes. I'll just take a couple of things in the suitcase."

"Better bring up another wardrobe box," Frank told Bill. "No need to crowd the threads." He reached out a finger, surprisingly tentative, and touched the nubby surface of a silk shantung jacket. "Stuff like this, you want to take care of it."

Bill departed to bring up a box, and Donovan selected a dark suit, the shantung jacket, a pair of pants and a handful of ties, fitting it all into a garment bag on the bed with the practiced ease of a frequent traveler. With Frank's help, he started filling wardrobe boxes with the rest of his dress-for-success life. It didn't take long to empty the closet.

"What line of work might you be in," Frank asked, sealing up one of the boxes. "Investment banker?"

"Venture capitalist," Donovan said absently, opening his biggest suitcase and tossing underwear into it.

"You don't look it now," Frank remarked, with a skeptical lift of his eyebrows. Donovan looked down at his thick wool sweater, the comfortable cords and running shoes that completed his off-duty ensemble. The sweater was a concession to the chilliness that had plagued him during the past year. Perhaps, in Santa Cruz, he wouldn't need to depend on wool to keep himself warm.

"Guess even Donald Trump has to go off-duty once in a while," Bill reminded Frank. "Who knows what he wears when he's watchin' TV at night?"

Frank had a risqué answer to that hypothetical question. Donovan wasn't really listening to their byplay. He put a few shirts, stiff in their laundry wrappings, into the big suitcase, along with jeans and T-shirts, running sweats, shaving gear and the necessities for life on the road.

Frank nudged Bill. "Takes some kind of capitalist to have a tie like this," he said, his pudgy fingers smoothing the glowing red silk.

Donovan could see the wistfulness beneath the man's mockery. "I've got too many ties," he said, staring at the silk with dislike. "Take one, if you want. I never want to wear a red tie again."

"You mean it?" Frank's face brightened. "Don't wear 'em much in my line of work," he added, "but the missus and I like a night out now and again."

"Help yourself." Donovan took the picture of Thea off his dresser and slid it carefully between layers of undershirts. "Makes less to move, doesn't it?"

He carried his suitcase out to the living room, leaving Frank behind in an agony of blissful indecision. He was finished with the bedroom now. It was empty of his belongings.

But it had been empty anyway, even before he'd stripped the bed and closet.

He added suitcase and garment bag to the pile of things to take down to his BMW. Bill was loading boxes of books onto the hand truck. Already the living room had a waiting look, ready for the next tenant. He picked up the audio gear he used in the car and his garment bag and headed for the elevator.

There was a garage attached to his apartment, one reason why it had carried such an exorbitant rent. He'd rarely driven the BMW in the city, preferring not to risk its silvery paint in cutthroat city traffic. "We'll be on the road soon," he murmured, opening the car door and arranging his things. "Just you and me, baby." Grinning, he remembered the time Thea had asked him if it made him feel silly talking to his car. "Not at all," he'd told her. "I only feel silly when I'm overheard."

Cecily would have liked his car. Shaking his head, he waited for the elevator and wondered why thoughts of his ex-wife had intruded. He had made use of their failed marriage for years to keep women at bay, until Thea had slipped past his defenses. And even then, Cecily and the nasty divorce had been behind his refusal to think about marriage again.

"I was a chump," he muttered, pushing the elevator button again. Thea was nothing like his ex-wife, whose beauty and gaiety had concealed a greedy cunning that had finally obscured her lovely face and body for him. The divorce had been painful and emotionally costly.

Looking at it from a distance, he could see now that a marriage between them would have no chance of making it. But when he'd been fresh out of business school flush with his academic success, it had seemed merely the crowning glory that a beautiful, sought-after campus beauty queen had agreed to marry him. He had envisioned Cecily presiding at the dinner parties and cocktail parties that, according to business school, were an essential part of any rising executive's life. He had gloried in her excellent taste, her instinct for knowing what was suitable.

Cecily had shared those visions—but without realizing that at first, that was all they were. He had no influential family, no wealthy friends to help him into a prestigious job. He would get there, he knew, but it would take long hours of proving himself, working hard to get what was available to some of his classmates simply by making a few phone calls.

He'd been willing to work. He'd felt that it was all waiting for him. But Cecily couldn't wait. She complained that they'd only gotten six place settings of the expensive china she'd chosen as wedding gifts—all from her relatives, who were not much better off than he was, but knew how to make a show. Cecily wanted to buy more—more china, more crystal, more silver. She wanted a fancy apartment in Pacific Heights, not the small place he'd found near the Marina. She wanted expensive furniture, handmade rugs and the equivalent in her own wardrobe. It was a full-time job to plan the entertainments they couldn't afford and do all the work herself, since he was too stingy to hire a caterer.

Even now, he could call up the memory of her voice, turning shrill, needling him about his unpolished upbringing, his lack of money. Her scent had begun to seem heavy and unappealing. She had not been interested in making love very often, so he'd been astonished when at last he learned that she was involved in the well-publicized divorce of a prominent San Francisco attorney, whose wife of twenty-three years was not reticent in blaming her husband's infidelities on Cecily.

He'd been lucky, he realized now, that the attorney's divorce had made his own easier. Cecily had retained the things she'd wanted so badly—the silver, the furniture, even the car. He didn't want anything around to remind him of her anyway. He'd kept his fledgling investments and worked like a demon.

Now he had achieved the success that she'd craved when they were married. And he recognized that somewhere in the past year, when all his emotions had been focused on Thea, the spector of his ex-wife had ceased to have the power to make him reject marriage.

The elevator arrived, finally, and Donovan got on, feeling light enough to ascend without it. He pressed the button for his floor. "That's all behind me," he said aloud, his voice echoing strangely in the empty elevator. Cecily and marriage had been inextricably mixed in his head. But at last she had receded into the dim corner where unhappy events of the past were transformed into the wisdom of experience. Now he was free to link marriage with someone else— Thea. He couldn't wait to get out of New York and on his way back to her.

It took three more trips before he'd stowed everything away, and by that time there was just room enough inside the car for him. The movers were carting their last load out the door. "Fast job," Bill told Donovan. "We got time for a cup of coffee now."

"I should have left the coffee maker out," Donovan said, realizing that the finer etiquette of moving had escaped him.

"We'll get some around the corner," Bill said.

"That's right." Frank patted his pocket, from which a flash of red silk could be seen. "We could even get into the Stork Club, with our power ties."

Bill was above this sort of frivolity. "All this stuff goes to storage in California, right?"

Donovan signed the bill of lading and copied the address of the storage facility into his pocket notebook. He handed Bill and Frank each a ten-dollar bill, clapped them heartily on the back and took his last survey of the apartment that had not been home for the past year or so.

There was one more unpleasant duty in front of him. After handing in his keys and arranging with the manager to send the deposit to Thea's address, he climbed into the car and eased out onto the street. One more drive in the crazy gridlock that New Yorkers knew as traffic. Then he'd head for the interstate, plotting a course directly to Santa Cruz.

He found a parking garage close to the World Trade Center and walked the rest of the way to Gaskell Associates's office near the stock exchange. Brice Tobin was in the reception area, haranguing the secretaries. He broke off when he saw Donovan.

"So what are you doing here? Change your mind?" Brice smoothed the thinning blond hair that was leaving his forehead behind. "I told Metlock you would."

"Sorry to disappoint you, Brice." Donovan smiled easily. "Just came in to sign off on the Torobitshu project, and then I'm out of here."

A door opened down the hall and Bob Metlock came toward them. "You remember, now, Donovan," he said fussily, fingering the knot on his red silk tie. "Two months, that's all. We can't really spare you that long, but considering the circumstances—"

"I'd just as soon hand in my resignation right now," Donovan told him. "There'd be no ambiguity then."

"Nonsense." Metlock looked alarmed. "Don't be hasty, now. If you must have time off, we'll consider it a leave of absence. Irregular, of course, but we don't want to lose you."

"Fine." Donovan wanted to tell Metlock to go ahead and lose him, but he'd tried already, and it hadn't worked. Besides, there was some security in knowing that he could come back to his job if things didn't work out. He'd never burned his bridges before, and he wasn't sure he was ready to start now.

"And remember, keep your eyes peeled." Metlock pumped his hand in farewell. "The start-ups are thick on the ground out there in California. Let us know what you find."

"I'm not going to be looking for business," Donovan said, keeping his voice mild with an effort. "I need to get away from that for a while."

"Sure. I understand." Metlock nodded, but clearly he didn't understand. He had a family, Donovan knew, but he seemed content to live most of his life at the office, engrossed in deal-making.

Brice Tobin watched the New York director of Gaskell Associates disappear back into his office and gave Donovan a malicious smile. "You may not be able to brownnose your way back in after that, buddy," he remarked. "Should have let him think you'd be scouring the hills for good prospects.''

"I don't really care," Donovan said, turning away to sign the papers the secretary presented him with. "There's more to life than Gaskell Associates." Saying the words, he felt the truth of it. Something tight inside him sprang loose.

"Big talk," Tobin muttered. Donovan thought he detected a flash of envy in the other man's eyes. "Talk doesn't pay the bills.''

"Yeah, but it's cheap, they say." Donovan stuck out his hand. "Look me up if you're ever out in Santa Cruz."

Tobin shook his hand. "Sounds like you're not coming back, after all."

"Maybe I'm not." He crossed his fingers, hoping he wouldn't need to eat those words, and headed for the door, unable to wait another moment to get out of New York. "Go ahead, Tobin. Step into my shoes. I'm sure they'll fit you fine."

Exultation filled him as he took the elevator, strode through the motley crowds on the sidewalk, fastened his seat belt. He crept through the traffic to the Brooklyn tunnel, catching a glimpse of the Statue of Liberty lifting her torch offshore. Grinning, he pushed a tape into the tape player and, in the confines of his car, shouted out his own freedom. A few days of driving, and he'd be back with his love, ready to besiege her until she found a place for him in her life.

Glancing down, he checked that the big package he'd stored in the passenger foot well was still intact. Its gay wrapping paper had been provided by FAO Schwartz. Inside the box was a brightly colored circus train, guaranteed by the salesclerk to have no piece small enough to harm a baby.

The picture in his mind was very clear. The living room of Thea's cottage, in front of the fireplace. Thea and him, sitting on the rug. Lucas reaching eagerly for the smiling circus clown, popping it into his mouth.

Donovan refused to entertain the possibility that it wouldn't happen that way. Now that he'd rearranged his life so drastically, things would work out. They had to.

The speakers vibrated when he turned up the volume. "I—I feel free," Jack Bruce blasted. Donovan sang along. "I feel free."

"HAWAII," HELEN SAID disgustedly. "She says he's in Hawaii."

"Who?" Thea lowered Lucas into the playpen at the rear of the kitchen. He sat up for a moment, grinning his broad, toothless grin, and then slowly toppled over. Still grinning, he wriggled onto his stomach and stared at the plump pink elephants that dangled over the side of the playpen.

"The cleaning lady," Helen answered, flipping furiously through the telephone book. "She said he's been in the South Seas, and she thought he was in Hawaii by now."

"Who is in Hawaii?" Thea plopped the diaper bag beside the desk and stared at Helen. "Who are you talking about?"

"Oh. I thought you knew." Helen found what she needed in the phone book and began punching numbers on the telephone. "This Guerneville person." She turned away, speaking into the receiver. "Yes, maybe you can help me. I want a list of all the places in Hawaii a yacht could be tied up."

Thea smothered incredulous laughter, eased one hip onto the desk and waited while Helen badgered the unfortunate person on the other end of the line. John Northrup Guerneville III, the object of her quest, owned the building that housed Babycakes. And Helen was leaving no stone unturned in her effort to locate him.

Since the real estate management firm had declared their intentions nearly two weeks earlier, Helen had miraculously managed to keep quality control at the bakery high. In fact, turmoil seemed to stimulate her to greater heights. Never had her custards been so smooth, her croissants so flaky, her cakes so feather light.

But when there was no baking to be done, Helen fretted. She had nagged and pestered the real estate people into admitting that their proposal to boot the bakery out was not directed by the actual property owner, but simply sound business practice—turning over a low-profit long-term lease in favor of a high-profit divestment.

This had led to interviews with lawyers, all unsatisfactory. With enough money, as the last attorney had patiently explained, Helen could fight the attempt to break her lease. But her lease, unfortunately, had been negotiated in a kinder, gentler time six years ago and was not ironclad. The property management firm had found a loophole and was busily engaged in trying to wriggle through it. Only large-scale legal maneuvering would stop them. And that, the attorney said, cost money. "Do either of you have a relative or close friend who's a lawyer?"

Sitting in his plush chairs, dressed in their best clothes, Helen and Thea had shaken their heads.

"Well, then." The attorney shrugged, clearly putting it out of his hands. "There are some tenant's rights organizations around, though they mainly focus on living space, not commercial arrangements. Give them a try. That's all I can advise."

As his own contribution to the cause, he had charged them only twenty-five dollars.

So Helen had taken the crusade to a higher level. If the actual property owner would call off the management sharks, she argued, they'd be fine. She'd researched the title deed at city hall, and turning up John Northrup Guerneville III had been initially a means of rejoicing. The name was vaguely familiar, and Helen remembered reading something about the Guerneville heir in the local paper years ago. But when the clipping had been found at the library, some of her jubilation had faded.

"He's nothing but a playboy," she'd stormed to Thea. "Sails a damned yacht around and leaves all his business to people like those property managers."

"But there is the Guerneville Library," Thea had pointed out, "and Guerneville Park, and the Marguerite Guerneville Auditorium. Someone in the family has had some concept of philanthropy."

"To hell with philanthropy," Helen had said. "I just want his goons to lay off my lease!"

With the tenacity she had developed in dealing with the IRS, Helen had spent the past few days on the trail of the last of the Guernevilles. Thea had come to regard it almost like a television serial. Every day Helen had some new fact to report, some fresh clue to follow.

"Thanks," she said now, and banged down the phone. "Too many yacht clubs to tell me over the phone." Her voice was gloomy. "She suggested I get a Hawaiian phone book and work my way through the islands."

"That could cost a lot if you do it long-distance," Thea said, watching Lucas as he batted one of the pink elephants against the side of the playpen. "And what would it accomplish? What will you say when you find him?"

"I'll think of something." Helen scowled at Thea. "After all the improvements we've put into this place, I would think you'd be excited about saving it. I know it would break *my* heart to leave this building now."

"I'm with you on it." Thea began to pace in the narrow space around the playpen. She couldn't tell Helen that everything, even the bakery, had begun to lose significance as she thought more and more about Donovan. She couldn't stop herself from daydreaming, and her subconscious was only too happy to provide the same topic at night. It was an effort to wrench her mind away and confront the bakery's dilemma.

"They did offer to compensate us, you know," Thea ventured. "That would be enough money to pay off the IRS, at least."

"And then what would I do? What would you do? We couldn't sell our equipment for what we paid for it. One of our assets is our low overhead here. We would pay a lot more for any other space we rented. Besides," Helen added, "this place is my home. I don't want to leave."

Thea shook her head. "I understand," she said. "But it's not really smart to feel like that about property you don't own. You're always at the mercy of someone."

"What about your cottage?" Helen demanded. "You sank money into that, and it's not yours."

"No, but I have an agreement with Miss Sophie." Thea handed Lucas the yellow plastic whale he'd just thrown out of the playpen. He gnawed on it for a minute, then tossed it overboard again. "She insisted on it, really. I have an option to buy the cottage and the part of her backyard that goes through to the street behind. I can buy it when I want to, at a rate below market value, and in the meantime I'm renting for a very reasonable amount."

"Yeah," Helen pointed out, "but Miss Sophie is old. What happens when she kicks off?"

Thea winced. "She's very healthy for her age," she protested. "And if she dies, I can choose to purchase the property from the estate, or to be reimbursed for the work I did. Really, it's a great agreement, no matter what Donovan says."

"What does he say?" Helen abandoned her chase for a moment. "You haven't told me what's happening between him and you."

"Nothing." Thea handed the toy whale back to her son and scooped him into her arms. "I mean, he left, like I told you."

Helen whistled. "I was sure he'd be back. He hasn't turned up yet?"

"He won't be back." Thea spoke as much to her yearning heart as to Helen. She smoothed her cheek against Lucas's silky, nearly invisible crop of hair. "If you can't take the heat," she added cynically.

"I don't know," Helen said, pursing her lips. "He didn't look like the kind of guy to bow out without a fight. And since he's Lucas's dad, he has rights, doesn't he?"

Thea didn't answer right away. "Biologically," she said, "he's a father. But emotionally, he isn't." Lucas banged her arm with the whale and then dropped it again. Still holding him, she knelt to dig a rubber bear out of the diaper bag.

Helen shook her head. "Mark my words," she said darkly. "You haven't heard the last of that guy." She tapped her fingers on the desk and dismissed Thea's personal problems. Watching her, Thea wished she could do it so easily.

"Who would know?" Helen muttered. "Who would know where this globe-trotting millionaire has parked his yacht?"

"The property managers can get in touch with him, no doubt."

Helen snorted. "I can just see them handing me that kind of information." She shook her head, sending the glossy black hair flying. "Other people know, I'm sure.... That's it!"

"What are you up to now?" Thea phrased the question with some apprehension, noting the gleeful look on Helen's face as she rummaged through the local phone book.

"I'm about to run the guy to ground," Helen announced, punching numbers on the telephone again. At least it was a local number, Thea noticed.

"Hello." Helen's voice was sweeter than usual. "Yes, I know you're the yacht club. Is Jack Guerneville tied up there? Not for another month? But he told me to meet him in Santa Cruz—oh, I see. I misread the itinerary. He's in Hawaii now, it looks like. But I can't quite read his writing here—yes, it is a dreadful scrawl, isn't it? Do you happen to know—oh, thanks. Yes, I've got it. Thank you so much."

This time Helen cradled the phone gently, smiling in triumph. "Got him!" she crowed. "The Harbor Club, on Maui." She chewed her lip for a moment, concentrating. "Should I phone, or telegraph? A telegram is more urgent."

Thea put Lucas back into the playpen. "There's no way he can sail back here in under a couple of weeks," she pointed out.

Helen shrugged, unconcerned. "He can fly, can't he? He's rich. I just have to figure out what will get him here."

"Helen, listen. Don't try anything too fancy," Thea begged, alarmed. "No fake paternity suits, nothing like that."

"Of course not." Helen looked up, indignant. "Do you think I'm crazy? I want him on my side, after all." She made shooing motions with her hands. "Run along and help them in the store. I think better by myself."

If it was a choice between remaining ignorant of Helen's probably harebrained plan or being involved in it, Thea knew what choice to make. She fled.

Business was brisk at the front counter, despite the dishevelment of remodeling. Thea had to go back for another tray of brownies. Helen was talking on the phone, but by judiciously clattering the trays, Thea could avoid hearing what she said.

Betty stood by the counter when she got back. "Roxie told me you'd be bringing more brownies," she gushed. Betty was in her midfifties, tall enough to carry off the ample hips and bosom that might have made a lesser woman despair. "The girls in the shop wanted me to pick some up. They all love your brownies."

"How many do you need?"

"Let's see—Carol's dieting, but she'll eat one, I bet. Melissa, Freddy, Bambi—better give me half a dozen, just to make sure."

Thea transferred the thick chocolatey squares into a pink box. "How are things down at the shop?"

"Oh, fine. Business is good. You could use a little trim, you know." Betty eyed Thea's flyaway hair professionally. "Is that some gray, I see? My goodness, honey, you should color that right away."

"It's just a little bit," Thea said defensively. "I'm too young to color my hair."

"Now where did you get that idea?" Betty giggled, accepting the box. "What are you, thirty, thirty-one? Take my advice, honey, and stay there. Get your moisturizer, your color rinse—just don't get a day older!"

"That might be a little hard to arrange." Thea leaned on the counter, wondering why Betty didn't take her own advice. Her hair, fearfully and wonderfully arranged, was growing out distinctly gray.

Betty caught the direction of her glance. "Honey, I'm getting on for fifty," she said, shaving, Thea suspected, five or six years off her age. "I decided it was time to face up to it. I'm gonna let my hair grow out natural, and then decide what shade of silver complements me. You know?"

"You'll look magnificent." Thea accepted Betty's money, operating the complicated new cash register without a hitch. "To tell you the truth, I like the way people's faces look when they let their lives show through."

Betty turned this over, clearly skeptical. "I don't know about that. But after that Raymund business, I realized there's no fool like an old fool. From now on I'll act my age." She sighed. "If it wasn't for that, I'd cozy up to that nice fellow from the IRS. He's a real cutie pie."

"Patrick?" Thea said cautiously. "Did you get the same one we got?"

"That's him." Betty nodded. "Patrick Lasswell. I always did have a soft spot for the Irish. And he's so charming, isn't he?"

"You couldn't prove it by us," Thea muttered. She had been thankful the past couple of weeks that Patrick had ceased to badger them for the time being.

"He just gets the girls at the shop in whoops," Betty said, removing her elbow from the top of the display case. "I know he's going to find that rotten Raymund and get my money back. See?" She dug into her bag and pulled out a flyer. "I went and had these made and I'm handing them out to all my customers."

Thea stared at the flyer. In the center was a picture, fuzzily reproduced, of the same dapper young man she remembered in the picture Helen had flushed away. His hair shone, his teeth flashed in a winsome smile. Below the picture were the words, "If you see this man anywhere, call 408-555-7577 Right Away."

"It's something, isn't it," Betty said proudly. "I just know one day the phone will ring and it will be someone that's spotted the louse."

"You think this will work?" Thea handed it back.

"You keep it, honey." Betty left the flyer on the counter. "Put it up in the bakery. You never know when it will ring a bell."

"Helen wouldn't stand for it," Thea said regretfully. "And I can't help but wonder if it's a good idea. Suppose someone who looks like Raymund got hounded by this?"

"Honey, no innocent person has anything to fear." Betty chuckled. "Of course, there are some people who have seen him everywhere—one lady said she was positive she spotted him in Monterey, and another customer said she saw him in San Francisco, but doesn't remember just where." She shook her head. "What a thing to go through. But it'll come out right in the end. That nice Mr. Lasswell will get things straightened out."

"I hope so," Thea assured her.

"Well, I'll be going," Betty said, dangling her pink box by the string. "The girls will be wondering where their treats are."

She swept out, leaving Thea feeling bemused. Encounters with Betty were so full of related incident that it took a few minutes for your ears to stop ringing, she decided, straightening the tray of croissants and rearranging the basket of whole wheat baguettes.

"This will fetch him," Helen cried, bouncing in from the kitchen. Thea folded the flyer hastily and shoved it into her purse, which was under the countertop, while Helen read from the piece of paper in her hand. "Your property managers are really destroying the Guerneville reputation for philanthropy in Santa Cruz. If this matters to you, lose no time in checking out the situation at Babycakes across from the Boardwalk.''

Thea shook her head. ''Maybe he doesn't care about his family's reputation for philanthropy.''

Helen's face hardened. ''He will care, after I've finished with him, if he doesn't get his butt over here. I give him one week max, and then I go to the newspapers. Judging from the tone of that old article I found, they'd love to pitch dirt about a Guerneville.''

''Helen,'' Thea said worriedly, ''it's one thing to try to save the bakery, but when you blacken someone's name— isn't that going too far?''

''No,'' Helen said, still in that hard voice. ''This bakery is my life. I'm fighting for it.''

Thea gazed at her for a minute and then smiled. ''Okay, partner. Shoulder to shoulder!''

''That's the spirit!'' Helen laughed, waving her piece of paper. ''Watch out, Jack Guerneville! You haven't got a prayer.''

Like an echo of Helen's triumphant cry, Lucas raised his voice. Thea consulted her watch. ''I need to take him home for a nap,'' she said, frowning. ''Guess I'll do the payroll at home.''

''Sorry to monopolize your desk so long.'' Helen folded her message and stuck it into her pocket. ''He should get it sometime this afternoon, or evening, in Hawaii. He could be here by Monday.''

''Don't get your hopes up too high,'' Thea warned. ''See you later.''

LUCAS FELL ASLEEP in his car seat, and Thea decided not to stop at the market, reluctant to wake him. She carried him into the cottage, car seat and all, and put another load of the omnipresent diapers on to wash while he slept.

R.J. came to the back door as she was adding the washing soda. "Do you have any juice?" R.J. didn't look good. Her eyes were heavy and her normally ruddy face was pale. "Extra juice, I mean. We're out at the big house, and I don't feel like going to the store."

Thea rummaged in the refrigerator. "All I have is one bottle of apple juice, and some frozen lemonade."

R.J. accepted the apple juice. "Keep the lemonade," she said, turning her head aside to cough. "You'll need it when you get this flu bug."

"I won't get it," Thea said, finding a bag for the juice. "I never get sick. How's Miss Sophie doing?"

"She's better." R.J. didn't complain when Thea added a packet of chicken noodle soup to the bag. "But Mr. Castigliano's sick now."

"Oh, no." Thea looked at R.J., concerned. "You're not trying to take care of all these people, are you? You've got it yourself."

"Not too bad," R.J. said stoutly. "And Mr. C. doesn't want to be tended. He was pretty good," she admitted grudgingly, "with Miss Sophie. That's how he got it, I guess."

"Well, this time next week you'll all be well," Thea said bracingly. "What can I do for you?"

"Just keep away. Keep Lucas away." R.J. coughed again and headed for the door. "If either of you got it, we'd all feel ten times worse."

Thea watched R.J. totter back to the big house and decided to make some chicken soup. "I never get sick," she told Lucas when he woke up, "but chicken soup will taste good, and maybe R.J. would like some."

Lucas sat up, strapped into his high chair, and gummed away at a piece of hard toast while Thea chopped vegetables and simmered chicken. The soup's aroma made both of them hungry. Thea joined Lucas with a piece of Baby-cakes' French bread, spread with unsalted butter and honey. Lucas grew tired of his toast and demanded to be nursed, and Thea poured herself a glass of milk to take into the living room. Cuddling him in the rocker, she sipped her milk and paged through a magazine. She'd lit a fire in the fireplace, and the flames seemed brighter as dusk stole through the room.

Lucas drowsed at her breast. The fire crackled, mingling its incense with the homey smell of chicken soup. And Thea felt lonely.

She thought of the big house, where even with everyone stricken by illness there was always companionship nearby, if you wanted it.

"I've got Lucas," she said out loud. And Lucas was a lot of fun. But he wasn't really a companion. "Maybe when he gets older."

Perhaps she would find a kitten. "You'd like that, wouldn't you, sweetie?" Lucas rolled a sleepy eye up at her, and Thea had to recognize that what she needed was not a cat.

As they had for days now, thoughts of Donovan brought conflicting emotions to torment her. Picturing him made interesting sensations occur in the nerve-rich areas of her body. But thinking about his abortive visit was only good for heartache.

She'd almost managed to convince herself that his visit was a dream, that it hadn't really happened. If only she could feel, in the back of her mind, that he hadn't come yet. Then she could still anticipate that someday he would show up. Someday he would be thrilled to find that he was a father.

"What did you expect," she berated herself now. "You should have let him know. You should have prepared him."

But what could prepare a person for becoming a father, if he wasn't willing to be one?

Her musings were interrupted by a knock at the door. "That'll be R.J. again," she told Lucas, carrying him over to the door. "She can take soup back with her."

But it wasn't R.J.

Donovan leaned against the doorjamb.

Perhaps she was still daydreaming. Thea gaped at him, noting the hectic flush on his pale face, the way his hair fell lankly over his forehead, without its usual healthy springiness. "I'm back," he croaked feebly, thrusting a big brightly wrapped package toward her. "For Lucas."

"Donovan! What's the matter?" Thea juggled Lucas and the big package while Donovan collapsed into the nearest chair.

"I got a fever in Truckee," he muttered, passing a hand over his eyes. "Gave me the shakes. Thought I was . . . too tired."

"Have you been—good grief, did you drive from New York?" Thea perched on the chair arm next to him, keeping Lucas away from the source of germs. She put her palm on Donovan's forehead and nearly jerked it away again. "You're burning up! What is it?"

"Flu, probably." His eyes looked glazed. "I couldn't stop on the road. Had to get here. Thea, you're all I've been thinking about, you and Lucas—"

"You shouldn't drive when you feel so bad," she said, smoothing the hair away from his face. "But I'm glad you're here safely."

"I couldn't see having the flu in a motel when I could expose you to it," he said, smiling weakly.

"I wouldn't want you to stay in a motel." She got up. "Let me get you some aspirin."

"Fine," he said trustingly, and turned his face into the cool, smooth surface of the upholstery.

Thea strapped Lucas into the high chair again, providing him with an ice cube to chase over the tray while she rummaged in her cupboard. Aspirin, she decided. Some of that frozen lemonade, made up and warmed. Chicken soup, if Donovan could be made to eat it.

When she went back into the living room, he was limp in the chair, sleeping with the deep concentration of the utterly exhausted. She hated to wake him, but he felt so hot that she knew he needed the aspirin. "Donovan," she said, shaking him gently. "Take your medicine, now."

After a moment he sat up, disoriented. "Mustn't fall asleep. My God!"

"It's okay." Thea handed him the pills and the warm lemonade. "You're safe. You're here. Take these."

Obediently he swallowed. "I've got a leave of absence," he said, blinking up at her. "Family reasons, I told them." He shook his head. "Feels funny to have a family, just like that."

Thea felt guilt clutch at her again and resolutely stifled it. It was enough that Donovan was back of his own free will, after finding out about Lucas. She still hadn't forgiven him for leaving in the first place.

And if he'd come back well, in full possession of his senses, she'd have made sure he knew he would have to find his own place to stay. But given his state, it would be cruel to turn him out.

"How long is your leave of absence?" She didn't want to get her hopes up once more and have him walk out again.

"Couple of months, they say, but I dunno." Donovan's eyes were bleary as he tried to focus them on her. "I say to hell with Bellevue. Any of those other places, too."

"Right." Thea looked at him warily. "I'm going to make up the sofa bed. Then you can get some rest."

He sat, docile, while she pulled out the bed and swiftly made it up with her softest sheets and a warm wool blanket. "There you go. Need any help?"

"Are you offering to undress me?" Despite the tiredness in his eyes, a spark glowed there suddenly.

"Only for medicinal purposes," Thea said firmly. "I don't know what you expect by coming back, Donovan, but you can't just waltz into my house and my bed as if the last year didn't exist."

"I don't expect to." He headed for the bed, sitting wearily on the side and pulling off his shirt.

Thea watched him for a second and then turned away, arranging the warm lemonade and the aspirin on the side table. When she turned back, he was already under the covers, shivering at the contact with the cool sheets.

Somehow the sight of his long, lean body, even concealed by sheets and blankets, gave her the shivers, too. She scolded herself for having sexy thoughts about a sick man, but when Donovan turned his head, she caught a reflection of her own thoughts in his eyes.

He beckoned her down, and she sat gingerly on the edge of the sofa bed. "You know," he said, his voice an exhausted thread, "this isn't how I pictured our reunion. I'm sorry to land on you like this, Thea."

"You couldn't help it," Thea assured him. "The flu doesn't pick and choose who gets it. You'll be on your feet in no time." *And out of here,* she added silently. The unexpectedness of his return took her aback; she wasn't ready yet to deal with all the ramifications, and certainly not ready to live with him again.

Lucas was banging on the high chair tray in the kitchen. "I've got to go get him," she murmured, pulling the blanket up around Donovan's shoulders.

"You do that," he mumbled. "I'm going to sleep for a week or so."

Lucas babbled happily at her, patting her face with wet, ice-cold hands. "Time for your bath," she told him, carrying him through the living room. A glance at Donovan showed him motionless, eyes closed, chest rising and falling. The bakery would be closed the next day. She'd have to spend the whole day alone with Donovan. Maybe he would be well enough to tell her why he'd come back. Had he come to stay or just to get to know his son?

She was turning out the lights in the living room when she noticed the package, shoved behind a chair. Undecided, she hesitated, then went on into the bedroom. "We'll open it when Daddy can watch," she said. Daddy. It had a nice ring.

CHAPTER EIGHT

OPENING HIS EYES, Donovan stared up at the unfamiliar ceiling. Dark wood beams crossed the white plaster, and the whole effect was much lower than the ceiling in his New York apartment.

New York. His car. A blizzard near Elko, Nevada. Coming down I-80 from Donner summit on the western side of the Sierra Nevada in a late snowstorm, while fighting debilitating chills. He didn't remember much of the final ascent and descent of the Santa Cruz mountains via the curves and strains of Highway 17.

But somehow he'd made it. He was in Thea's living room now, tucked up in the sofa bed he recognized from their San Francisco condo.

Lying there, he felt oddly disconnected from his body. His hand, when he tried to lift it, moved reluctantly, heavily. Somewhere in his head was the memory of stabbing pain. In fact, he felt much like he had at fourteen, when he'd run afoul of a gang during a brief stint in a group home. The gang members had very physical ways of greeting newcomers and making them feel part of the community. He had ached all over for a week.

Light came through the diamond-paned windows in pleasant patterns, washing over rose-print chintz curtains and white-plastered walls. Donovan enjoyed the sense of early-morning peace, of homecoming, that permeated the room. After his exhausting drive, all he wanted to do was lie there and make like a log.

But there were other, more urgent forces at work. He would have to get up soon.

He sat up in the bed and swung his legs over the side. Immediately dizziness assailed him. "Damn it," he muttered. "I'm weaker than day-old coffee!"

His voice sounded loud in the stillness of the living room. Evidently no one else in the house was up. On the floor beside the sofa bed was his clothing. His watch lay on the lamp table. It told him it was nine-thirty in the morning, and he had to stop and figure out what that was in California time. Six-thirty, and it was Sunday. No wonder he was the only one awake.

Yawning, he sat for a minute on the edge of the sofa bed, scratching his unshaven face and pushing the hair out of his eyes. The fever must have really pummeled him. His legs wobbled when he stood up on them, and he had to grab the back of the sofa to steady himself.

But nature was calling him to the bathroom. Gritting his teeth, he tottered into the hall, retaining a vague memory of the bathroom being to the left. Blessedly, it was.

He took a few seconds to stare into the bathroom mirror. The Donovan who stared back was unfamiliar, unfocused somehow. He was used to seeing his reflection while he shaved or knotted his tie. He searched his foggy brain for the difference and had almost given up when he realized that on the reflected features there was no sharp sense of purpose. This was not the face of a man who intended to slash his way through the financial jungle.

Wearying of speculation, he turned away and thought instead about taking a shower. But the effort seemed exhausting. He contented himself with splashing water on his face, cupping his hands and greedily drinking some to assuage the desert that had grown in his mouth.

After that he was unaccountably tired. He rested for a minute, staring vacantly at the black and yellow tiles that marched around the bathroom walls. Those thick blue towels with their yellow borders were from the San Francisco condo, too. It was strange how just the recognition of little things like that could shake him, bring him to realize how far he was from regaining what he'd lost.

He got to his feet again, puffing as if he'd run miles. Cool sheets and a soft bed were beckoning. But he didn't want to be there alone.

Thea's bedroom door was open. Donovan stood in it for a minute, bracing himself on the frame. Shades were drawn against the early light, but gleams of it stole in and highlighted the crib in one corner, caught crystal glints from a bottle on the dresser top, accented the soft flower print on the down comforter.

Thea was curled up in the big bed, one arm thrown protectively around Lucas, who slept facing her, his tiny hand resting on hers. Donovan figured she must have brought the baby into bed to nurse; her nightgown was unbuttoned down the front, and one rosy nipple was exposed.

His longing to crawl into bed with her, to clasp her to him and join her dreams, was powerful. He knew how she would mutter drowsily and make room for him, without waking up. He knew how her hair would smell and how the sheets would be warm from her body.

You've got germs, he told himself. *Bad ones.* There was no point in spreading them around. Perhaps even now Thea could escape this nasty flu, and certainly he didn't want to give it to the baby.

He turned and made his way back to the sofa bed. At least, he thought, pulling the covers up as a chill shook him, he was here, with Thea. It wasn't the way he had pictured it—not yet. But it beat the hell out of shivering alone in his car.

THEA WOKE SUDDENLY, as if Lucas had called her. But he was still sleeping peacefully next to her, his breath coming out in little puffs. She pulled a fold of blanket more securely around his shoulders and buttoned up her nightgown. Though he started the night off in his crib, when he woke to be fed around two or three in the morning, she usually ended up bringing him into her bed, where the process of nursing him interrupted her sleep less. Some mornings he didn't wake until it was nearly time for her to be at the bakery.

She looked at the clock, wondering why the alarm hadn't sounded at five. It was nearly seven, far later than she usually slept. Of course, it was Sunday, and she didn't have to go pour bags of flour into the big mixer.

Then she remembered Donovan.

She had gone to him in the middle of the night, when Lucas woke her, and found him tossing feverishly. She'd gotten some more aspirin down him, and another tot of lemonade. She'd changed Lucas and taken him with her into bed and from then on hadn't stirred.

Wedging pillows on either side of the baby, she slipped out of bed and put on a warm robe. Some impulse she didn't want to name made her stop at the dresser and pull a brush through her hair.

Donovan lay sprawled among the sheets and blankets on the sofa bed. She sat down beside him and put her palm on his forehead. He felt cooler than he had the night before, and his breathing was easier.

Thea studied his frowning brows and the sweep of long lashes that lay along his cheekbones, the tight mouth and uncompromising jaw shadowed by incipient beard. She had to school herself to remember that this was the man who'd walked out two weeks ago rather than come to grips with the change in her situation. What was he doing back, when she'd already started writing him off again?

Those long lashes flicked open and steel-gray eyes stared straight at her. She watched the confusion in them change to emotion and looked quickly away. She wasn't ready—she might never be ready—for what those eyes were saying.

"Good morning." His voice was husky. "I'm not dreaming, am I?"

"If you are," she said, turning back to him, "I'm having the same dream."

"I feel better." He stretched, unfolding his long length beneath the covers. "Last night is kind of a blur to me. Did I tell you how sorry I am for getting sick on you?"

"Several times." Thea bit back a smile. "Don't worry about it. But you shouldn't have been driving when you were so sick."

"I was too sick to realize that, I guess," he said, grinning up at her. "I remember getting this blinding headache going up the Nevada side of the Sierra. I just thought I'd been on the road too long, and took some aspirin. I remember having the chills while I was coming down that steep part of the freeway on the other side—the part with the truck break-away lanes. I was talking to myself after every curve, telling myself it was just like flying."

Thea shivered involuntarily. "You idiot. You should have gotten off the road!"

"I was too close to stop," he said simply. "I kept having this picture in my mind, of you, of your living room—" his eyes traveled around the cottage "—and a nice fire on the hearth." He shook his head. "I could almost feel that fire."

"You were on fire," Thea said tartly. "If you'd been any hotter, I would have called an ambulance to take you to the hospital."

"No!" Alarm showed in his face. "I'm fine now, really. Let me fix breakfast. I won't be any bother." He swung his legs over the edge of the sofa bed.

"Idiot," Thea said again, pushing him back. "You'll stay in bed the rest of the day, and take what you get." Her voice softened. "You'll be just fine later today. Though why you should get so upset about going to the hospital—"

He was quiet for a minute. "Institutions," he said at last. The bitterness in his voice surprised her. "I've had enough of them to last a lifetime. I'd have to be dying before you could get me into a hospital."

Shaken in spite of herself, Thea got up. "In that case, you'd better stay off the road while you're sick," she said briskly. "You might have woken up there this morning. Or not woken up at all."

"Right." His face relaxed into a smile, trusting and open. "I'm sorry to be such a bother."

"It's okay." Thea tightened the belt of her robe, hesitant. But now was not the time to cross-examine Donovan on his motives. He had pulled the covers up around him again, with a hand that seemed almost too weak to grasp them. "I've got plenty of chicken soup and peppermint tea. Do you want some tea and toast?"

"That sounds good," he said drowsily. "I'd like that."

"As soon as I have my shower," she promised. She half expected him to make some remark about showering with her, but his eyelids drifted down and a gentle snore was her only reply.

She checked on Lucas before heading for the bathroom. He was asleep, too. Climbing into the hot water, she felt a little aggrieved. "I must be lacking in charisma," she grumbled, lathering her hair. "All the men fall asleep on me."

Lucas was still snoozing when she got out of the shower, but he woke as she moved around the bedroom getting ready for the day. She spoke softly to him as she changed his diaper and dressed him in red cotton overalls and a white T-shirt. "Your daddy's here, you know." Lucas gurgled, his gaze fixed on the wooden climbing bear that hung by the changing table. "He's come to visit you."

Was a visit all that he'd come for? Thea guessed that his leave of absence had to do with investigating the state of their feelings toward each other—and checking out family life. Maybe he wanted to see if he could put up with Lucas. She raised her chin a little at that idea and then told herself to calm down. After all, this time he'd driven. That meant something, she was sure. And he'd brought that big box for Lucas—another meaningful thing. Trouble was, she didn't know what those meanings added up to.

Donovan was sleeping again when she took Lucas out to the living room. She was sure he'd want a change of clothes, and he hadn't brought anything in the previous evening. "Like it or not, we've got a houseguest," she muttered to Lucas. He was entranced when she fished Donovan's car keys out of the jeans on the floor, and made loud demands to have the keys given over into his keeping.

Thea carried Lucas out the door and up the path to the big house. Donovan hadn't parked in the driveway, she saw. His silver BMW was behind Marlon's transportation, a Volkswagen truck that was at least twenty-five years old and had the paint job to prove it. The two vehicles could not have provided greater contrast. Even through the mud and highway dirt, the BMW gleamed elegantly.

Donovan had not locked it, Thea discovered. It was difficult to tell if anything had been stolen, however. The car was so packed and crammed it had probably daunted any potential thief. The CD player was still there, she saw, and the case of CDs. She was overcome by nostalgic remembrance of cruising in the Silver Bomb, as she'd called the car. Often she'd teased him that he cared more for it than for any person in his life.

Grabbing a suitcase with one hand, she hauled it out onto the sidewalk. Certainly with Lucas, one was all she could manage.

Marlon came bounding down the front steps of Miss Sophie's house. "Let me give you a hand, babe," he called good-naturedly. "Some wheels you got here."

"Not mine," Thea explained. Marlon didn't stagger under the weight of the suitcase, so she added another smaller case and a garment bag to his load and locked up the car. "I have a houseguest for a few days."

"I see." Marlon's blue eyes twinkled in his tanned face, and Thea had to repress the impulse to explain.

She felt vindicated when he brought the bags into her living room and saw Donovan sprawled on the couch. "He's sick," she whispered, "or I'd ask you in."

"Hey, no sweat." Marlon backed cautiously from the room. "If it's the flu that everyone's got at the house, he isn't going to be any fun to take care of." He shook his head. "R.J. nearly bit my head off this morning when I took her up some tea."

Thea followed him out to the front steps. "How is R.J. today?"

"Grouchy." Marlon buttoned his shirt a little farther up his chest and grinned at Thea. The shirt, she noticed, had lurid pink flamingos interspersed in a bloodthirsty way with yawning crocodiles colored an improbable grass green. "That must mean she's getting well, huh?"

"I hope so." Thea crossed her fingers. "If she would only take it easy until she's over it! But she always wants to be up and doing."

"Well," Marlon said cheerfully, "I stole her tool belt when I took her the tea. Have it locked up in my closet right now. If she asks you where it is, you don't know, okay?"

"Very clever." Thea smiled at him. "Without her belt she's helpless. Let's just hope she has the sense to know it."

"Gotta split." Marlon prepared to bolt. "Me and the dudes are going to shoot the curl off Pillar Point today." Marlon did not like, Thea had discovered, to be thanked for the nice things he did. Call him a slob, berate him for leaving the kitchen in a tumult, and he would smile amiably. Mention his bringing a beautiful shell to Miss Sophie, and he was out of there.

"Thanks, Marlon," she called after him, and received a backward flap of the hand in acknowledgment.

Lucas was getting fractious, and before she could move the luggage out of the way in the living room, she would have to feed him. Sitting in the rocking chair where she could keep an eye on Donovan, she pulled up her shirt and gave Lucas what he wanted. While he nursed, she tried to plan the day. Donovan would need juices and bland food, and she made a mental shopping list of invalid comforts. R.J. would not be on hand to spell her with Lucas, "but that doesn't matter, does it, sweetie?" she asked her greedy son, cuddling him closer. "I'll have you all to myself." He grunted, tearing himself away, and she shifted him to the other side.

She was in the kitchen, fixing a pot of tea, when Donovan awoke. Lucas was strapped into the high chair, working on a piece of toast. Thea heard the rustle of bedclothes from the living room, and a faint groan.

She carried a tray into the room, with the tea, some toast and the bottle of aspirin on it. Ignoring the way Lucas trumpeted when he saw her leave the room, she smiled at Donovan. "Feeling better?"

"Some," he allowed, stretching again. "I don't ache so much, but I'm damnably weak."

"It'll pass." She put the tray down on the lamp table and poured a cup of tea. "Here's a hot drink, and some toast if you feel up to it."

He picked up the cup and sipped gingerly. "I'm sorry, Thea. I didn't intend to turn your place into a hospital ward."

"Don't worry." She moved over to the door and picked up his garment bag. "You couldn't help getting sick."

"Wait a minute," he said as she hung the garment bag in the hall closet. "You didn't have to go out and get my stuff."

"I didn't carry it in," she assured him. "Marlon gave me a hand."

"Marlon. The surfer boy with all the muscles?"

She wondered if he could hear the jealousy in his voice. "That's the one," she said cheerfully. "Those muscles come in handy at times."

"I'll bet," he muttered. She pretended not to hear, dragging his suitcase over to the closet and laying it on the floor so it could be opened.

"There," she said. "Sorry I don't have a better spare room for you, but space is kinda tight here."

"That's fine." He ran a hand over his jaw. "Maybe I'll take a shower."

"Good idea." She wrinkled her nose at him. "You could sure use one."

"Wretch." He lurched to his feet, and she went over in alarm to stand next to him.

"Be careful. You're weak, remember?"

"Hard to forget."

She pulled one of his arms around her shoulder. "Is that better?"

"Much better." His hand tightened, cupping her shoulder, making her feel all too aware that he was wearing only a T-shirt and briefs. She moved toward the bathroom, and he perforce had to follow.

With Donovan safely stowed in the shower, she folded up the sofa bed and arranged pillows and blankets on it, with the coffee table full of magazines and books nearby. Lucas was ready to abandon his toast, so she brought him into the living room to roll around. She sat on the floor herself, pulling out the basket of toys that occupied one corner.

Watching Lucas bang the stacking rings against the post they were supposed to go on, she tried once again to decide what tack to take with Donovan. Should she confront him head-on about his recent desertion, demand to know his intentions? Should she lead up to the subject with gentle questions? Should she wait for him to broach it himself?

"Head-on," she decided, taking the plastic ring Lucas handed her and fitting it over the post. "No more shilly-shallying for me."

The bathroom door opened, and she looked around, only to gasp, words deserting her.

Donovan strolled into the living room, naked, drying his hair with the towel.

"Forgot to get any clothes out of the suitcase," he explained, catching her openmouthed stare. "What's the matter? Did I grow something new the past year?" He glanced down at himself.

"No—no," Thea stammered, turning away, and then berating herself for behaving like a schoolgirl. *For heaven's sake,* she thought, *it's nothing I haven't seen a thousand times.*

When she turned back he was hunkered down by his suitcase, pawing through it. "Wouldn't you know," he said conversationally. "What I want is always on the bottom."

"That's the way it goes," she agreed faintly, her eyes riveted to the broad, sculpted muscles of his back. He'd stayed in good shape, that much was obvious.

When he stood up, briefs and undershirt in his hands, she looked away involuntarily. "Something bothering you?" His voice was genuinely curious. "Neither of us was so modest when we lived together."

"Yes," she gulped. "But that's been a while. I mean—"

"You mean the only male parts you've been seeing lately are a few sizes smaller than mine," he said gently. She met his eyes, seeing understanding and not a little blatant masculine satisfaction.

"Well," she said, irked by his smugness. "Of course, I've seen quite a bit of Marlon." At the look in his eyes, she hastened to add, "We all have. He usually wears the legal minimum of clothes."

"Does surfer boy put the moves on you?" Now attired in briefs and T-shirt, Donovan could still be an intimidating sight. Thea longed to let him stew, but the thought of Marlon coming on to her was too funny.

"Are you kidding?" She laughed. "In his eyes I'm a kindly old aunt. He classes me right up there with R.J."

"I'll bet." Donovan no longer sounded intimidating. He was pulling on clean jeans, groping in his suitcase for a shirt. But his hands came up empty, and he held them to his head.

"Does your head ache again?" Thea abandoned Lucas to the plastic blocks and crawled over to Donovan. "You'll be getting a fever all over again if you're not careful," she scolded, laying her palm against his forehead.

He pressed it to his head. "Your hands are cool," he said, his voice muffled.

"Why don't you rest?" She pulled at his hand, guiding him toward the couch. "You can sleep, or read. You never did finish your tea. And you should really try to eat something. You'll never get your strength back this way."

Obediently he stretched out on the couch, propping his head against the pillows she'd arranged. She pulled the blanket over him and picked up the thermometer. He eyed it with suspicion.

"What's this? We playing doctor now?"

"Just my way of shutting you up," she said graciously, inserting the thermometer into his mouth. "Keep still, now, or I'll get out the one I use with Lucas. It goes in a different place."

He glared and tried to talk around the thermometer. "You'll be shorry you shaid that—"

"Hush up." She looked over at Lucas, who began a long string of babble, waving one of the blocks around.

Donovan's eyes followed her gaze. "Fackage," he said.

"What?"

"Fackage!" He pointed to the big box he'd brought in the night before. "For Lucash."

"Of course. We waited to open it until you were better." She took the thermometer out of his mouth. "You've still got a fever," she announced. "One hundred and one degrees. That's not good. You've been overdoing it."

"I won't do another thing," he promised. "I'll just lie here. But why don't you open the package?"

"Okay." Thea felt excited about it. She pulled the big box out into the middle of the room, and Lucas inched right over to investigate. With a little prompting he got very good at ripping the paper off it, crowing loudly. Thea helped with the ribbon.

The box inside had a brightly colored picture of a circus train, with an engine and several cars that hooked together and could be pulled around. Thea took her time unpacking it. Lucas was ecstatic over the animals and a squatty ringmaster, all big enough for him to gum without hurting himself.

When it was all unpacked and she had hooked the cars together for Lucas, she gathered up the wrapping, giving herself a minute to blink the tears out of her eyes. It touched her that a man so ambivalent about fatherhood as Donovan should have selected such a present.

"He likes it, doesn't he?" Donovan was watching Lucas as he picked up one of the cars and dumped all the animals out. Painstakingly he grasped them in his chubby fists and brought them one after another to his mouth.

"He certainly does." Thea scrambled to her knees and gave Donovan an impulsive hug. "You were sweet to bring it."

At the look in his eyes she backed off again, seizing the wrappings to take out to the trash bin.

When she came back she had a grip on herself. Donovan was still watching Lucas from the safety of the couch, not getting down on the floor with him. But, Thea reflected, he was sick, not wanting to spread his germs around.

He turned, and his gaze collided with hers. She squared her shoulders. "So why did you come back?"

"Did you think I wasn't?" His brows drew together. "I left a note, didn't I?"

"You didn't say anything about coming back," Thea pointed out. "You just said you couldn't handle it, see you later."

"I said I'd see you for dinner another time." He leaned back, folding his arms across his chest. His eyes, she noticed, looked heavy, and she felt a moment's compunction at drilling him when he was obviously still under the weather. But it was important for her to know where they all stood. "That implied my return."

"Not in so many words," she said stubbornly. "I had no idea what you really meant."

He ran a hand through his hair, pushing that stubborn piece off his forehead. "Neither did I, at the time," he admitted. "You threw me for a loop, you know." He shot a glance at her. "I'm still steamed that you kept it such a secret. What was I, the big bad ogre? You could have told me."

"And have you sacrifice the job you wanted? No way." Thea shook her head firmly.

"Isn't that what you did?"

He kept his voice neutral, but Thea could hear a faint trace of guilt. "Never," she exclaimed. "I could have stayed at MSC. I didn't want to. I didn't want to even before I found out I was pregnant. Lucas gave me a good excuse to change direction in my life. Otherwise I might have been there forever, growing more and more discontent."

Donovan didn't scoff at this, as she'd half expected him to. "You really find it satisfying," he said, probing. "You're not just telling me that."

"Helping to run a small business is very satisfying," Thea said quietly. "Or at least it was," she added, remembering the IRS and the looming presence of eviction. "There are problems that crop up, of course."

"I'm not surprised, with that ditzy woman for a partner," Donovan muttered.

"Helen isn't to blame for it," Thea said loyally. "She trusted her accountant, and he wasn't to be trusted. Lots of people have had the same problem."

Donovan clearly wasn't interested in Helen's troubles. He gazed broodingly at Lucas, who had discovered that the monkey's head tasted delicious. "I've been thinking about what you've done," he said finally. "I told myself that everything that was wrong with my life this past year was because you weren't in it. But maybe it was more than that. Maybe I need a change, too."

"Is that why you came back?"

"I always meant to come back." He scowled at her. "If you think I'd let a child of mine grow up without a father, you're nuts."

"Donovan—"

"Shut up for a minute." He sat up straighter on the couch. "I may not have been keen to bring a child into this wretched world of ours, but I don't shirk my responsibilities. I expect to share in Lucas's support."

"Donovan—"

"I'm not done." He brushed one hand across his forehead, and suddenly he looked desperately tired. "I want to share other ways, too, Thea. He's half my son. I want to help bring him up. If you don't want to live with me, I won't press it. But I am going to be around. I am going to raise my boy."

Words crowded Thea's mouth, but she couldn't say them to a man who looked so utterly spent. "We don't need to talk about this now," she said instead. "You need some rest. Why don't you lie down on my bed?"

"Will you lie down with me?" He summoned a feeble grin.

"And catch your germs? No way," she retorted. "I'm even going to make you take your own pillows in there to keep mine safe."

"Whatever you say." Suddenly docile, he got to his feet and leaned over to collect the pillows.

"I'll carry them, silly." Thea pushed him into the hall. "You just get yourself in there. You look about to collapse."

"It comes over me," he admitted. She arranged the pillows on her big bed and got out an afghan. He sank into the covers as if drawn there by a magnet. "I hate feeling so weak." His words were interrupted by an enormous yawn.

"Three-fourths flu and a quarter travel fatigue, if you ask me," Thea said severely, covering him. "You need your rest. And when you wake up, maybe you'll feel up to some chicken soup."

"Maybe," he muttered drowsily. "Sorry to be such a drag."

"Don't mention it." She closed the door softly behind her.

In the living room, she played with Lucas and the circus train for a little while, feeling at loose ends. Donovan's words echoed in her head, filling her with a conflicting mixture of elation and worry. On the one hand, he had renewed her confidence by declaring himself ready and willing to help support Lucas. At some level a stress and worry she hadn't acknowledged, even to herself, was assuaged. She didn't have to be the sole support of a child any longer.

On the other hand, she wasn't ready to relinquish Lucas into Donovan's care. It wasn't as if he were R.J., pleased to take care of him, but no threat to the mother-child bond.

Thea shook her head. It was awful to think of Donovan as a threat. She knew her son would always love her. But it was impossible not to view Donovan as a rival for that love.

And what did he know about babies, anyway? Thea had been immersed in baby care for the past six months, and she still felt astounded at all there was to learn. Donovan hadn't even begun yet.

Besides, she argued, setting up some blocks for Lucas to demolish, when would Donovan even get to see his child? He spent the hours from early morning till late night working, and many weekends, too.

"He's planning to make a change," she said, wiping a little drool off Lucas's chin and exploring briefly along his gums to see if that tooth had finally appeared. "Soon," she told the baby. "Soon you'll have weapons in there. It'll be a whole new ball game, nursing a baby with teeth."

Lucas seemed enchanted by the idea, but it raised another area in Thea's mind where Donovan would have trouble with his son. Lucas didn't like bottles. It had been her intention to wean him to a cup.

"You're begging the question," she told herself sternly. "Is he going to stick around? What if he turns out like his father?"

That wasn't really a fair question, she acknowledged. Donovan showed every sign of being ready to shoulder the burdens of parenthood, even though his father had deserted him when he was seven. Donovan's mother had died when he was three. And even if he couldn't take the day-to-day stuff, Thea knew he would always make himself financially responsible. Lucas was in no danger of needing a foster home.

There was one more question burning inside her. Did Donovan want her—or not?

She examined herself in the mirror over the fireplace. She had never been a beauty, but in her city days, she'd felt that she had style and sophistication.

There was nothing left of the style, unless you counted it stylish to wear blue jeans with patches shaped like hearts and stars. There was nothing sophisticated about her scrubbed skin and shoulder-length hair, with the nearly invisible silver threads that Betty had so considerately pointed out.

"I'm not even wearing earrings," she told Lucas, who seemed uninterested. It was his fault, really; he found earrings fascinating, and his attempts to make them his were painful.

Did she want Donovan? Shivering, she remembered the feeling of his hand on her shoulder. It had been a long time since her body had responded sexually—since Donovan's departure, actually. The excitements of pregnancy and birth had superseded the need for physical closeness with a lover.

But it seemed that his presence could awaken that need.

What if they made love? Thea felt herself go hot all over at the picture that thought conjured up. But Donovan the venture capitalist didn't fit into her placid life. Was she willing to cast her lot in with his, go where his fast-paced job took him, be the domestic half of his high-powered life?

She looked around at her cottage. It was small; with Donovan in it, it seemed much smaller. But she loved it so. She had worked hard to bring it into line with her vision of it. In her present life with Lucas she was important, needed, both by him and by her work.

"I'm not going to be just someone's wife, just someone's mother," she vowed, staring into the mirror again. "Thea Willits is in charge here. No love-'em-and-leave-'em guy is going to make a fool of me."

There was laundry to do, but Thea didn't allow it to repudiate her vow. "It's my laundry," she told Lucas, passing him with an arm load of towels. "And yours. I don't have to do any man's laundry, just because I'm at home during the day and he's out being important at work. And that's the way it will stay."

When she thought of that lean masculine form stretched out in her bed, her resolution quailed a bit. But she talked herself back up. Donovan sounded interested in changing his life. Fine. When he was finished, if she liked it and he wanted her to, she might consider getting back together. But until then, he was on his own. She didn't need any man messing in her life, dictating to her what to do, how to get along. She could manage just fine, just her and Lucas, like they'd been doing before.

When Donovan was well enough, he would have to leave the cottage.

The phone rang, and she hurried to answer it before it could wake him up. Helen was on the line, sounding harried. "Those property managers are here," she said, her voice low. "I can see them on the sidewalk outside—two guys and a woman in business suits, even on Sunday. They're pointing at stuff and making notes. They really mean business, Thea!"

"Of course they do," Thea said briskly. "We knew that before. But you've taken appropriate action and we'll be ready to deal with them as soon as we hear from the owner. Don't worry, Helen, everything will be fine."

But when she hung up the phone she didn't feel so confident. If Guerneville didn't turn up and intercede, they could be in real trouble.

Sighing, she went to the desk in the living room where her computer was kept. Thanks to the modem, she had access to the latest market information twenty-four hours a day. She called up screen after screen of figures, hoping to spark that sixth sense of hers, to find some way to turn the little that remained of her personal investment fund into a fancy profit.

Because if Babycakes went down the tubes, all her fine talk of independence was just so much hot air.

CHAPTER NINE

PATRICK LASSWELL STOOD on the sidewalk in front of Babycakes and peered cautiously through the window. He had chosen his time carefully, assuming that the partners would be upstairs at their late breakfast. He didn't want to confront that fiesty little Helen again while there were cakes and pies in reach as ammunition.

There was no sign of her behind the counter, so he walked on in. The young woman on duty was the one with spiky purple hair and three earrings in each ear. He was surprised she didn't dangle one from her nose, as well.

"Good morning," he said breezily. "Now, you must be—"

She gazed at him dispassionately. This one, he could tell, was not to fall victim to his fatal Irish charm.

"Can I help you?"

"Yes, you can." He glanced along the trays of muffins. "I want the best muffin you make. Which one would that be, now?"

The girl shifted her weight onto her other skinny hip. "They're all good," she said flatly. "And they're good for you, too."

"Well, give me that one, then," he said, pointing at random into the glass case.

"Cranberry oat bran," the girl said. "Right. Anything else?"

"Coffee," he decided. "A big cup."

She poured it, put it on the counter beside the paper bag holding his muffin and told him the price. He pulled out the money and said teasingly, "Aren't you going to tell me I shouldn't drink coffee?"

"Drink it or not," she said without cracking a smile. "No skin off my nose."

"True. And speaking of your nose—"

"Yes?"

"Never mind." He glanced around casually, through the door into the kitchen. "Where are the owners this morning?"

"Upstairs. Strategy planning," the girl told him. "You're the IRS guy, aren't you?"

"As a matter of fact, yes." He cradled the coffee cup in his hands. "Name's Patrick Lasswell. What's your name?"

"Roxie."

He waited for a moment, but she didn't volunteer anything else. Another woman came out of the kitchen, holding a baby in her arms. Patrick thought the baby looked familiar.

"Hey, isn't that what's-her-name's baby?"

Roxie turned, and for the first time a slight smile lifted the corner of her mouth. Her voice, when she spoke, was different, softer.

"So he's awake? I'll take him, Maria."

"No," the other woman said. "I get him until he cries the first time. Then you can take him."

Patrick glanced around the room. There were a few people scattered at the tables, reading newspapers and sipping coffee, but no one seemed to need anything. He'd never heard of the counter people in a bakery or coffee shop passing the time with a baby before, but stranger things had happened.

If the baby was awake, Thea Willits would probably be winding up her breakfast to come and care for it. He judged it a good time to go upstairs and have a brief chat with Ms. Willits.

And with her cake-throwing partner, too. Strange how when he thought of the bakery or the mounds of paper he'd brought away from it, it was Helen's face he saw, and not the other one, who had the most to do with the books.

Picking up his coffee and muffin sack, Patrick left by the front door, going through the alley to the back stairs. After a few more chats, he should have Helen Macaphee pinned down in his mind where she belonged, with the others who'd counted on their looks or their money to get them through the hard places in life. He met a lot of those people, women and men, in his line of work.

It just remained to get Helen classified there, in her proper place with the rest of them. Then she'd cease to take up so much room in his head.

THEA INSPECTED her almond croissant gloomily. "I didn't realize how much child care R.J. does for me until I had to do it all myself," she told Helen across the little table in Helen's upstairs kitchen. "She's still knocked out with the flu, or I wouldn't have had to bring Lucas along. I know he got in the way this morning."

"Not enough to worry about," Helen said, her voice polite.

"I worried about it, obviously." Thea shook her head over the croissant's less-than-perfect half circle. "It's a relief that he finally went to sleep down there. Thank goodness Maria promised to listen for him to wake up. I feel like the two of us have been surgically attached for the past twenty-four hours."

Helen nodded sympathetically. "That's the worst of these rug rats," she said, with a hearty attempt at lightness. "You can't just shove them in the doghouse and leave 'em alone, like a pet."

"It doesn't help for Donovan to be around, either," Thea said in an outburst of honesty. "Sick as he is, I need to tend him, but all the while I feel like he's assessing my mothering skills."

"You're just paranoid." Helen assembled a handful of vitamins and popped them into her mouth, washing them down with a glassful of some vile-colored juice. "No doubt he's marveling that you keep it together so well. I know I do."

"Well, if the man hadn't had such a temperature this morning, he'd be out the door by now," Thea declared. "He's got a lot of gall, to waltz in and expect me to hover over his fevered brow after walking out on me two weeks ago."

"Does he expect that?" Helen asked curiously.

"Probably not," Thea admitted. "But I'm not feeling rational today. All my trials just sort of came down on my head, and I'm sunk." She eyed her partner. "You seem mighty chipper for someone who was in such a sweat yesterday."

"I got it off my chest," Helen said airily. "Now it's bothering you instead of me." She picked up a muffin, turning it over and over. "Actually, I just decided that it would all work out, and if it doesn't, something else will." She put down her muffin and stared at Thea. "I'm a quivering, trembling mess inside," she said, her expression serious. "But I'm tired of carrying that around. And I'm sorry I've been dumping it on you. This morning I resolved: no more whining. I'll take my punishment like a woman and go on."

"Right on!" Thea raised her teacup in a salute. "You cheer me, partner. I was beginning to feel that if we couldn't pull out of this you'd head for the nearest cliff."

"Well, so I might," Helen said placidly, taking a big bite from her muffin. "But only to learn to hang glide. New challenges are everywhere. One has only to meet them to overcome them!"

They clicked their cups together solemnly.

"So, debauchery above the bakery." Patrick Lasswell stood in the doorway, studying them with amusement. "Now I know what you're really doing up here, when your staff swears you're planning the daily strategy. What's in those cups, rum?"

"If only there was," Helen said haughtily, "it would render this moment easier to bear. Couldn't you just call us on the phone when you want to make our lives miserable?"

"Now, now," Patrick said, his smile growing. "Then I wouldn't be causing my quota of misery in a day." He shook his head in wonder. "Other folks find it comforting to put their tax problems in my hands. What is it with you ladies?"

"Just natural contrariness, I suppose," Thea said, kicking Helen under the table. "What can we do for you, Patrick?"

"Well, for starters, I'm going to need the files going back three more years." Patrick came over to the table, plunking down a white paper bag and a cup of coffee. "You see," he said to Helen, "I paid for my own. I was afraid you might start throwing baked goods at me again, and that would be a clear-cut attempt to offer an agent of the IRS a bribe."

Helen choked on her herb tea.

"She wasn't trying to bribe you," Thea hastened to say. "She's just generous with samples. That's all it was."

"Yes," Helen chimed in, fighting to repress a smile. "Just a sample. Our kind of hospitality, you might say."

"I see." Patrick bit into his muffin and sighed. "Delicious," he said when he could speak. "Your hospitality has a lot to recommend it." He turned to Thea. "That's a mighty cute baby you have, ma'am. The women were passing him around downstairs like a box of candy."

"Is Lucas awake?" Thea jumped to her feet. "I'd better go on down." She hesitated, looking from Helen to Patrick.

"If you could hunt out those records for me," he said smoothly. "I just have a few things to check with Ms. Macaphee here, and then I'll be down to collect them."

"Fine." Thea didn't sound as if she thought it were fine. She gazed sternly at Helen, who interpreted the look with ease. It said, *don't throw anything else at this guy, or he'll throw the book at us.*

Helen smiled to reassure her partner, but something inside her recognized that Patrick was good at goading her into her worst behavior. So it behooved her to play it cool, refuse to be goaded. No doubt every display of temper went into his notes, to be used against her in the future.

Patrick took the lid off his coffee and had another bite of muffin. "I will say this," he mumbled around it. "You ladies know what you're doing in the kitchen."

"And we don't in the office, I suppose." Helen drank the rest of her tea. "Thea is an expert in financial matters. She used to be an investment counselor for a big company in San Francisco."

"Well, keeping the books straight in a small business these days can be complicated," Patrick said. "I suppose that's why you hired this—" he pulled a little notebook out of his pocket and consulted it "—Raymund Neves."

"I told you so," Helen said, shifting in her chair. "He had references from several shops in the neighborhood. I thought he could keep track of things for me."

Patrick nodded. "I need your old books," he explained, "so I can compile a payment record. So far, it looks as if you've had trouble several times meeting your quarterly payments."

Helen glanced down and noticed that she was twisting her fingers together. She forced herself to relax. "I never pretended to be on top of that stuff. If I had been I wouldn't have fallen for Raymund's line of chat." She glanced mockingly at Patrick. "Is that what you want to hear from me? Poor, stupid woman lets a man turn her inside out? Well, it galls me to admit that the shoe fits. And in fact, I'm tired of wearing it."

"So you're saying that Mr. Neves is guilty of making you default on your taxes." Patrick's voice was even, but she felt a quantity of hidden scorn in it.

"I'm saying he cheated me," she said irritably. "Why is that so hard for you to comprehend? Men are doing it to women every day of the year. He cheated me. He cheated Betty, the hairdresser. He cheated the Molinaris down at the corner grocery." A bitter laugh escaped her. "At least he didn't screw those two around emotionally. Just ripped off their money, not their love life."

Patrick flipped through his notebook. "You're asking me to believe—" he began.

"I don't give a damn what you believe," Helen, said, her hands itching for something to throw. She remembered that she was going to control herself from now on. Taking a few deep breaths, she shut her eyes and visualized herself calm, reasonable. Opening her eyes, she met Patrick's fascinated gaze. "Listen." She leaned forward, pointing at his notebook. "And write this down, because I don't want to have to go through it again. I hired a crook as an accountant. I didn't know he was a crook. He seemed like a nice fellow. He appeared to fall passionately in love with me." She closed her eyes again, briefly. "I was a fool. I trusted him. He left, taking with him all the money he could get his hands on. Before he left, he evidently took money intended for you." She inhaled again. "You didn't write that down. I guess you still don't believe me."

"It's not a question of me believing you or not," he said, clearing his throat. "But I must confess, a smart, beautiful woman like you—it is hard to believe that you were on the losing end of that scenario."

Helen had to laugh. "Mister, women always lose. We're suckers for a smooth-talking fellow, didn't you know? Ask Betty if you don't believe me." She sent him a mocking smile. "At least I don't have to worry about that with you. You aren't wasting any smooth talk around me."

He didn't seem to be paying attention. "Wait a minute," he said, flipping back a few pages in his notebook. "You're telling me that Betty Arboline down the street also had an affair with Raymund Neves?"

"Didn't she tell you?" Helen clutched her hair. "Maybe I didn't have to tell you, either," she moaned. "Here I've been spilling my guts to the IRS for no good reason."

Patrick scribbled wildly. "So that's why—" He got up from the table. "I'd better have a few words with Ms. Arboline." Shaking his head, he looked down at Helen. "Didn't it bother you to snatch the old girl's boyfriend out from underneath her?"

Helen jumped up. "You just never quit, do you?" She balled her hands into fists to keep them from going for his throat. "Get out of here," she snapped. "I don't believe it's any part of your job to make these remarks to me." She whirled around and grabbed her own notebook off the kitchen counter. "What's your superior's name? I'm going to report you. I'm going to have you taken off this case."

Patrick smiled grimly. "My superior," he told her, "is in Fresno. I'm the ranking field agent in the Santa Cruz office. But report me, by all means." He rattled off a phone number, and Helen wrote it down. Then he stalked over to the door.

She watched him, wondering why she wasn't angrier over his allegations. There was emotion raging around inside her, all right, but it wasn't anger. A vast, aching hurt filled her. It hurt to have someone think so badly of her that no matter what she said, she appeared to be the villain.

At the door Patrick turned, stuffing his notebook into his pocket. "You're right," he said formally. "I apologize for the tenor of my remarks. It's none of my business what goes on in your life, except as it applies to the case." He made a little flourish with one hand. "But go ahead and report me. I'm sure it will afford you some amusement to put a spoke in my career."

He left, and Helen, impotently fuming, tore up the piece of paper with the phone number he had given her and threw the pieces at the door.

PATRICK STOMPED down the outside staircase, calling himself every kind of fool. What was it about that woman? He just couldn't stop his mouth when he was around her. He had to keep picking, picking, hoping to expose something about her that didn't fit in with the profile of a tax evader, hoping that he had her all wrong.

Well, maybe he did. If Betty Arboline confirmed what Helen had said—but that made Helen look even worse. She'd had an affair with this Neves person, knowing that nice old Betty had fallen in love with him. That sounded pretty callous. When he stacked it up with the rest of the evidence, it just proved him right once again. People like Helen were takers, in it for what they could get. Once in a while they got taken, but generally when the money was missing, you only had to look as far as their own interests to find it.

When he went into the kitchen downstairs, his mood was as bad as it could be. It didn't help to interrupt Thea Willits while she was discreetly nursing her baby. All he needed was to feel like a heel for hounding a Madonna over tax difficulties.

"The records are there," Thea told him, nodding toward the desk. "I won't be needing them, since I've copied all the pertinent information into my computer files." She frowned. "How long will it be before you come to a determination? This is very disruptive to our long-term plans, as you can well imagine. We've halted our remodeling in case we have to use that money to pay the IRS."

Patrick opened his briefcase and began putting in the files on the desk. "I can see your point," he hedged. "The fact is, this case is tangled up with others if we approach it as possible fraud on the part of the accountant. It could take a couple of months before we've sorted out any criminal charges to be filed."

"And that would let us off paying the arrears," Thea said.

"Right." The door behind him opened, and Patrick turned to see Helen stalk in, her black eyes blazing at him. He stared back. "On the other hand, if we simply use the evidence to date and look at it as a straightforward case of tax evasion, things become much simpler," he said, talking as much to Helen as to Thea. "Then the quicker you pay your bill, including interest and penalty, the easier things are for everyone. It is probably in your best interest to assume that things will work out that way. We'll refund the money if we decide to file criminal charges down the road."

"Yes," Thea said, before Helen could spit out the words Patrick was sure were on the tip of her tongue. "But payment seems to me to be admission of fault on our part. We don't agree to making such an admission. And will you continue to investigate if we pay, or will you just close the case?"

Patrick shut his briefcase and looked from one woman to the other. "We are not out to get anyone, regardless of the common perception of the IRS as a terrorist organization," he said with exasperation. "If the evidence warrants an investigation, there will be one." He turned to pin Helen with his glance. "Despite any attempts to alienate the agent."

Helen sputtered. "I like that! Let me tell you, Mr. Agent, that if I reported to your superiors one-half of the slanderous things you've said to me, I could have your hide nailed up to the federal building! If you goad me anymore, I won't be able to resist!"

So she wasn't going to report him. Patrick felt a flicker of relief. He wasn't ready to give up this job, not yet. Not until Moira was finished with her residency and earning her keep, like the rest of them. Then maybe he could thumb his nose at the government.

"Suit yourself," he told Helen curtly. It wouldn't do to let this woman get the idea she had power over him. But he knew he was flirting with danger. He made her angry—and she wasn't a peaceable sort to begin with. Rile her any further, and he might be pounding the pavement before he was ready to.

Thea detached the baby, pulling her shirt down. Patrick found it amazing that a woman could nurse a baby in public without displaying even half an inch of strategic skin.

And the baby was cute, he supposed. He himself had had enough of children. His mother had delivered nine of them, starting with him and growing progressively weaker with each new baby. He remembered, after Ryan's birth had made seven, railing at his father with a twelve-year-old's passion. "Can't you do something about it? Mama shouldn't have any more!" His father had given him a troubled shrug and turned away. "It's the way things are, Patrick, lad. And it doesn't really concern you."

Well, Moira had been the last. And a couple of his sisters were already populating their own houses, Bridget with a brood of four, and Elizabeth with three. But as the oldest, he had felt responsible for them all, while his dad was working and his mother occupied with the latest small one. Even when struggling through college, he'd felt obliged to major in economics because the job prospects were better, confining his real interests to his minor in anthropology.

Now, gazing at Thea's baby, he was profoundly grateful that he'd finished playing father. Somewhere inside him there was a crazy teenager who'd never been allowed out. He'd never had time for a steady girlfriend, never put his own selfish interests first. It had always been someday with him—someday he could doff his mantle of officialdom, someday he could indulge his dream of becoming an anthropologist and not worry about the small salary or uncertain funding. Someday he'd really start to live.

But perhaps he was too far gone into bureaucracy to get out, now. Maybe he was stuck working for the government for the rest of his life.

Thea was staring at him curiously. He pulled himself together and picked up his briefcase. "I'll be in touch when I've verified that information," he said to Helen.

Thea transferred her gaze to Helen, who had actually blushed. "I mentioned about Betty and Raymund," she explained, "and do you know, Betty didn't tell him about it. About anything but the money part, I mean. She might be so upset with me—"

Thea frowned. "She was certainly broadcasting it around here, after he split. I mean, that's how you found out what a two-timer the guy was. She probably didn't think it was germane to the IRS investigation."

"It's not," Helen wailed. "Why did I tell? Why didn't I keep my big mouth shut?" She rounded on Patrick. "If you breathe a word of it, if you put in your report that I let that crook make love to me, so help me . . ."

Patrick felt a slow smile spread over his mouth. So it cut both ways, did it? "Why, Ms. Macaphee," he drawled. "I wouldn't dream of mentioning any irrelevant bits of information in my report." He paused for a moment. "Provided, of course, that you also maintain a judicious reticence."

Helen squinted suspiciously. "Are you blackmailing me?"

Patrick shook his head. "Such an ugly word," he murmured. "And as I've pointed out to you before, madam, the IRS is not susceptible to blackmail, bribes or coercion."

Thea was smiling, too, but she interrupted, looking at Helen's clenched fists, "Perhaps you'd better leave, Patrick. Before Helen gets the urge to offer you any more samples."

"Excellent idea," Patrick agreed, and bowed mockingly to Helen. "Top of the morning to you, my dear."

But when he turned to go, the back door was blocked. The man who stood there looked like a bum. He had three days' growth of golden stubble on his deeply tanned face, and long, untidy, bleached-blond hair. His clothes were rumpled and stained, with holes in the elbows of his sweater and more holes in the knees of his blue jeans. He wore ancient loafers with no socks.

"So this is where everyone is," he said, entering the kitchen and smiling vaguely around. "You're the owners here?"

"Yeah," Helen said, transferring her hostility to the ragged apparition. "We've already arranged to donate the leftovers to a food distribution group for the homeless. Sorry."

The man glanced down at himself and then back at Helen as if surprised. "How amusing!" When he laughed, his teeth were very white against his brown skin, transforming him. He pulled his hands out of his pockets to smooth back his hair, and Patrick noticed a glittering signet ring on one finger. The watch that was exposed when his ragged cuff rode up was no five-and-dime cheapie, either. "I didn't come to beg, although it might be fun to try sometime," the man explained. "I'm Jack Guerneville. Someone here sent me an urgent message." Those lazy blue eyes scanned each of them in turn, dismissing Patrick before moving on to Thea, and then to Helen, where they lingered with an appreciative sparkle. "Which one of you is Helen Macaphee?"

Patrick found himself forgotten. Helen's attention fastened on the rakish stranger who, despite the deep creases around his eyes, Patrick judged to be in his early thirties, a good few years younger than Helen. Now that he thought of it, he was younger than she was, too, by almost two years. But he felt so much older than his years. There was no real discrepancy between them, agewise.

She was smiling up at this Guerneville person as if he had brought the Holy Grail with him. Patrick took a firmer grip on his briefcase. Maybe the bum had, at that. He must belong to the locally prominent Guernevilles, who had lots of real estate named after them. Maybe Helen was counting on him to bail her out of her tax troubles.

Thea remembered him, then. "And this is Patrick Lasswell, Mr. Guerneville."

"Please, call me Jack," the young man said, his eyes crinkling up as he smiled. "No one calls me Mr. Guerneville unless they've got a clipboard in their hands."

"Well, Mr. Lasswell almost does," Helen said, shooting Patrick a glance that made it clear he was not forgiven for his trespasses. "He's from the IRS."

"Heaven forfend!" Jack Guerneville stretched his hands out in front of him, shaking back that overlong blond hair. "I didn't do it, honest! It's all up to my tax accountants."

Another one of the it's-not-my-fault crowd, Patrick reflected bitterly. He managed a brief smile. "It's not yourself I'm investigating now, Mr. Guerneville, although if you'd like I'll be pleased to check how your accountants are managing."

"No, no," Jack Guerneville said hastily. "Joke, man, joke. Don't worry about it for a single second."

"I must be going," Patrick said, acknowledging the joke with another forced smile. "I'll be in touch, Ms. Macaphee. Ms. Willits."

He marched through the back door, closing it gently behind him, but not soon enough to drown out the murmur of Jack Guerneville's voice and Helen's laugh.

For a few moments he felt an overpowering urge to stalk back in, take Helen Macaphee by the ear and make her pay for the trouble she was giving him.

But then sanity intruded. He had work to do, after all. Consulting his notebook, he went down the alley and back onto the street. Only a few buildings away was Betty Arboline's beauty parlor. He would stop in there, take Betty back into her office and find some way to verify that Raymund Neves had made a habit of seducing the ladies whose accounts he handled.

It wouldn't make him wholly believe in Helen's story. But it would go a long way toward it.

CHAPTER TEN

DONOVAN FELT a little guilty, rummaging around in Thea's computer while she was at work. But he had an excuse. He wanted to transfer some funds, and Thea had conveniently given him a deposit slip two weeks ago, which made it easier for him to put money into her account. True, there was a map to her house drawn on one side, but the bank wouldn't care about that. As long as he put in the check made out to Thea, they'd deposit it. He'd already talked to the bank on the phone.

And he had other business to transact. There were bank accounts in New York to close, accounts in Santa Cruz to open, and he could take care of it all with a couple of letters to his bankers. He left a token amount in his New York account, but he knew he wasn't going back there, no matter what happened. His future now was near Lucas, and Lucas's mother had made it clear that she was settled in Santa Cruz.

It would be nice to have his investments liquid, he mused, hands poised over the keyboard. Then he'd be in a better position to help Thea out of her financial difficulties.

Not that she'd asked for his help.

"She's proud," he muttered, staring at the screen. It displayed a list of files, files that were none of his business. "She wouldn't ask for help unless she was on her last legs. I'll have to offer it."

But he was a businessman. And he didn't just give away money. True, he was depositing a nice lump sum in her account, but that was for child support. And judging from what she'd said, it wouldn't go far to bail out the bakery.

If he was going to do that, it would have to be on his terms.

He stretched, willing himself to feel a surge of his usual energy. He did feel much better that morning, though he wasn't going to let Thea know it. In fact, he'd dunked the thermometer into the tea she'd brought him, to make his temperature higher. It had worked, too. She hadn't booted him out. As soon as he was well, she would.

Turning his attention back to the computer, he sternly resisted the temptation to go through her files. He wrote his letters to the bank quickly, and another one to his broker, printed them out and then purged them from the computer's memory. No need to leave evidence that he felt good enough to sit up and take care of business.

He was licking the stamps he'd found in the desk, when the sound of crunching gravel came to his ears. Darting to the window, he could see Thea trudging down the path, carrying Lucas, diaper bag, grocery bag and briefcase. He wanted to go to her, relieve her of her burdens, help her along her path in every way. Instead he hid the letters in one of the magazines on the coffee table and lay down on the couch. Just in time.

When Thea pushed open the door, he allowed his feigned sleep to be interrupted. She was tiptoeing toward him when he opened his eyes, blinking in what he devoutly hoped was a drowsy, feverish way.

"Hello," Thea whispered. Lucas stared down at him solemnly from his mother's arm. "You look better."

"I feel a little better," he said feebly, struggling up on one elbow. "Don't worry, I'll be out of here as soon as I can."

"I'm not going to kick a sick man out," Thea retorted, putting one hand on his forehead. "Your fever seems to have gone down, though."

"Oh, yes, I'm much better." He made his voice as weak as possible and was rewarded by her quick frown.

"You really do sound terrible. Chicken soup," she said. "Here, I don't suppose you're contagious anymore. You can entertain Lucas while I heat up the soup."

She plopped Lucas beside him on the couch and carried the bag of groceries into the kitchen.

Donovan was surprised at the eagerness with which he put an arm around the baby, who seemed a little wobbly. He eyed his son, and Lucas gazed at him in interest. "You look like Thea," Donovan said on a note of discovery.

Lucas liked being talked to. He smiled a wide baby smile, displaying pink gums and one tiny sliver of white. "Hey," Donovan told him, "you're getting teeth."

That was funny, evidently. Lucas gurgled with laughter, and Donovan couldn't help smiling back. Those big gray-blue eyes reminded him of his own eyes. They were fixed now on the knitted snowflakes that patterned the front of Donovan's sweater. Lucas reached for one of the snowflakes, overbalanced and fell on his face against Donovan's chest.

"Uh-oh," Donovan murmured, righting the baby and gathering him closer. "That's torn it." There was no laughter now in the little face that stared indignantly up at him. Lucas's mouth opened again, this time to emit a loud wail.

Thea came running out of the kitchen. "What happened?" She picked up Lucas, and he clung to her, still staring down at Donovan in accusation. "What did you do?"

"He fell into my sweater," Donovan tried to explain. "He's fine, Thea."

Unconsciously she cuddled the baby closer, and he stopped crying. "I'll just bring him in the kitchen," she said, backing toward the door. "He's probably hungry."

Alone in the living room once more, Donovan settled back against the couch cushions, mulling over his brief encounter with his son. Thea had swept Lucas away from Donovan as if he was the big villain, just waiting to pounce on a little baby. If she really felt like that, it would be uphill work to get her to issue an invitation to join the family.

Drawing a deep breath, he studied his options. He could demand his rights as a father, threaten custody battles, blackmail her into letting him in. Was that likely to get him what he wanted?

"Not a chance in hell," he muttered. Where Lucas was concerned, Thea was hardly rational.

What if he asked politely to spend some time with his son? Would his son's mother come meekly along in a package deal?

"Probably not."

"Who are you talking to out here?" Thea stood in the kitchen doorway, hands on hips, staring at him. "Are you delirious?"

"Just hungry," he said, springing off the couch and then staggering a little. His invalid pose was not really a fiction. He still didn't feel up to par. "Hope I can keep some food down today."

Thea led the way to the table, where two places were set with bowls of soup, a basket of crackers, some carrot sticks and glasses of milk. His lips quirked. "This looks very wholesome—almost like a soup commercial."

Thea sat down and shook out her napkin. "It's homemade," she protested. "And nursing mothers have to watch their nutrition."

Lucas was in the high chair, gumming on something. "Isn't he a little young to eat solid food?" Donovan asked. The soup smelled wonderful. He wanted to dive into it. It was an effort to hold himself to one languid spoonful.

"He's six months old," Thea said. "He doesn't really eat, although I give him some rice cereal in the mornings, and mash up a veggie or two for dinner. He's teething, so he likes to gum that hard toast."

"Zweiback," Donovan said knowledgeably. At Thea's look of surprise, he added, "I've had a lot to do with babies in my life."

"More than you wanted to, I know," Thea said, glancing away as she crunched into a cracker.

He put down his spoon. "Thea," he began, trying to choose his words carefully. "People go through life updating their attitudes about things. I remember a time when you were totally uninterested in children. Obviously, you've changed."

"I had to," Thea pointed out. "You haven't."

"Why do you think I left so abruptly a couple of weeks ago?"

She seemed to find the bottom of her soup supremely interesting. "I have no idea," she muttered. "Or rather, I guessed that you wanted to escape. That you found the whole idea of Lucas too frightening."

"Not frightening," he corrected. "Stunning is a better word. It's not every day a man is confronted with the six-month-old evidence that he's a father. I needed to assimilate it."

"And now you have?" Her gaze was skeptical.

"I've started to," he said quietly. "I've gotten so far as to accept the responsibility. I've deposited an amount in your account to cover a share of your pregnancy expenses and child support for the last six months. I'll be giving you monthly payments.''

She laid down her soupspoon with a decisive click. "You can't buy your way into Lucas's life, Donovan. He's mine. I haven't made any claims on you, and I don't intend to.''

Her words pierced his heart. "I'm not trying to buy his affection or yours," he protested. "For God's sake, Thea. I'm trying to do what's right. After all," he added vehemently, "he's my son. You can't deny that. You tried to keep me from knowing I was a father, but now that I know, you can't deny me my rights.''

Thea's face was without color. Only Lucas, banging a spoon on the high chair tray, seemed oblivious. "I didn't mean—" she whispered. "Oh, Donovan. What are you going to do?''

"I don't know." He pushed away the half-eaten soup. "But I won't stay here any longer, to trespass on your hospitality and endure your hostility." He passed a hand over his forehead, no longer faking the sick feeling that rose up inside him. His hand trembled, and he dropped it into his lap to hide it, but not before Thea noticed.

"I'm sorry for snapping at you," she said, putting her hand over his. "We're both under a considerable strain, here." He searched her face and saw the contrition there. "I don't want you to leave, Donovan, until you have someplace to go to. Don't just storm out of here. You'll get sick all over again.''

"Thanks," he mumbled. It would have been a nice gesture to sweep grandly out, but he doubted his ability to sustain it. "Maybe I'll lie down for a while right now.''

"You do that." Thea patted his hand and withdrew her own. "Use my bed if you want.''

He wanted more than that, but he didn't have the strength to follow through on any of those desires, either. Clasping her hand, he brought it to his lips briefly before he got to his feet and left the room.

THEA WANDERED around her living room, at loose ends. Lucas had been fed, changed and was down for a nap, sleeping in the same room as his father. Diapers were churning in the washer, wet laundry had been hung out, the payroll for the bakery was finished, and she could no longer suppress the guilt that dogged her when she thought of that disaster of a lunch.

"He asked for it," she muttered, but it didn't assuage her conscience. After all, he was right. She'd concealed her pregnancy and Lucas's birth from him, cut him off from his child and had flatly told him he wasn't wanted. "Bad," she chided herself, stopping to look at the front window. "Very bad."

She would have to watch her step. She didn't want to make an enemy of Donovan. The courts these days were much more liberal in awarding privileges to fathers. Her actions would not look good if it came to a custody hearing. Donovan would appear to be the wronged party. She could lose Lucas.

Chilled, she rubbed her hands along her arms. "Donovan wouldn't do that," she told the window. And he wouldn't, she knew, unless she drove him to it.

But it was hard for her to voluntarily hand Lucas over to him. "Look what happened today," she said, trying to justify her maternal anxiety. "Five seconds later the baby was crying. Donovan just doesn't know how to take care of a little baby."

She heard a noise from the bedroom, the creak and rustle of a large body turning over in bed. Moving quietly to the door, she saw that Donovan had kicked off the quilted throw. He had his face buried in a pillow, and seeing him sleeping that way brought a host of memories to her—the way he would always seek her side of the bed, wrapping himself in her warmth, the way he slept with such concentration, as if it were the most important thing in the world.

To replace the cover, she had to crawl up on the bed. As she was tucking it around his shoulders, his arm came up, toppling her down next to him. She found herself snugly imprisoned between his arms. His eyes remained closed, but she wasn't fooled that he could still be sleeping. "Donovan—" she whispered fiercely. Then he kissed her.

He kissed her like a man waking from a nightmare, like someone drinking after long thirst. The heat and the sheer unexpected intensity poured over her. His body was warm beside her, its hard planes and angles achingly familiar. His lips moved on hers, tender, persuading, insistent. She found herself wondering how she had been able to do without this amazing sensation, the flame that seared down through her body and out along every nerve ending in her skin. Her hands stopped pushing at his shoulders and curled around his neck.

When he took his mouth away, she moaned softly before opening her eyes. He was propped on one elbow, gazing down at her with a dreamy smile on his face. "Good afternoon," he whispered. "Shall we go back to square one?"

"You must be feeling better," she said, groping for some way to put things back where they belonged. Something seemed to tell her they belonged here, the two of them together.

But no. There were three now. That made all the difference.

Donovan brought his hand up to smooth the skin along her cheekbone, then wrapped it briefly around her neck. She shivered at the needs that uncoiled within her. "This is a bad idea,'' she said faintly, unable to do what she should do and get off the bed.

''It's the best idea I've had in a long time,'' he assured her, his palm traveling down her arm. ''Now, there's an interesting phenomenon.''

He was staring at her chest. When she looked down, she saw twin patches of dampness on her shirt.

''I'm leaking,'' she muttered. The sight galvanized her. She sat up, pressing her arms against her breasts.

''Milk?'' Donovan glanced over to the crib in the corner. The only evidence of Lucas was the faint sound of his breathing. ''Does that mean it's time for him to eat?''

''Guess so.'' Thea rolled off the bed. Lucas had nursed before his nap. It wasn't overfullness that caused her breasts to let down when Donovan had kissed her. It was stimulation of a quite different sort.

He didn't press her for an explanation, luckily. ''I feel a lot better,'' he said, stretching. ''Must have been the flu's last gasp.''

''You'd better be careful,'' Thea warned him, getting a fresh shirt out of her drawer. ''R.J. got up too soon and now she's back in bed.''

''I'll pamper myself,'' he said. ''Thea, about what we said at lunch—''

On her way out the door to the bathroom, Thea tensed. Without turning, she said, ''I'm sorry, Donovan. I got defensive. I didn't mean it . . . most of it.''

He was quiet. Then his voice came from directly behind her, and she felt his hand on her shoulder. ''I meant what I said just now,'' he said. ''Let's start over. Neither of us wants to threaten the other. We have a lot of happiness at stake here, Thea. Let's not throw it away.''

She couldn't speak. Instead she nodded and took her clean shirt into the bathroom.

When she came out, Donovan was in the living room, putting on his shoes. "I'm going to get some stuff out of my car," he told her. "I need fresh air."

She glanced back into the bedroom, where Lucas was sleeping, and he interpreted the look correctly. "You don't have to come with me," he said. "I promise not to strain myself."

"Fine," she said, standing in the door, watching him walk down the path toward the big house. He looked very masculine and confident, but his stride was slower, without its usual healthy swing.

Touching her lips, she turned away and closed the door.

THE SALTY WIND felt good against his face, and Donovan breathed it in deeply when he straightened after pulling his briefcase out of the car. The sky was very blue, dotted here and there with fat white clouds. Gulls wheeled and squawked overhead, and the tulips along the front walk of the big old house danced in the wind.

It was a far cry from New York City.

He wondered if there were many jobs around for people like him. Scotts Valley had some high tech companies, he knew, but venture capitalists were more often found where the money was than where the businesses were.

Shrugging, he picked up his compact disc player and the briefcase and started back to the house. To be around Thea, he'd do just about anything. Maybe he would go back to the construction skills that had earned him a college education. Maybe he'd attend classes at the university, get another master's or a Ph.D. But whatever he did, he wasn't leaving to work anywhere else without Thea.

Miss Sophie came out of the front door of her big old house and sat down in an ancient willow rocker. "Young man," she called. Glancing around, Donovan realized she meant him. He hadn't felt young for a while. Harried people never felt young.

"Afternoon, Miss Sophie," he said, stopping beside the porch and squinting up at her. "I heard you had the flu."

"It was terrible," she said, nodding. "But I brushed through it better than poor Rosalie Jane." She looked curiously at the things he carried. "Are you, ah, moving in with Theadora?"

"No, no," he hastened to assure her. "She's been taking care of me—I had the flu, too, you know."

"I didn't know." Miss Sophie got out of her chair and came over to the porch railing. "Are you sure you're quite well?"

"Not quite," he told her, "but almost. Then I'll find my own place."

"Forgive me," Miss Sophie said hesitantly. "That is—we were wondering—well, you are Lucas's father, are you not?"

"That's right." Donovan made the admission cautiously. He didn't know what Thea had told her friends here—not much, evidently. But it was up to her to make explanations. He certainly didn't know how to go about it.

"And you don't plan to marry Theadora?" There was distinct disapproval in the old lady's face.

Donovan shook his head. "I would like nothing better," he said. "She doesn't appear to see it that way."

"Hmm." Miss Sophie's eyes took on a faraway look. "You seem like a nice young man."

"I'm very nice," Donovan told her, smiling. "Actually, I've been a selfish bas—fellow. But if Thea would let me, I'd love to take care of her and Lucas."

"Perhaps," Miss Sophie said, "you would care to look at my room?"

"Your room?"

"The rent is really most reasonable." Miss Sophie peered at him earnestly. "And it's one of the nicest rooms in the house."

"Thea didn't tell me you had a vacant room," Donovan said, understanding at last what she was offering.

"Would you care to see it? I always prefer to rent to people I know. It's much less risky that way."

Still clutching his briefcase and CD player, Donovan came around to climb up the stairs. "Yes," he said, reflecting that living in the big house would be extremely convenient. "Yes, I would like to see it."

THEA HUNG the last diaper on the line and bent to pick up the basket. It seemed heavier than it should, and she grunted as she lifted it to her hip.

She was overdoing things. Looking after Lucas while R.J. recuperated was fun, but a lot of work, as well. And adding Donovan to her patient load hadn't made things easier.

Nursing mothers, according to the book on her shelf, were supposed to drink lots of liquids, rest every afternoon and spend their time doting on their offspring. Instead, she was cooking, cleaning, doing a ton of laundry and looking after an invalid. If she wasn't careful, she'd get the flu, too.

She set the basket atop the washer and tiptoed into her bedroom. Lucas was still sleeping, but he wouldn't stay down much longer, she knew. Still, even a short rest would help. She picked up *The Wall Street Journal* and propped herself on the pillows. Briefly it crossed her mind that Donovan was taking a long time to get a few things out of his car. But she wouldn't worry about him. He could take care of himself.

The *Journal* wasn't as absorbing as she usually found it. She read through an article on trusts and decided the one she'd set up for Lucas was adequate. Halfway through an editorial excoriating the Securities and Exchange Commission, she felt the pages slipping out of her hands. She made an effort to rouse herself, but it hardly seemed worth it. Snuggling deeper into her pillows, she slept.

THERE WAS MOVEMENT in the room, and hushed whispers, and baby gurgles when she woke up again. It was late afternoon, judging by the sunlight that slanted into the bedroom. She squinted sleepy eyes and saw Donovan standing by the changing table, wrestling with Lucas's plastic pants.

"For heaven's sake," she said, sitting up. "I went right to sleep."

"You must have been tired." Donovan turned around to face her and brought Lucas over to the bed. "He was just waking up when I came in," he said, snapping the legs of Lucas's overalls, "and you were dead to the world. So I changed him."

"You changed him. Well, thanks." Thea rubbed some of the sleep out of her eyes and folded up the *Journal*. "I must have needed a nap, too."

"It's been a lot of work for you, having me here," Donovan said contritely. "I'm sorry. I'll be leaving as soon as I get some furniture."

Lucas squirmed and wriggled, laughing as Donovan tickled his neck.

"You—you found a place already, then?" Thea watched Donovan's hands, intrigued by their gentleness when he touched the baby. "That was fast."

"It found me, you might say." Donovan shot her a look she couldn't interpret and changed the subject. "Since I'm feeling better, let me take the two of you out for dinner."

Thea shook her head. "I don't think you're ready for that yet. Learn to walk before you try to fly, buddy."

"I could handle it," Donovan insisted.

"Later." Thea grinned at him mischievously. "When you're recovered from the flu, maybe I'll let you accompany us to Mr. Popper's Pantry, where the waiters wear gorilla suits and ride unicycles around the dining room, and at least four birthday parties are going on at one time, and the menu features five variations on peanut butter and jelly—"

"Enough!" Donovan put his hands over his ears. "You've convinced me. We don't go out to eat until Lucas graduates from college. But there's always take-out food. Where's the nearest Chinese?"

"I'll call it in," Thea said, adding magnanimously, "but you can pay for it. A little wonton soup is good for an invalid."

"Fine." Donovan went back to tickling Lucas, discovering that even tiny feet had sensitive spots. "I'll baby-sit while you pick it up."

Thea phoned an order in to her favorite Chinese restaurant, washed her face and admitted, looking at her reflection in the mirror, that she'd needed a rest. It was nice not to have to cook dinner. It was enjoyable to have another adult to talk to.

And it worried the hell out of her to see Donovan getting so close to Lucas. She knew, rationally, that he wouldn't just pick up and go after making them both depend on him. But given his admitted lack of a good role model for being a father, and given the fact that venture capitalists weren't in much demand in Santa Cruz, a logical person would be forced to the conclusion that Donovan would be unemployed if he stayed, and without a family if he left.

"So where is your new place," Thea asked casually, on her way out the door to pick up the dinner.

"Not far away." Donovan sat on the living room floor with Lucas, busily exploring the circus train. When he looked up, she recognized the devilish glint in his eye. "Just up at the big house, in fact. We'll be neighbors, Thea. Isn't that nice?''

She had completely forgotten Miss Sophie's vacant room. ''Neighbors?'' Stunned, she gaped at him. ''You're going to live right here?''

''Handy, isn't it?'' He smiled blandly. ''While R.J. is laid up, I can spell you with child care. It'll be nice to be so close to my son.''

''You—you—''

''Our dinner's getting cold,'' he reminded her, getting up to give her a gentle push out the door. ''I'll set the table while you're gone.''

She drove to the restaurant on automatic pilot, wondering why his news put her in such a dither. On the one hand, she'd expected him to put up much greater resistance to moving out. On the other hand, she'd been resenting the effort of nursing him, stepping around his suitcases, getting used to having a man around. Really, she tried to convince herself, this would be the best of both worlds. Companionship without the companion being underfoot.

Unless he felt free to be someone else's companion. Maybe she should let him stay in the cottage after all, to keep an eye on him.

''Straighten up, Willits,'' she admonished herself. ''Don't make plans for Donovan until you know what you want yourself.''

It sounded so simple. Why couldn't it be that simple?

At any rate, Donovan wanted to be a father to his son. She found great consolation in that fact, until she got back with the food.

Donovan met her at the door, his expression grim, holding Lucas in his arms. Lucas twisted and arched his back, screaming at the top of his lungs, his fists going furiously to his mouth.

By the immediate heaviness in her breasts, Thea knew that she had forgotten to nurse Lucas before she'd left. And twenty minutes with a hungry baby could seem like hours.

"What's wrong with him?" Donovan demanded. "Right after you left he started to cry, and he hasn't stopped yet."

"He's hungry," Thea said, trading Donovan the sack of food for the wailing baby. "That's all."

She sat down in the rocking chair and lifted her shirt. It took a little while for Lucas to calm down enough to eat, but after a few more cries he latched on, sucking hungrily.

"I figured he was hungry," Donovan said, his voice defensive. "I even found some bottles of formula in the fridge."

Thea could see the bottle on the coffee table, with the nipple screwed on a little crooked. There was a pacifier there and a whole assortment of toys. Evidently Donovan had tried everything.

"He wouldn't take the bottle."

"He doesn't like it much," Thea agreed. "Did you warm it in the microwave?"

"Of course." Donovan looked injured. "I'm not stupid, Thea. I know babies can't drink cold stuff. I warmed it, I tested it on my wrist. It was just the right temperature. He simply wouldn't take it."

"Even R.J. can't always get him to take a bottle," Thea murmured soothingly. "You did fine, Donovan."

He paced through the room, still holding the bag of takeout food. "I felt so helpless," he said finally. "It was awful, Thea. He cried and cried and there was nothing I could do." He passed one hand through his head. "I—I swore at him," he admitted, low voiced. "I said, 'damn it, Lucas, shut up!'"

Thea smothered a smile. "If that's the worst thing you ever say to him, he'll be a lucky child," she told him.

"Donovan, give yourself a break. Lucas is a good baby, but even good babies cry sometimes. For the first two months of his life he had colic. He cried every evening from five-thirty to seven. I called him a lot worse things than you did, believe me."

He stared at her in wonderment. "How did you survive? That crying just goes through my head until I think I'll go crazy!"

"R.J. came to the rescue finally," Thea admitted. "She took care of him for an hour every evening while I went for a walk. For some reason he didn't cry so hard with her. Maybe I made him nervous, because I was so nervous about what to do for a little baby." Lucas finished with one side. She sat him up on her lap, patting his back. "Also, I learned the importance of burping," she added. "Listen, why don't we eat? I'm starved."

"Me, too."

They ate Szechuan prawns and snow-white chicken while Thea regaled Donovan with more tales of Lucas's early months. He listened, enthralled, and even volunteered to burp the baby after Lucas had finished his second course.

Why it should upset her to see Donovan jiggling his son on his lap, encouraging him to burp, Thea didn't know, but she was meanly pleased when Lucas spit up on him. It wasn't that she didn't want Donovan to love his son, she reasoned, clearing up the dishes and stacking them in the dishwasher. She just didn't want Lucas to love him—at least, not as much as he loved her.

"Okay, so I'm petty," she muttered, listening to the splashes that came out of the bathroom. Donovan hadn't even asked if he could give Lucas his bath—he'd just gone ahead and started doing it while Thea cleaned the kitchen.

The part of her that was ashamed of her pettiness wouldn't let her go into the bathroom, to hover over Donovan and correct him when he did anything differently than she did. But the other part, the mean-spirited part, expected him to run into trouble somewhere. When he emerged into the living room with Lucas in a clean sleeper, his hair tousled and his eyes already heavy with sleep, Thea looked up from her book and managed a smile.

"So you got through it okay." She tried to make her voice sound less grudging. She loved giving Lucas his bath. He sat up so straight in the tub, and he enjoyed splashing so much.

"We found everything we needed," Donovan said proudly. "Does he get a bedtime story, or what?"

"He's not really up for stories yet," Thea replied, laying down her own book. "He just wants to tear the pages. Here, I'll take him."

Donovan relinquished the baby reluctantly. "Is he going to eat again? Seems like he spends all his time there."

Thea looked at him sharply, wondering if that was jealousy she heard. It was a little reassuring to know that she wasn't the only one with those irrational emotions. "He does nurse more often in the evening—maybe he gets less milk at a time then."

Donovan paced restlessly around the room while Thea nursed Lucas. After watching him for a few minutes, she felt her own impatience build. "I'm sorry it's so quiet and domestic here," she said. "Things must have been much more exciting in New York."

Donovan looked surprised. "Oh, no," he assured her. "By the time I got home from work, or from meeting some client for drinks, I was too exhausted to do more than flop into bed." He illustrated by casting himself onto the couch. "Do I look restless? Guess I must be getting my energy back."

"And then what?" Thea met his gaze straight on. "What are you going to do with your energy here, Donovan? It's wonderful that you plan to be part of your son's life, but he's only part of your life, too. What will you do when your leave of absence is over?''

Donovan stared back at her. "Believe me," he said, sighing. "When I've figured that out, you'll be the first to know."

Thea dropped her gaze. "It's so unlike you to be without a plan," she muttered. "I'm just warning you, Donovan. If your plan is to get me and Lucas to go back to New York with you, it won't work."

His jaw tightened. "I wouldn't dream of it. You've already made it clear you're calling the shots on location, Thea."

"Have I?" She glanced at him again, uncertainly. "Well, good." Lucas was asleep. She rose to her feet, cradling him against her shoulder. "I think I'll put the baby down and go to bed myself."

"Good idea." Donovan followed her down the hall. "We could all use an early night."

She laid Lucas in his crib, patting him gently back to dreamland when he stirred. When she turned around, Donovan was sitting on the edge of the bed, removing his socks and shoes.

"What are you doing?" She stared as he pulled off his shirt, then stood up and stripped off jeans and briefs.

"Getting ready for bed," he whispered back. "I'm tired, too. After all, I'm still convalescent."

"But in here? And naked?"

"I always sleep naked." He turned an innocent face to her. "Have you forgotten already?"

"The sofa bed," she began.

"It bothers my back." He pulled back the blankets and lay down, turning his back back to her, giving her a good view of the broad shoulders and long muscles she had so often run her hands over.

"But—you can't—"

"Hush, you'll wake the baby." He looked over his shoulder at her. "And don't try to put any moves on me. I'm a sick man, remember. Just stay on your own side of the bed."

"You won't get any rest in here," she tried. "I get up often, with the baby."

"I'll sleep like a log, away from that lumpy sofa bed," he said, snuggling his head into the pillows. "Don't worry, you won't bother me." His eyes drifted closed, and when she moved around the bed she could see his chest rise and fall in deep, rhythmic breaths.

Feeling ridiculously prudish, she nevertheless took her nightshirt into the bathroom and changed there, brushing her teeth with more vigor than was necessary. "I can't just throw him out," she told her reflection. "That sofa bed isn't too comfortable, after all."

What would she do if he tried to make love to her? She felt a treacherous weakness inside at the thought of his sweet caresses.

But there won't be any of that, she assured herself, turning out the lamp and sliding cautiously into her side of the bed. *Not until things are straightened out between us, if ever.*

So it was odd that she was disappointed when Donovan, after briefly rolling over to kiss her forehead and murmur "Nighty night," went promptly back to sleep.

WEAK MORNING LIGHT seeped in around the blinds when she woke, wondering groggily why her alarm hadn't gone off.

But she felt no inclination to move. She was very comfortable, very warm. Lucas was snuggled in the crook of her arm, nursing drowsily, though she didn't remember bringing him into the bed. And of course Donovan was at her back, as usual, his arm around her waist, his hand cradling one of Lucas's small rounded knees.

Donovan. She woke up in a rush. For a moment it had felt so right, the three of them together in the big bed. But it was all wrong, really.

His voice came over her shoulder, thick with sleep. "Morning, love. Lucas all done?"

"He seems to be." She sat up carefully. "How did he get here? What time is it? My alarm—"

"Relax. It's not quite five." Donovan smothered a yawn. "Lucas woke me up a little while ago, making some weird kind of noise. I didn't know if he was all right or not, so I went over to look, and he was gnawing away at his fist. That means he's hungry, right?"

"Right." Thea slipped out of bed, leaving Lucas drowsing there. Donovan slid across until he was next to the baby.

"So I brought him to you, and he did the rest." Donovan sounded proud of himself. Thea thought about asking who'd unbuttoned her nightshirt, but decided the whole subject was best ignored.

"I'll be back to get him dressed in a minute," she whispered, gathering up clean underwear and jeans. "I just need a quick shower."

"Let him sleep, why don't you?" Donovan yawned again. "I'm going to."

"I have to take him in to work with me," Thea began.

"I'll take care of him." Donovan opened his eyes, giving her a searching look. "I'll do my best. Don't you trust me?"

"Of course," she said reluctantly. "But you've been sick."

"I'm well now." His look sharpened. "Too well to spend another platonic night with you. Lucas can help me get some furniture today."

Shrugging, Thea went to her shower. When she returned, the bedroom was quiet, with both the male occupants apparently asleep.

"Fine," she muttered, sweeping out the door. If Donovan wanted to take care of a baby all day, she wouldn't say a word. "He'll be begging for help before the morning's half over."

Well, he knew where to find her. And meanwhile, there were muffins to make.

CHAPTER ELEVEN

THE SUN POURED IN through the front-facing windows of the big room on Miss Sophie's second floor, throwing sharp black angles from the big packing boxes across the new rug.

Donovan whistled as he moved around the room, putting his things away. Thea, sitting on the bed he'd had delivered from the sleek high tech furniture store downtown, felt decidedly disgruntled.

"It's nice and low," he pointed out, watching Lucas inch to the bed and reach up to the top. "He'll be pulling himself up on it pretty soon."

"Right," Thea muttered. She had come back right after lunch to rescue Donovan from his son, only to find both of them in the room upstairs at Miss Sophie's, unpacking boxes and screwing together furniture. Lucas had been happy to revel in bubble wrap and big cartons, and Donovan had seemed perfectly capable of getting his bed assembled with a baby for company.

"I just hope you don't find this room too small, Donovan." Thea tried to keep the petulance she felt out of her voice.

He smiled at her easily and lifted a small speaker out of a box. "At least I'll be out of your hair," he said, unpacking the speaker's mate. "You seem content in a small space, at the cottage, so I should be able to hack it here. I got the feeling I was crowding you there."

"Did you?" Thea felt just a little guilty. She'd tried to give him that feeling, and now she wondered why she was sorry. "Three rooms doesn't really hold a baby and two adults very well."

"Especially if the adults have to have separate beds." Donovan opened his briefcase, took out a roll of tools and unrolled it on the floor. Selecting a screwdriver, he started hooking up a complicated network of speakers, compact disc player and tuner.

"Donovan," Thea began, and then pressed her lips tightly together. It was the emotional vibrations that made the cottage seem too small for both of them. Now, watching him work, his eyebrows drawn together in concentration, the lock of dark hair springing over his forehead, she was washed with sensations. His hands, so competent with his task, would be knowing and gentle on her body. His mouth, now set in lines of concentration, would trace damp, delirious patterns on her skin. His eyes would glow with the fire of need she remembered so well. He would say—

"Hand me that socket wrench, would you?"

Pulled abruptly out of her imagination, Thea scrabbled around for the socket wrench, smiling a little—and sighing, too. Donovan could certainly exert a powerful pull on her senses.

But making love with him would just complicate things, she told herself, arguing with her rebellious body. She didn't know how anything stood between them. And she had a shrewd suspicion that Donovan didn't, either. Drifting into intimacy, allowing things to develop, would not work now that a baby was on the scene.

"So how's things at the bakery?" Donovan leaned back on his heels and fished for the instruction sheet. "Any more unexpected revelations this morning?"

"None. In fact, Helen is having lunch with the landlord. He already sent around a big bouquet of roses, so it should go well."

Donovan raised his eyebrows. "I see. You're hoping she'll be able to seduce a new lease out of him."

"Not at all!" Thea glared at him. "I assumed the flowers, which were incidentally addressed to both of us, were in the nature of an apology for the actions of his management firm. Helen will simply point out the advantages of allowing us to remain, and that will be that."

"If you say so." Donovan looked up from the instructions. "You know, I have some discretionary money right now. I might be interested in investing in the bakery, if I was convinced there was a future in it."

Thea blinked. "You might?"

"Of course," Donovan went on, glancing at her from the corner of his eye, "I would want some say in running the business. I wouldn't be a silent partner, Thea."

"Well, I'll pass the news along to Helen," she temporized. "We'll think about it. If the IRS investigation turns out right, we won't need to look for outside money."

"Fine," he said absently, reaching for his tools again. "Let me know what transpires."

There was silence for a moment. Lucas was involved in studying the green plastic handle of a nut driver, and Thea watched Donovan attach the speaker wires. "You don't even have a place to put that rig," she said at last, as he made some adjustments to the tuner.

"I'll get some stuff out of storage," he told her casually. "That bookcase—remember the one we bought in Port Costa that time, with the gingerbread along the shelf edges? And the antique commode—"

"I'm using that," Thea told him. "Didn't you notice, in the living room?"

"You have the marble-topped washstand in your living room." Donovan finished his work and turned on the tuner. The voice of a radio announcer filled the room. Selecting a CD, Donovan replaced the voice with music and adjusted the volume. "There! Tunes for my lady." He bowed ironically in Thea's direction. "I was talking about the walnut commode with the burl finish."

The old disagreement made Thea smile nostalgically. "You'll never get me to agree. And don't try telling me that morris chair is a Stickley again. It's just generic mission oak, that's all."

Donovan got to his feet and roamed around his new room. The big bay window in front looked out over the street, with a glimpse of the curving white shoreline and silky blue ocean. It was a large room with a walk-in closet, and he'd managed to unpack his car almost completely. Thea noticed that he'd even had time to set up his lap-top computer at a small streamlined desk that matched the bed.

"Antiques will look funny with this furniture," she commented, not sure why she wanted to find fault with the arrangement. It wasn't that she wanted Donovan to stay with her in the cottage. No, that would never work. He disturbed the very air with his presence, that subtle challenge she could never resist.

"What have you decided about your job?" She tried to make the question casual. "How much longer do you have on your leave of absence?"

"More than a month." He leaned against the wall and watched her with a faint smile. "But actually, I'm writing a letter of resignation." He gestured toward the little computer. "I'll need to down load it onto your printer, though."

"You're going to resign?" Thea tried to take that in. "Donovan, I can't believe it. You have never in your life resigned from one job without a better one lined up. You're a vice president at Gaskell Associates. What will you do if you throw that over?''

He shrugged. "I don't know, yet. I only know that resignation feels right."

Thea fixed him with a troubled gaze. "If you're doing this because I said I wouldn't move, then don't. It's your life, Donovan. I don't want the responsibility of being involved in your decisions."

He came to crouch in front of her, taking one of her hands. "Don't worry." He squeezed her fingers. "I understand. You don't need to take the slightest responsibility for my resignation."

"But what will you do, without your job?" She could see the insecurity in his eyes beneath his show of nonchalance.

"I don't know, exactly. But I couldn't work there anymore. They wanted all my life, and I realized I need to keep some for you, and for my son." He turned to look at Lucas and found him reaching a curious hand toward the CD player. "No, you don't, big guy. Babies aren't allowed to play with my sound equipment." Scooping Lucas up, he blew gently into his neck, grinning at the delighted response he provoked.

This simple act gave Thea a queer ache in her heart. "I wish it was as easy as you make it sound," she whispered finally.

"So do I." His mouth twisted in a half smile. "The two of you are a closed corporation. You won't even give me a seat on the board of directors, let alone take me into partnership."

"That's not true," Thea began. But her voice lacked conviction. Certainly she had tried to give him that impression. Evidently she'd been successful. Why was it that now she regretted it?

Standing there with Lucas in his arms, he looked so right, so much like the father her son needed. She had not let herself admit that before. She had been enough for Lucas, wanting to provide everything. But she could never be a father. And there was a basic satisfaction in seeing her son with his father that no one else, not even as wonderful a baby-sitter as R.J., could engender.

She opened her mouth to tell Donovan what she felt, but a crash that reverberated through the walls of the old house distracted her. "What was that?" She jumped to her feet. "Earthquake?"

"Relax," Donovan said, opening the door to the hall. "I think it's just plumbing."

Thea crowded out after him. Marlon was already running down the steps. "Radical, man," he said as they joined him at the door to the back porch. "This is really torn."

"That's putting it lightly," Thea muttered into Donovan's ear. Mr. Castigliano had nearly disappeared into the wall that divided the porch from Miss Sophie's kitchen. There was another tremendous clank and Mr. Castigliano's hand emerged, holding a section of ancient galvanized pipe.

"Is the rethreader connected now?" His booming voice was only slightly muffled by the wall. Faintly from the kitchen came Miss Sophie's reply.

"Oh, Mr. Castigliano, I'm not sure—"

"I'll go check," Donovan said, taking in the situation. "Is the pipe breaking off before you can reconnect it?"

Mr. Castigliano withdrew his head and shoulders and pushed back his crest of wavy white hair. "That would be obliging," he said, smiling placidly at Donovan. "These old pipes, now, always do make some trouble. But I just borrowed a rethreader, and if the pipe breaks, I'm prepared."

Donovan lingered for a moment, taking in the array of tools spread out on the floor with a fascinated eye. "You certainly are. Looks like a major job here."

Mr. Catigliano shrugged deprecatingly. "Just a favor for Miss Sophie. A grand woman like that certainly deserves to have her plumbing up-to-date." He surveyed the pipes that dangled forlornly out of the wall. "I'm thinking of replacing all this with copper," he confided. "Never wears out, copper. And then I can do the bathrooms."

"Well," Thea said, rather staggered by all this ambition. "First things first. Is the water turned off now?"

"Of course, missy." Mr. Castigliano turned a kindly smile on her. "We never work on the plumbing unless the water's turned off."

Marlon came out of the kitchen in time to hear that remark. "I wondered why nothing came out when I went to take a shower," he said philosophically. "Hey, Mr. C. Need some help?"

"Well," Mr. Castigliano conceded. "If Lucius here will man the kitchen side of things, I could use your brawn, Marlon. Guess it would be smart to make tracks and get the water back on."

Thea could see that a baby wasn't an asset in the work they were doing. "I'll take care of Lucas," she shouted at Donovan as she passed the kitchen door. "We're going to visit R.J."

He nodded and turned his attention back to the pipes. Miss Sophie fluttered over with a loaf of banana bread.

"Take this up to Rosalie Jane," she said, with a nervous smile at Thea. "I declare, I'm afraid to leave the kitchen, for fear of what these men might do to it."

"Don't worry, Miss Sophie," Thea told her. "I'm sure they'll get it all working." She headed for the back stairs, carrying Lucas and the banana bread. After checking on

R.J., she would go into the bakery and wait for Helen to return from lunch. At least there, she could be in charge of things, even if her personal life was running out of control.

R.J. was feeling much better, but indignant at her forced rest. "They won't let me down there at all," she complained to Thea. "Just marched me right back up the stairs." A loud bang reverberated through the pipes in the wall, and R.J. winced. "I should be helping."

"Everyone's helping," Thea said soothingly, putting the banana bread on the table beside R.J.'s little sink. "Don't worry, they don't need you."

"Someone stole my tool belt." R.J. looked at Thea broodingly. "Do you know where it is?"

"Not a clue," Thea replied. "Listen, I'm late for the bakery. See you." She escaped before R.J. could ask any more questions.

It was quiet at the bakery. The back room was deserted, and Thea spent a productive half hour getting receipts in order for the monthly statement.

When Helen breezed in, she was in a good mood, Thea could tell. "How did it go?" Thea looked up from the papers she was organizing. "Is he going to renew the lease?"

Smiling, Helen reached for her apron. "Looks like he might," she admitted. "He seemed like a human being, too."

"Great!" Thea jumped out of her chair, and Lucas, catching the excitement, clapped his hands from the playpen. "There's one hurdle down!"

"Not so fast," Helen cautioned her. "Jack Guerneville is really under the thumb of those management guys. I could see he thought it would be tough to get them to let him have his way."

"It's his building, isn't it?" Thea frowned. "Can't he just tell them to go fly a kite?"

"That's what I said." Helen looked at the production schedule posted above the sink. "Is the sourdough sponge set for tomorrow?"

"Yes, and I did the ordering, too. What's Guerneville's problem?"

"I dunno." Helen shrugged and got herself a glass of water. "Just a slave to his money, I guess. Maybe he's afraid if he throws his weight around, all those guys who know how to manage things for him will quit, and he'd have to do it himself."

"Well," Thea said, "let's hope he's going to stick up for us. I'd hate to get so close and have everything fall through."

"He'll come through," Helen said, her jaw set mulishly. "If he thinks he can let us go down the drain so he doesn't have to confront those real estate vultures, he'll have to think again." She drained the water and set the glass down with a thump. "I'm having dinner with him day after tomorrow," she added casually. "We're going to hammer out some details."

"That's nice." Thea examined Helen's poker face. "All business, I take it?"

"Of course," her partner agreed. "I wouldn't have it any other way."

HELEN LOOKED ACROSS the candlelit table at Jack Guerneville. He had cleaned up really well, she admitted. It was hard to believe now that she'd thought he was a bum when he'd walked into the bakery a few days ago.

He turned away from consulting with the sommelier to smile at her. "We need something special tonight, don't we?"

"Why?" Helen smoothed down the skirt of her one nice dress, which wasn't quite nice enough for the fancy restaurant Jack had chosen. Left to herself, she would have been just as happy to dress in jeans and eat burritos at Mi Corazon down the street. But here she was, afraid of spotting her green silk, wearing high heels no less, at Monsieur Paul's.

Jack seemed a little taken aback by her blunt question. "Because," he said. "It's our first date."

"We had lunch the other day," Helen pointed out. "And I didn't think this was a date. We were going to discuss business, I thought."

He leaned back in his chair, gazing at her. "Helen," he said, his voice soft, "you're a beautiful woman. Did I tell you how great that color looks on you? When you look so beautiful, so desirable, it's impossible to discuss business."

Helen shut her menu with a snap. "I don't have anything else to talk about." She lifted her chin a little, wishing that her one good dress wasn't cut quite so low. She wasn't used to exposing skin for men to ogle.

Not that Jack did anything so vulgar. He merely swept his gaze down her body, giving the impression that she was wearing nothing at all and he found it delightful.

"Let's talk about you," Jack suggested, and the tired old line sounded fresh, coming from those lazily smiling lips.

Helen leaned her elbows on the closed menu and smiled back. "Great idea," she enthused. "I'm going to be forty in October, did you know? How old are you, Jack?"

His smile wavered for a moment. "Forty? My God, you sure don't look it." He cleared his throat. "I'm, uh, thirty-four."

"Ah." Helen did her best to look maternal and wise. "That explains it. You have so much to learn, my boy." She shook her head.

The amusement reappeared on Jack's face. "If we're talking experience," he drawled, "I think I have a few years on you."

"That depends on the quality of the experience." Wine arrived, and Helen watched the golden light it gave off when the waiter poured it into her glass. "Thank you."

Jack murmured something to the waiter and the man moved away. "You were saying?" He raised his glass to his lips, savoring the bouquet.

"My experience," Helen said, taking a gulp of the wine, "is that when a man brings a woman to a place like this and begins to ply her with wine, he has seduction in mind."

"Your experience is probably accurate on that point." Jack reached across the table, taking her hand, and began to stroke lightly along the tendons.

"Well," Helen said, watching his long, tanned fingers, "I won't be seduced." She detached her hand to pick up her glass again. "Does this stuff have sulfites in it, do you know?"

"Does it matter?" Jack sounded impatient. "Helen, from the moment I walked into your bakery and saw you standing there, so adorable in that white apron, I knew what it was I've been searching for."

"A good piece of bread?" Helen said brightly. The wine was beginning to go to her head. "I think I'd better have something to eat."

Food arrived even as she spoke, like magic, she thought. There were little dishes of artichoke hearts, water chestnuts in bacon, pastry shells filled with creamy dilled shrimp. The waiter arranged them on the table, added a basket of rolls, curls of fresh butter, and topped up the wineglasses.

"This looks good," Helen said. "I didn't know they would bring you a bunch of stuff like this." She glanced around the restaurant, where the tables were discreetly tucked into padded booths and the lighting was so low you couldn't really see who was dining a few feet away. "But then, if you've got the money, you can get anything, I suppose."

Jack lounged back against the padded seat, his arms stretched on either side. One hand touched her shoulder. "Anything?" He shook his head. "Why do you think I spend my time sailing instead of hanging out near my money? It's depressing what you can't buy."

Helen bit into one of the shrimp cups, closing her eyes at the taste. "Tons of butterfat," she moaned, taking another bite. "But it's worth it. I'll eat oat bran tomorrow."

"You have grains on the mind." Jack inched a little closer around the edge of the booth. "What if I told you I'd already gone a couple of rounds with the money managers about extending your lease another ten years at the same terms?"

"I'd say you were nuts." Helen put the remains of the shrimp cup on her plate and gazed, narrow eyed, at him. "Either that, or you expect some return besides money."

"I don't expect anything," he said, his voice deepening. "No, that isn't true. One does expect the inevitable, and it's inevitable that you and I will be lovers."

Helen selected one of the artichoke hearts. "No animal fat at least," she observed.

"Is that all you have to say?" Jack flung himself back in his seat, arms crossed over his chest.

Helen put down her fork and looked at him kindly. "Jack," she said at last. "You're a nice guy. I appreciate how difficult it is for you to tell your money people to jump in the lake—"

"You don't know the half of it!" Jack eased his collar away from his throat, looking nervous. "I thought they'd threaten to have me locked up as certifiable for failure to maximize profits."

"Just don't go overboard," Helen said soothingly. "I don't object to a graduated increase—that would be fair to you, and my business could stand it over the next ten years."

"That might make it easier for them to take," Jack agreed, reaching for her hand again. "But I want you to have the best possible deal, honey."

Helen regarded him for a moment. "Jack, I'm not selling anything here. If you keep the building out of the hands of the developers, I'll be ecstatic. I'll even go as far as to provide you free bread for life. But that's bread, not bed."

She slid her hand out of his grasp and went back to the artichoke, bridging the silence by helping herself to another shrimp cup. "If you want to take me home, I'll understand," she said finally.

That won a smile from him. "You're impossible," he grumbled, finishing his wine. "I thought you were so anxious to save your bakery. You should be more grateful than this."

"I am anxious," she said quietly. "My bakery means everything to me. Too much to tangle up with the kind of gratitude you're talking about." She slapped her palm on the table. "And you should be ashamed of selling yourself so cheap!"

"Me?" He blinked at her.

"Yes, you!" She pointed her fork at him, disregarding the piece of artichoke heart that was still impaled on it. "If you want the kind of relationship money can't buy, you're going the wrong way to find it."

"You think so?" There was an expression in his eyes she couldn't interpret.

"You're a handsome, intelligent fellow who happens to be rich. Forget your money. Find a woman you can offer the rest of you to, and stick with her." Helen grinned at him and put down her fork. "Just a little motherly advice."

"Don't be ridiculous." His voice was sharp. "The difference is our ages doesn't matter." He transferred his gaze to the wine bottle and poured some more into his glass. "It's the other differences I wonder about."

Helen watched him raise the glass to his lips. "You should eat something," she said.

He shook his head when she offered him the plate of hors d'oeuvres. "I meant what I said about the lease," he told her intensely. "First thing tomorrow, I'm going to bat for it, and I won't take no for an answer." When she would have spoken, he held up his hand. "Listen, forget the rest of it. There are no strings attached."

"You mean it?" Helen could hear the sincerity in his voice. Her face split in a wide grin. "Yahoo!"

He didn't seem as elated as she was. "You really see me as a wishy-washy kind of guy, don't you?" His voice was accusing.

Helen shrugged. "Not really, Jack. You're a sweetie pie, I can tell. But all that money—it's intimidating. Not just to me, but to you, too, evidently."

The waiter brought a vast tureen of cioppino, serving them with an assortment of shellfish and spicy tomato sauce. After arranging plates of asparagus and endive salad, he finally left. Jack poked moodily at a clam with his fish fork.

"It's kind of awful," he said at last, looking at Helen without the man-of-the-world suavity she'd expected. His eyes were open and vulnerable, making him appear younger than his thirty-four years. "For as long as I can remember, the money's been like a—a thundercloud on the horizon, always threatening to move in and blow me away, the real me, I mean, and just leave this empty financial kingpin person in my place—like my father is." He drained his wineglass. "I've been running from it for years," he added. "This is the closest I've come to dealing with it since my grandfather died and the lawyers spent three weeks telling me about all the stuff he left me."

"I guess it is hard," Helen said, trying to understand. "But, frankly, I can't imagine it. Never having to worry about working, or whether all your work is going to go down the tubes—sounds great to me." She speared a crab leg and attacked it enthusiastically. "Cioppino every day if you want it! Some thundercloud!"

Jack smiled a little. "Right. It's all in your perspective." Watching her, he leaned across suddenly. "You're going to have tomato sauce all over you if you're not careful. Here." His fingers shook a little as he tucked her napkin into the neckline of her dress.

"Thanks." Helen pushed his hand away. "I can do it myself. And it's not too gallant of you," she added, "implying that I'm a messy eater."

"Cioppino is like that," he retorted. "Makes pigs of all of us."

"You won't emerge unscathed," Helen crowed, pointing a bread stick at him. "It's on your shirt already."

He peered down. "So it is. Aren't you going to tuck my napkin in for me?"

"Nope." Helen found a shrimp inside one clamshell. "I don't have to do that in a business relationship, which is all we have going for us."

Jack sighed. "I'm going to change your mind, you know."

"I doubt it." Helen spoke calmly. "What's for dessert?"

THEY EMERGED from the restaurant sated and, in Helen's case, a little sleepy from so much food and wine. The night air was moist and balmy. It was cool, though, and she hadn't brought a jacket. "Let's get moving before we freeze," she said, wrapping her arms around herself.

Jack put his arm around her shoulders. "Cold? Where did I leave my car? We'll get out of the breeze."

Helen shrugged away, laughing. "It's behind the bakery. Don't you remember? It was nice out when we left, so we decided to walk."

She set a brisk pace down the sidewalk, Jack following. The street was lined with restaurants and bars, shops and businesses, some still open for the evening trade. In the distance the lights of the Boardwalk glistened like fallen stars. Over the constant, slow murmur of the ocean, Helen could hear the Giant Dipper rattling its cars up its wooden rollercoaster framework, and the downhill swoosh and resultant screams of the passengers. Thin wisps of fog veiled the sky seaward, but just overhead stars blazed with a festive gleam.

They went on, past Mi Corazon, past the Vietnamese restaurant next to it. Helen felt suddenly in charity with the rest of the world. "You did mean it," she asked Jack, "about negotiating our lease tomorrow?"

"As soon as the lawyers are in their offices," he assured her. "I'll give you a call midmorning or so—it should be ready to sign then."

"Wow!" Helen flung her arms around him. "Croissants on the house. Sourdough on demand. Muffins whenever you want them. You name it, buddy."

"I already have." His arms tightened around her, and before she could draw away, his lips found hers.

Helen stood still in the circle of his arms, curious about his kiss. It was pleasant, she supposed. She hadn't been kissed in a while, and there was comfort in being held by a man. With the right man, she might even have liked to reciprocate.

But there was no magic. At last, reluctantly, his arms dropped and she withdrew, reaching up one hand to cup Jack's cheek. "I'm sorry," she whispered.

He stared down at her, his face unreadable in the dark. "So am I."

The restaurant door behind them swung open, emitting a gust of warm air and laughter. A group of people came through it and along the sidewalk toward Helen and Jack. It was a big group, all together, and in the midst of them, arm in arm with a lovely young redhead, was Patrick Lasswell.

His eyes found Helen's, flicked to her companion and then back to her, with an expression she couldn't immediately read. Helen found herself blushing, fervently grateful for some reason that the door hadn't opened a moment earlier, when Jack had been kissing her.

As the group came abreast of them, Patrick gave her a tight nod. One or two of the people in his party noticed and glanced at her curiously. She received a confused impression of intimate camaraderie from the group around him, which seemed to range from one elderly couple to the pretty girl on Patrick's arm.

Her own lip curled, seeing those melting blue eyes turned up adoringly to Patrick.

The group swept past them, and Helen found Jack watching her. "Wasn't that the IRS guy?" he asked, glancing after the noisy throng. Following his eyes, Helen saw that Patrick had looked back, his gaze assessing Jack's arm around her waist. Then he was gone, and she realized that she knew what it was she'd seen in his eyes before he'd veiled them. Hurt.

More than hurt. Jealousy. She knew, because those emotions stirred within her.

"Hey, wasn't it him? That IRS agent?" Jack poked her gently in the arm, bringing her attention back to him.

"I didn't notice," she said, shrugging.

"He noticed you." Jack's eyes were shrewd.

Helen pictured again that lovely young redhead—and then scolded herself for paying the least attention to such a man or his companion.

"Just checking to see if I was spending my ill-gotten gains, probably," she said, unable to keep the bitterness out of her voice.

"So are you really in trouble with them?" Jack emitted a low whistle. "Once they get their claws into you, it's doomsville."

Helen found herself telling him about the mess as they walked back to the bakery. Jack listened intently. "So now you're short of cash," he said as they stopped beside his car in the back alley at Babycakes.

"Not really." Helen put a good face on it. "Thea's digging up some stuff that'll help."

"Sure." Jack stopped her when she would have gone up the steps. "I'll say goodbye here," he murmured, cupping her face in his hands. Standing on the second step, she was just about at a level with him.

"You want to come up?" After she'd said it, she was sorry.

He seemed to pick up on that. "Not tonight." In the starlight she could see his twisted grin. "I might be too maddened by desire to restrain myself."

"Jack—" Helen put her hand on his shoulder. "You're a nice fellow, really. It'll be easy to have a business friendship with you, maybe even a real friendship. But that's all I'm interested in."

"Well, that's laying it on the line." He dropped a kiss on her hand. "At least you didn't call me a nice boy. I'll get under your skin yet, Helen Macaphee. Just you wait."

He climbed into his low-slung sports car, and Helen leaned on the railing, watching him drive away. Wasn't that just the way it went, she thought, a little melancholy. *The bird in the hand is never the one you really want.*

"In fact," she said out loud, climbing up the steps, "a bird in the hand is really just a big mess."

CHAPTER TWELVE

THERE WAS SUSPENSE in the bakery the next morning. While they were fixing up the muffins and baking the raisin bread, Helen filled Thea in on Jack's comments about the lease. "I really think he'll get it for us," she finished. "We'll be locked in for another ten years."

"Great," Thea said, scrubbing the Hobart. "How are we going to wait until he phones?"

"We'll play with Lucas," Helen suggested, looking around. "Hey, where's my main man?"

"His daddy has him." Thea tried to make her voice noncommittal, but Helen wanted more information.

"He's taking care of Lucas, all by himself? Diapers and everything?"

"He's done it before," Thea said, feeling defensive on Donovan's behalf. "He seemed to like it, but I think he'd be taking care of Lucas even if he didn't like it, because it's a father's duty, and he's a father now."

"Like that, is it?" Helen lifted a knowing eyebrow.

"No, no!" Thea abandoned the Hobart. "Really, it's touching. He even changes the poopy diapers, although he doesn't put them on tight enough and it can really make a mess. He showed up this morning before I left, before Lucas was even awake. I left him making some rice cereal."

"No kidding." Helen bit back a smile. "Your Donovan is not exactly the person I would picture being domestic."

"He's working on it." Thea stared at the racks of bread waiting to be pushed into the store. "He's practically leaving me behind. In the last week alone, he read six books about baby care."

"Well, maybe he'll concentrate on that and leave my bakery alone." Helen took the wooden peel and began opening the ovens, checking the loaves and turning some of them to brown more evenly. "I saw him sniffing around the place the other day." Her scowl deepened. "He was so gracious as to tell me I was doing everything wrong."

"Not wrong exactly," Thea said placatingly. "Just differently from how he would do it." She tried a hesitant smile. "He's offered to invest, if we need money for the IRS. But he intends to be involved if he buys in."

"Do you want to let him in?" Helen's gaze was direct. "I thought you had a few bones to pick with him yourself."

Thea sighed. "I do. I don't know." Looking up, she met Helen's eyes. "I don't feel particularly decisive today."

"I never do," Helen admitted, taking a cloth and rubbing some of the flour off the legs of the nearest baker's table. "How anyone can make a decision knowing that they'll have to live with it the rest of their days—"

"Not necessarily true," Thea protested. "If you're talking about Donovan, anyway. We could draw up contingency papers—his investment contingent on our having to pay off the IRS. That way, if they decide to prosecute Raymund, we won't have to take in another investor."

Helen's expression brightened somewhat, only to fall again. "Raymund," she muttered. "They'll never find the bastard, and then they'll want to take it out of my hide. That's what Mr. Patrick Lasswell will think, anyway. Mark my words, Thea. He believes the worst about me, and he'll use the IRS to see that I get what he thinks I deserve."

"Hold on, now." Thea leaned back in her desk chair, stretching out one hand to Helen. "Where did all this come from? I don't get that idea from Patrick at all."

"You have to admit," Helen said, her back turned to Thea, but with a suspicious quaver in her voice, "that he's never been in here except to criticize me."

"No, I don't have to admit that."

"And he saw me out with Jack last night—"

"Really?" Thea tried to contain her grin.

"It wasn't a date," Helen growled. "Why, the lad hardly needs to shave!"

"Nonsense." Thea straightened. "He's a couple of years older than I am, and I hope you don't feel there's that much difference between the two of us."

Helen looked away. "I'm sorry to be such a bear today. This tax thing has just put me in a terrible mood."

"I understand," Thea said, beginning to have a faint glimmer of the problem. "Maybe it'll be resolved soon. Maybe we won't need Donovan to invest, either."

"Maybe." Helen didn't sound optimistic.

Thea arranged baguettes and loaves in the baskets at the counter, pulled cakes and pastries out of the racks to stock the refrigerated display cases and let Roxie in when she knocked at the door just before opening. There was already a line of customers outside before they opened the doors, and time moved briskly for the first couple of hours. By ten o'clock, though, both women were pacing around the kitchen, waiting for Jack Guerneville's call.

They jumped when there was a knock on the back door. Helen answered it and let in Patrick Lasswell. "Oh, it's you," she said, disappointed.

"And were you expecting someone more exciting?" His usually smiling mouth was set in a firm line, his eyes hooded and somber. Thea wondered what had happened to take the lively humor from his voice.

"Not really." Helen turned away just as the phone rang. "There he is! I'll get it!" She leaped for the receiver that hung by the door into the front. "Jack! How did it go? Really? Fabulous!" She turned to give Thea a thumbs-up sign and then, still talking on the phone, moved into the store, stretching the extralong cord behind her.

Thea, grinning broadly, found Patrick Lasswell's eyes fixed on her.

"Good news? Someone getting married, maybe?"

There was a fierceness in the way he said the words that got through to Thea.

"Nothing like that," she said, smiling. "We just got our lease renewed, instead of getting kicked out so they could sell the building."

"Great," he said, relaxing enough to sit at her desk.

"Can I help you with anything?" Some of Helen's joy spilled over, making Thea feel that even the IRS deserved her patience.

"I've been looking at your balance sheets," Patrick began, taking them out of his briefcase. "Just checking the paper trail. Where exactly did the money come from for these renovations of yours, if you don't mind me asking?"

"They came from my personal savings and investments," Thea answered, her good humor beginning to evaporate. "I'm afraid I don't understand how that's germane to your investigation."

Patrick frowned. "In this kind of affair, everything is germane until I've arrived at the truth." He glanced over his shoulder through the door into the front, where Helen was still talking on the phone. "From the way the two of you act sometimes, you wouldn't think I'm doing my best to keep you out of jail for tax evasion."

"We're all rather tired of this endless investigation."

Patrick appeared to agree. "I'll be wrapping it up soon," he said, gathering the balance sheets.

"I need those back," Thea told him. "When are you going to be done with them?"

"Soon," he said again. "And don't try to tell me you haven't got it all in your computer." He glanced around. "Where is this famous computer, anyway?"

"At my place," Thea explained. "I do a lot of the book-keeping at home."

"Ah, yes." Patrick injected sympathy into his voice. "You do the bookwork, and work at the bakery, and put in the money. And Ms. Macaphee goes out to expensive restaurants with that young playboy that was here the other day."

"Wasn't that nice?" Thea said mildly. "You know, she hadn't gotten out at all since the Raymund episode."

Patrick's fingers clenched on the balance sheets, but his voice was smooth. "Perhaps she's planning to bring in a little investment money herself. By all accounts, Guerneville drops a bundle on his lady friends."

Thea frowned at him. "It's hard to believe that with all your poking and prying you didn't know Jack Guerneville owns this building. He's the one renegotiating our lease this morning. And you must really keep your ear to the ground to hear so much gossip."

"It wasn't ears I needed, but eyes," Patrick muttered, stuffing the balance sheets into his briefcase. "It didn't take twenty-twenty vision to see the two of them twined together so shamelessly last night."

Thea raised her eyebrows. "Is that so? He's a fast mover."

"Very convenient for you both." Patrick shut his brief-case with a snap. "You need money, and money appears in the person of Mr. Rich Boy."

Thea tossed a stray plush elephant back into the playpen where it belonged and looked at Patrick through narrowed eyes. "Helen isn't selling herself or her bakery for the money to pay you off, Patrick. We have already made arrangements to find the money."

"Indeed." Patrick picked up his briefcase and directed a hostile look over her shoulder. Thea glanced around to see Helen coming back into the kitchen.

"So you're leaving already." Helen sounded sweetly sarcastic. "Nice of you to take time out from your busy social life to attend to our little matters, Mr. Lasswell, but you shouldn't inconvenience yourself for such a paltry visit."

"Your social life appears to be thriving, too," Patrick said, with his smile forced. "Has your new boyfriend been by yet today, or is he drying behind his ears still?"

"Really," Helen spat back before Thea could say anything. "The lady on your arm last night didn't appear too far removed from the playpen herself."

Patrick looked blank for a moment, and then a smile of real amusement lit his face. "She's a fair lass," he drawled, "and wouldn't thank you for leaving off one of her twenty-four years."

"Twenty-four." Helen's eyes were flashing, her fists clenched at her sides. Thea looked around automatically to identify and remove possible missiles, but the only items close to hand were of the soft fuzzy variety that Lucas took such pleasure in throwing. "You like them young, I suppose? You must be old enough to be her father."

"I'm thirty-seven, as it happens," Patrick said. Thea got the notion that he was beginning to enjoy himself. "But I've known her since she was born, though it's not a father I am to her, but a brother."

Helen frowned. "What do you mean?"

"She's my sister, Moira." He smiled once more and opened the back door. "That was my family I was out with last night. Moira's residency begins soon, you see, and we were celebrating."

"Good grief," Helen said involuntarily. Thea was glad to see her hands relax. "You must have an enormous family." There was a faint trace of wistfulness in her voice, but Patrick either didn't hear it or chose not to acknowledge it.

"Nine of us," he said, reverting to curtness. "I'm the oldest, so they're partly my responsibility. Mother and Dad see over us, but it's me they all turn to." His expression softened slightly at the mention of his parents, but when he looked back at Helen his scowl was firmly in place. "I don't suppose Jack Guerneville is your long-lost brother, though."

"Of course not." Helen tossed her head. "He's a perfectly nice man, however, and more trustworthy than nine-tenths of the male population."

"Just get it in writing," Patrick said cryptically, and left.

Helen stared at the faintly swinging screen door. "Now what did he mean by that crack?"

Thea coughed and swung her own briefcase up on the desk. "I believe he thinks you're expecting to get the money to pay the IRS from Jack."

Helen snorted. "He's a shortsighted moron," she said heatedly. "Jack offered, but of course I turned him down. I don't take money from men, especially not . . ." Her voice trailed off.

"Not what?" Thea gave up rooting around in her briefcase for the papers she needed. "He said he saw you two in a hot clinch last night."

Helen looked uncomfortable. "Well, I told you about that. Jack *was* wining and dining me—I guess trying to get me into bed, but I made it clear I wasn't interested. He's a nice boy, though."

"You're probably the only woman he's chased that hasn't run straight to his wallet," Thea surmised. "Did he really offer you the money for the IRS?"

"I told him we didn't need it, that you had it under control." Helen grinned, shamefaced, at Thea. "Sorry. I just couldn't take his money. He's a nice guy, but I don't want to be under that kind of obligation to him. He might ask for something that I can't give."

"Not to him, anyway," Thea said softly.

"Not to anyone." Helen scowled. "Despite what that blarneying revenuer has to say. So was that all right, Thea? Can we manage without Jack's money?"

"Sure," Thea said staunchly. "We'll use Donovan's, instead."

Helen looked at her, worried. "You don't sound too happy about that."

"I'm not, actually." Thea mustered a smile. "Not that it's the same as taking Jack's money. Donovan is a different kettle of fish. He certainly doesn't have Jack's fear of involvement in the business side of things."

"That's all I need," Helen muttered. "Mr. High-and-Mighty Donovan poking his nose into my business." She made a fist and pounded it into her hand. "He makes me feel so stupid, so helpless. I know he despises me for endangering your investment, and I don't really blame him. But I don't like his attitude." She looked at Thea apologetically. "Sorry. I know you probably have a soft spot for him."

"One or two," Thea admitted, and changed the subject quickly. "At any rate, we can breathe easy about our lease. Why don't we celebrate and have lunch out?"

"Why not?" Helen caught her mood. "Jack's not bringing the lease over for us to sign until after one. Let's go down to Mr. Sprout's and dig into a tofu burger with all the trimmings!"

"Lead on, Macaphee," Thea said, laughing. "Tofu it is."

DONOVAN OPENED the back screen door of the bakery and peered cautiously in. He had no desire to run into Helen. They'd already exchanged words a few days ago.

It was Thea he was looking for. Though he hated to admit it, he needed some help with the baby.

Thea was there, sitting at her desk. What he hadn't counted on was the handsome young jackanapes who perched beside her, smiling down at her. She was laughing, too, the treacherous woman.

Donovan strode through the door, wishing that Lucas didn't thrash around so much when he was hungry. It was hard to be threateningly macho to another man with a baby in your arms.

Thea looked up, still smiling. "Oh, Donovan. Were you looking for me?"

"Always," he said, deepening his voice. He'd discovered long ago that a deep, resonant voice had a demoralizing effect on the opposition at meetings. He took Thea's hand in his free one and pressed a lingering kiss on it. The moment was spoiled by Lucas's wail.

Thea looked up at him, her eyes wide, before holding out her arms to the baby.

"Donovan, meet Jack Guerneville. Jack is the landlord here."

The laughing young man held out his hand. "Landlord sounds so dull," he protested. "It's not as if I actually work at it."

"Glad to meet you," Donovan said, letting up a little on the resonance. "Guerneville—you invested in Tri-Gate, didn't you?"

Jack wrinkled his forehead. "Did I? Probably. I let my financial people handle most things, to tell you the truth."

Donovan shrugged. Tri-Gate had run through a lot of money before the investors realized that the payoff wasn't going to materialize. He hoped Jack Guerneville's financial people hadn't been in it too deep.

The younger man was perceptive. "I gather from your expression that it was a bad investment," he said ruefully. "But if I involved myself, things would just be worse. Or at least that's what the financial people tell me, anyway. I have no head for business, none at all."

"That's not really true," Thea protested. "You've taken an interest in the management of your real estate."

Jack looked a little uncomfortable. "Yes, but they're all mad at me," he reminded her. "They just don't understand why I'm throwing a very nice profit to the winds. I should have chucked your lease and sold this parcel to an office developer."

Donovan pursed his lips. "I can see why they would be mad," he admitted.

"Now just a minute." Thea jumped to her feet, Lucas tucked up against her hip. "Maybe you're not taking quick profits, Jack. But the land is still here. It doesn't decline in value just because you don't sell at the first opportunity. And you're investing in the community by allowing a small business to stay in place. Babycakes generates sales taxes. It draws shoppers to the whole area. An office building can be anywhere, but this property is ideal for commercial enterprises. It's shortsighted to think in terms of immediate monetary profit. What you're doing is far more satisfactory over the long haul than an office building.''

Jack had an arrested expression on his face. "You know," he said, "you're right. There's justification for what I'm doing." He seized Thea's hand and pumped it up and down. "Next time they start screeching at me in a meeting, I can come back at them with some of your points, instead of letting everyone think I'm just a whimsical know-nothing."

Donovan kept his thoughts to himself. In his opinion, though Thea's suggestions were fine, noble and even made sense, they were no way to run a business, unless the business was philanthropy. He rested his gaze on his woman. She was so different now that it would be hard for a bystander to guess that a year and a half ago she had worn sleek business suits, had her hair carefully styled and moved through the crowds on Montgomery Street with the confidence of belonging in the financial district.

Now her hair was long and carelessly tied back. There were hollows in her cheeks that hadn't been there before and shadows under her eyes. Her air of business propriety had given way to one of—well, he would have to say, a grownup, maternal authority. She wasn't the same woman.

And his love for her wasn't the same, he discovered. Despite her evasions and concealments, she was still Thea, a woman of honesty and integrity. Her stubborn need to manage everything about their child herself didn't diminish her in his eyes. He admired her for it. He wanted to help her. He loved her even more.

She held her squirming son, and gradually his cries lessened. Turning her chair a little away from Jack Guerneville, she raised her blouse discreetly. Lucas latched on.

"Was he giving you a hard time about the bottle?" She looked at Donovan, and he had to nod.

"He took one this morning, but the last one he simply wouldn't take. I couldn't do a thing with him," he admitted. "You've really got the goods in that respect."

"Is this your first child?" Jack Guerneville probably thought he was just making polite conversation, but Donovan could see Thea stiffen at the implication that they were a couple.

He smiled casually, holding the younger man's attention on himself. "So far," he said. "You have any children, Guerneville?"

"No, I don't even have a wife." Jack laughed, but his eyes strayed to the door into the front, where Helen's apron-clad figure could be glimpsed waiting on customers.

"Neither do I," Donovan assured him, but now his gaze was fixed on Thea, sending her a message. "Not yet, anyway." He willed her to say something, to respond some way, but she simply looked at him before dropping her eyes to Lucas.

"But—I thought," Jack stammered.

"You don't have to have a marriage license to procreate," Donovan said airily. "It would be nice, though."

"Jack isn't interested in our little problems, *dear*," Thea said, her lips twitching. Donovan couldn't tell whether she was amused or annoyed at his blatant pitch. He looked at Lucas, sucking contentedly in her arms, and experienced the new and exciting rush of emotion that came over him as he watched his son. This baby wasn't like all the others he'd reluctantly cared for, reluctantly been fond of. What was it that made Lucas so much cuter, smarter, more responsive? Donovan had to grin. Must be his superior genes.

"Didn't you, Donovan?" Thea was speaking to him, a quizzical smile on her face. He must have been wandering for a while.

"Sorry. I was watching the baby," he said, meeting her grin with one of his own. "Just thinking how superior he is to the general run of babies."

Warmth bloomed in her eyes, but also a kind of wariness, which disappointed him. She still had doubts. He would have to fix that.

"I was telling Jack that you have a lot of experience with investments," she said, taking a deep breath.

"So do you," he returned, watching when she tugged her shirt down and draped Lucas across her shoulder for a burp. Her body was different, too. Softer in some places, more voluptuous in others—but just as wonderful, just as dear.

Her cheeks grew delicately pink, as if she could sense his thoughts. "I don't deal in hard investments, like real estate and businesses," she said quickly. "Just the soft stuff— stocks, bonds, mutual funds—"

Jack looked at her in surprise. "You do that?" He swept his hands around, indicating the bakery. "What are you doing in here, then?"

"Investment is a sideline now," Thea tried to explain. "I keep my hand in with a few portfolios, but nothing else. Donovan is the man to talk to about placing your capital."

Sighing, Donovan accepted the inevitable. "Why don't we go out front and get a cup of coffee, Jack? I'm sure your financial people could help you better than I can, but I'll be glad to chew the fat with you for a while."

He heard Thea snort as he led the way into the store. But he figured that the sooner he heard what Jack Guerneville had on his mind, the sooner he could get back to his family.

The smile broadened on his face. He was wearing her down, he knew. Pretty soon she'd get tired of pussyfooting around the issue of their future, and they could hammer it all out. He was a family man now, but he had the game without the name. He wanted it all—and he would get it, too.

Turning abruptly, he stuck his head back into the workroom. "Say, Thea..."

She was nursing Lucas on the other side now. "Hmm?"

"Bring him in when you're through and I'll take him off your hands."

She stared at him, speculative. "Sure, if that's what you want."

"He'll pass out pretty soon, after that high octane you fill him up with." Donovan felt just a little twinge of jealousy—different, this time, from the first time he'd seen Lucas making himself at home in Thea's arms, nursing from her breast. Now he wasn't so much envious of Lucas. He envied the closeness of the nursing couple, the fact that she could feed their son from her body, and his father couldn't even get him to take a bottle.

"He's getting a little drowsy," Thea crooned, patting her son's bottom.

Donovan cleared his throat around the lump that had risen there. "Listen, I called Rob this morning, and he asked if we wanted to go up there for dinner tonight. We could take Lucas along."

"That sounds like fun," Thea said, her face brightening. "I haven't seen Pam in a long time."

"Great." Donovan nodded briskly. "We'll need to leave by four-thirty or five."

He went back to join Jack at a table. This evening he could talk to her in the car, going up to the city and coming home again. Perhaps they could reach some agreement.

He felt so cheerful he even smiled at Helen.

THEA TRIED to do some of the paperwork one-handed while Lucas drowsed at her breast, but her mind wasn't on it.

There had been an air about Donovan that spoke of determination and purpose—the kind of air he had worn when going after an important acquisition. She had a few minutes of nervousness trying to decide what that meant for her. Was he planning to resume his high-powered career? He wouldn't be able to do that in Santa Cruz—not without a long commute, anyway.

Perhaps that look was directed at her. Was she the acquisition he had in mind?

The thought sent a shiver through her, a compound of pleasure and apprehension. Lucas roused briefly, disconnecting from the nipple. She gathered him up and carried him into the store.

Donovan and Jack were finishing their coffee. "We're going to roll," Donovan told Thea. "Jack wants to show me a few places, and we have some talking to do." He gave her a proprietary peck on the cheek and took Lucas from her. "Sleeping like a baby," he said with a grin. "Once we get him into the stroller, he won't budge for a couple of hours."

"That's right, you got a stroller, didn't you? And a car seat." Somehow it really brought home to Thea how involved Donovan intended to be, that he had put a car seat on the nice leather upholstery of his Silver Bomb. "And I bet you'd let him eat zwieback in it and everything," she muttered.

"Not ice cream," he said, smiling down at her. "I draw the line at ice cream. See you later, honey."

He and Jack went through the back door. Helen came over to stand by Thea. "I see what you mean," she said grudgingly. "The guy is turning into Ward Cleaver right here before our eyes."

"Better than Ward Cleaver," Thea said softly. Suddenly she was anxious to start the evening. "Do you need me here? I've got some stuff to do at home."

"Go on," Helen said, glancing around the store. "The baking's done, and Maria will be here in a minute. And Thea—"

"Yes?" Thea turned, her mind already occupied with thinking over the contents of her closet.

"Have fun, okay?"

Thea smiled at her partner. "I intend to."

JACK AND DONOVAN PUSHED the stroller down the Boardwalk and up a couple of blocks, and Jack stopped in front of a vacant storefront. "Here's one," he said. "The realestate management people have given up on this one. Evidently you can't tear down a one-story building in Santa Cruz anymore and put a two-story building in its place. That's why they want Babycakes. It's already two-story, so you could put a bigger office building there."

Donovan studied the building. "It doesn't look rundown," he remarked. "Just a little paint and some fix-it work."

"That's what I said." Moodily Jack kicked at a broken edge of the sidewalk. "I get so tired of them always wanting to tear things up, build new things. In other countries, in other places, they fix what they have instead of insisting on replacing it. Why can't we?"

An idea began to evolve in Donovan's head. "You know," he said, advancing to peer in the front window, "you could get tax write-offs for providing space to nonprofit organizations."

"Could I?" Jack brightened. "That's another thing I always need. Unearned income is a drag sometimes."

Donovan kept his thoughts on this to himself. Growing up poor, he reflected, would have done a lot to change Jack's attitude about unearned income.

"There's a woman at the house where I live," he said, "who runs a low-cost women's health clinic. They do home births, exams, stuff like that. They can't pay much, and as a result they're always losing their clinic space."

"A woman's clinic." Jack thought about it for a minute. "Do they have nonprofit status? I wouldn't get the tax break without that."

"They've got it," Donovan confirmed. "I had a talk with Faith last night, and she told me quite a bit about it." He didn't mention that he'd been pumping her for information about Lucas's birth. But he'd been impressed with Faith and her single-minded vision of providing women of all races and income levels with the kind of services they needed.

Jack rubbed his chin. "You know, it kind of appeals to me," he said finally. "In fact, maybe there's more in it than this." He looked at Donovan. "Would you say that there's a lot of nonprofit stuff needing capital? Like venture capital, but with a different focus?"

The question took Donovan by surprise. "I wouldn't know," he said cautiously, "but you are always seeing articles in the papers about how there aren't enough day-care centers and low-income housing—stuff like that."

"And the one thing my money people have dinged into my head over the years is how great my tax liability is," Jack said ruefully. "Am I right in thinking there might be tax advantages to investing in a nonprofit-oriented venture fund?"

"You might be," Donovan said. He thought for a moment. "I'm not really up on tax stuff, but I know a guy in San Carlos who is. Are you thinking you would like to set up this fund?"

Jack nodded. "I wouldn't have to be the only investor. I can think of four more people offhand. Two of them would be in it for the write-off, and the other one was just moaning to me in Tahiti how he hates the rich getting richer while the poor get poorer. Maybe it was all talk, but I don't think so."

"You know," Donovan said, stepping back for a broad view of the vacant building, "it's a good angle. Socially responsible venture capital—going for the less tangible benefits instead of the maximum return, and getting a tax write-off, too." He grinned at Jack. "Those aren't so easy to come by anymore, you know."

"Really?" Jack was still thinking. "I don't keep up with that stuff so much," he said absently. "Hey, I'm really getting jazzed by this. I was tired of being run by my money. Maybe I'll run it for a change."

"You're going to administer your fund?" Donovan tried to keep his voice level.

"That would be a disaster, eh?" Jack clapped him on the back. "No, Donovan, old son. I just mean I'll have to wrest a tidy penny away from the business suits that take care of my affairs. They'll have a conniption." He regarded Donovan with bright eyes. "What about you? You've done venture funding before. How would you feel about running my fund?"

The idea sent a surge of energy through Donovan, much as he used to feel in his job before it had all gotten too overwhelming. "I like it," he admitted. "But these things don't happen overnight. Let's talk about it, and I'll talk to some experts. See if it would give you—us—what we expect from it."

"Great." Jack offered his hand to Donovan. "It'll work out. I can feel it." His white teeth flashed in a broad smile. "It's going to be great to help in something worthwhile, for a change, instead of watching my money make more money. And it'll give me a lot of points with her."

"Who?" Donovan's pleasure of a moment before knotted inside him. "Thea?"

"Thea?" Jack shook his head, staring at Donovan. "She's nice—gorgeous, too, if you like the Madonna type. No, I meant Helen." His eyes grew brooding. "She thinks of me as a kid, I know. And it's true I haven't had to take a lot of responsibility in my life up to now. But that's going to change." He turned briskly to Donovan. "About this clinic—why don't we go talk to your Hope."

"My what?" Donovan tried to clear his head. Jack Guerneville wasn't that much younger than he was—two or three years. But it was true, he did have a very youthful enthusiasm about him. Thank God it wasn't directed at Thea. "Oh, you mean Faith, the midwife."

"Whoever." Jack clapped him on the shoulder. "Let's go, man. I feel benevolence just spilling out all over me, and it would be a shame to waste it."

CHAPTER THIRTEEN

THEA LOOKED RELAXED when she opened the door at four-thirty that afternoon. It was nice, Donovan thought harriedly, that one of them was. Lucas had been awake for quite a while. And though R.J. had watched him at the big house while Donovan showered, he felt as if he'd hardly been parted from his son all day.

The cheerful grin on Thea's face faded somewhat. "What in the world has Lucas been into? His face is simply covered with dirt!"

Donovan's sense of harassment deepened. "I just turned my back on him for an instant," he said, digging out a handkerchief to take a swipe at Lucas's face. "I was on my way out the door—and R.J. had cleaned him up nicely—when Miss Sophie asked me to check out the washing machine. I just set him down for a second, not a moment longer—"

"Potted plant, right?" Thea took Lucas from him and pried open his mouth. "Did he get any of the leaves?"

"I don't think so." Anxiously Donovan followed her inside. "I turned around just as he was stuffing a handful of dirt into his mouth. Most of it spilled."

"I can see." Thea's lips twitched. "Well, we'll get him cleaned up again before we go. Maybe you should call Pam and tell her we might be a little late."

Donovan made the phone call and went on back to the bedroom, where Thea had Lucas on the changing table, talking softly to him while she used the washcloth on his face and hands. "Pam said not to worry," he reported. "She said anyone with a baby is automatically an hour late for everything."

Thea laughed, stripping off the soiled outfit Lucas wore. "Maybe that's true. You certainly have to take along a lot of stuff when you take a baby." She nodded toward the bed, and Donovan saw a big diaper bag bulging at the sides and a folded portable crib.

"You're going to take that?" He looked at it consideringly. "Likely Pam and Rob have one."

"Just in case," Thea said. "I want Lucas to go to sleep, so we can have some grown-up time with our friends. He'll sleep better in that."

"Fine." Donovan turned back to see her snugging the diaper around Lucas's rosy bottom. "Should you put that thing on so tight?" He felt a little distress in his own nether regions. "I don't think it's good for his, uh, parts to be so constricted."

Thea finished pinning the diaper and turned to glare at him, keeping one hand on Lucas. "His parts are fine," she said. "If you don't put the diaper on tight, noxious things leak out of it and get all over everything."

Donovan frowned. "Well, in *The Baby Care Handbook* they say—"

"I don't need the handbook to tell me," Thea snapped. "Anyone can see that a snug diaper is better than a loose one. Besides, in the diaper service newsletter they say—"

"That's no decent authority." Donovan shook his head. "You'd rather trust the diaper service than a book written by three doctors?"

Thea turned back, pulling on plastic pants and snapping up a clean jumper. "Trust me, Donovan," she said, picking Lucas up. "I know more about it than you do."

"Hey, I'm just trying to do my best." Exasperated, he put one hand on her arm. "It's not my fault I lost out on six months of experience."

Her lips tightened, and then she nodded. "Right. I'm sorry." She picked up the diaper bag and slung it on her free arm. "Can you bring the porta-crib? We'd better get going."

He carried the crib to the car silently, cramming it into the back next to the car seat and wincing only a little when one of its metal braces gouged a scratch in the leather upholstery. Thea, also silent, slung the diaper bag in and spent five minutes getting Lucas properly strapped into place. He wasn't too happy about it, but a squishy terry-cloth bear to chew distracted him.

"He'll settle down when we're on the road," Thea said, craning anxiously to peer into the back seat as Donovan started the car.

"I know. Relax." He slanted a look at her and had to smile. "We look like married people, we sound like married people. We even have the same fights married people have."

"Everyone has those fights," Thea said austerely, but he could see the smile lurking around her mouth. "Just like you always said, Donovan. We've got all the advantages without the disadvantages."

Donovan didn't reply right away. He headed for the highway, trying to decide how to phrase what he wanted to say. Thea shifted uneasily beside him, and he decided just to plunge right in.

"I was a jerk when I used to say that. I don't feel that way anymore."

She put one hand on his knee, briefly, but he could feel the warmth of it after it was gone. "You were not a jerk. You just did what you had to do. So did I."

"Well, then," he said, taking a deep breath, "right now I have to be Lucas's father. And since you're his mother, that involves the two of us spending a great deal of time together, right?"

"That's not necessarily—"

"And since we're living so close, spending all this time together, doesn't it make sense to go ahead and get married?" He tried to keep the pleading note out of his voice. It was important that she see this as a logical step.

She didn't answer for a moment. "I don't know, Donovan. As you've said before, marriage is a big commitment. It can go wrong. People don't always turn out like you expect them to."

"That won't happen to us," he argued. "We know each other very well."

Thea shook her head. "We knew each other once. I've changed, Donovan. Motherhood—parenthood—changes you. You'll find out. You feel differently about a lot of things."

"Not about you, about our feelings for each other." Donovan cleared his throat. "Those things will never change."

She sounded wistful. "Maybe. After you've been a daddy for more than a couple of weeks, we'll see."

The subject was closed, he could tell. Frustrated, he swooped around a curve, barely noticing the towering redwoods on either side of the highway. Thea rolled down her window a little. "You're not taking the coast road?"

"I figured we were late, so we'd better stick to the interstate."

She chuckled. "Traffic has gotten worse since you were here last, Donovan. Getting through San Jose will be a nightmare."

He shrugged. "So? Pam and Rob expect us to be late, and it just gives me more time with you." He smiled at her briefly before returning his attention to the road. "I wish we were going out, just the two of us."

"Without Lucas?" She turned sideways in her seat, glancing into the back. "He's sleeping."

"Finally." Donovan glanced into the rearview mirror, but he couldn't glimpse the car seat. "I waited all afternoon for him to take a nap."

"He must find you stimulating," Thea said with a laugh, brushing a strand of hair away from her face. "Usually he's out like a light by two."

Donovan shook his head. "It's really time-consuming, taking care of a baby. I'm amazed that you can do it and still find time for the bakery."

"I have R.J. to help," Thea began, her voice a little defensive.

"Hey," he said, holding up a hand. "I didn't mean you were shirking or slacking or anything. You do great, Thea. But I am glad I can help you from now on."

"While you're around, anyway." Thea was looking straight ahead, he could see.

"What does that mean?" He forced his gaze back to the highway. "Do you have some doubts about my permanence on the scene? Well, forget them. I'm in it for the long haul, just like you are. You won't be seeing the back of me, Thea."

Her breath came out in a heavy sigh. He was worried for a moment, and then she said simply, "I'm glad."

He took the exit onto 280, feeling light-headed with relief. "Not that I don't have a lot of mixed feelings," Thea added after a minute. "I guess I sort of resent it."

"Resent what?" Donovan was filled with tenderness for her, for their child, but he tried to keep his mind on the road and on her airing of her feelings.

"Resent that you can walk in and pick up a ready-made family, just like that." She snapped her fingers, half laughing, half serious. "When I had to agonize alone for all those months."

He didn't really know what to say. "I can understand," he told her at last, cautiously. "You went through heavy stuff, and I wasn't there to help."

"Of course, I didn't tell you I needed your help. I didn't need it, actually," she said, with a proud lift of her chin. "But irrationally enough I resent that you weren't there, even though I did everything I could to keep you from being there."

"Well, at least you concede it's irrational." He kept his voice dry and was rewarded with the sound of her laughter, quickly stifled.

"Sorry, Donovan." She patted his knee again. The brief touch made him catch his breath. "I don't mean to be a bitch, but you've got to admit there's provocation."

"We'll work it out, darlin'." He gripped the wheel tightly, wishing she'd put her hands on him again, wishing they were back at his place, with no distractions or interruptions.

The traffic was moving pretty well on his side of the highway, although the southbound cars were just inching along. Donovan concentrated on making the best time, finding the fastest traffic flow, slipping back into commute mode as if it hadn't been over a year since he'd needed those skills.

Thea watched him, his sharp gray eyes fixed on the traffic, his hands moving with sure competence to guide the car. "How did the Silver Bomb like driving in New York?"

"She didn't." Donovan shot her a look. "I kept her in the garage and only took her out once in a while when traffic was light." He patted the dashboard. "Couldn't risk something happening to this baby."

Thea felt the familiar mixture of indulgence and faint, unreasoning jealousy at the tender way he spoke of his car. It took her by surprise when he added, "I should get a good trade-in for her."

"You're trading in your car?" Thea stared. "Why in the world—"

"Not practical with babies." Donovan glanced at her. "You said it first."

"Yes, but—" She smoothed the leather upholstery with her fingertips. "You don't have to go overboard. You can drive my car when you take Lucas around."

He slanted a grin at her. "Thanks, sweetheart. But I need the right wheels for a father. A station wagon," he mused, "or a minivan."

"I'll miss the Bomb," Thea said, surprising herself. "Even though I've always thought of it as a rival for your affections."

"The other woman is a car?" He laughed. "It's too dangerous to keep her, then. Especially when Lucas gets old enough to drive—I wouldn't want him anywhere near my honey." He patted the dash again. "Better let her go now, and find some other guy to make happy, right?"

His glance was provocative, but Thea didn't rise to the bait. "You don't have to make that kind of sacrifice, really," she said earnestly. It frightened her a little that Donovan would give up his beloved car. What if he was sorry later and blamed her or the baby?

"It's not a sacrifice," he said, shrugging. "Fatherhood changes your perspective, as I believe you pointed out. I don't find it so important to put energy into worrying about my car. Maybe I'll get some old rust bucket and be trouble free about burglars and dents.''

"That'll be the day," Thea snorted. "I'll believe all this when I see it, buddy."

"You can see it tomorrow if you want to go car shopping with me," he said blandly. "As I recall, you're good at dickering."

She laughed. "You're the pits, that's for sure. Remember that time you were going to give that old geezer full price for the marble-topped washstand?"

"I remember you pushing me away and jumping in with all four feet," he told her, slowing down to accommodate the traffic coming onto 280 at Page Mill Road. "You found so many defects in that thing I wondered why we were buying it."

"That's the way it's done," she told him. "The old guy enjoyed bargaining, too."

"True." Donovan stared straight ahead. "It'll be interesting being on the other side of the table from you if we come to a deal over Babycakes."

Thea took a deep breath. "I talked to Helen about your offer," she said, trying to make her voice calm. "She had some concerns, naturally."

"I'll bet." Donovan gave her a brief glance. "I won't put up the money without demanding input in decisions, Thea."

"That's what I told Helen." Thea unclasped her nervous hands. "We thought of writing up a contingency agreement—your investment contingent on the outcome of the IRS investigation. If they decide to go after Raymund Neves—"

"The government likes to work on the handiest victim," Donovan said cynically. "And even if they do excuse you from payment, you could use extra capital to diversify into new markets, like restaurants and specialty stores, or to add new products to your line."

Thea shook her head. "See, you're talking like a marketing guy, not a baker. Helen's the baker. She has an instinct for what will sell, just like my instinct for investment. From her perspective, this is her business, her customers. She won't welcome suggestions like the ones you just made."

Donovan's jaw began to stick out in a way familiar to Thea. "Damn it, if I invest, those won't be suggestions. They'll be realities."

"That's what has Helen worried," Thea said dryly. "But since we're more or less over a barrel here—"

Donovan used one hand to rub the back of his neck. "I don't want to sound like Mr. Bad Guy," he said plaintively. "But I can't help working to maximize profit if I invest in something, Thea. Especially when it's my own money."

"I understand," she said soothingly. "Despite what you say, let's hope you don't have to bail us out. You can do something more fun with that money that's burning a hole in your pocket."

"Like work with Marlon," he retorted. "Marlon has a surfboard-resurfacing agent he's invented, did you know?"

"I know how it smelled in the kitchen for a while when he was cooking it up," she said, her nose wrinkling.

"He asked me about it, and I'm helping him write up a business plan. He's got a pretty good head on his shoulders, despite all that surfer-boy lingo." Donovan shrugged. "Maybe I'll put a little spare change into his cup, if he decides to get it together. And then there's Jack Guerneville."

"He doesn't have a business," Thea said. Donovan was glad to hear the slight disdain in her voice. Despite what Jack had said about Helen, he was a personable young man, and Thea might have been attracted to him. "He bums for a living."

"He's got ideas," Donovan insisted, but he didn't go into them. A glance at his watch showed him they were making good time. Another fifteen minutes and they'd be in San Francisco. "What does Pam have lined up for tonight?"

"I don't know." Thea stared at him. "You're the one who talked to them. I figured we'd have dinner together and then leave."

Donovan smiled secretively. "You're up to something," Thea accused him. "Why are you looking like the cat that swallowed the canary?"

"Am I?" His smile broadened. "Well, R.J. agreed to wait at the cottage for us. She'll look after Lucas for a while when we get back."

Thea frowned. "It'll be late when we get back," she protested. "After eleven, I'm sure."

"So?" He sent her a look that curled the nerve endings along her spine. "Shank of the evening. I thought we might go dancing for a while at the Coconut Grove."

Thea fell silent, biting her lip. Dancing with Donovan again would be heavenly, she admitted to herself. But it would lead to places she wasn't sure she was ready to go.

Not that she didn't want him. She stared again at his hands, strong but delicate in their touch on the steering wheel. His profile in the westering light was outlined against the car window, as familiar as if she had seen it every day of the past year.

Was he serious in his assertion that he would stay with her, with the son they had created between them? Thea guessed from remarks he'd let fall that one of the results of Donovan's upbringing had been a dislike of assuming responsibility. But, once assumed, he did not shirk his duties. That had been part of the reason why his marriage had gone sour, she knew. Cecily's demands had come under the heading of responsibility, and he'd done his best to fulfill them. Discovering that she did not render back equal honor had been devastating.

Now he was going to assume responsibility for Lucas. And if they got married, as he had suggested, Thea knew he would regard her as a responsibility, too. Maybe not to the extent he would feel toward Lucas, but he would expect to share in her decisions. She had not realized until that moment how much she had relished being in sole command of her life—and her son's. It had been lonely, certainly; it had also been challenging.

Absorbed in her thoughts, she was surprised when Donovan turned off the freeway. "Good grief, we're almost there," she said, sitting up and smoothing her hair. Lucas stirred in the car seat. "It'll be great to see them again."

Pam met them at the door, dispensing enthusiastic hugs. Her feathery blond curls were as perfect as ever, her ensemble well coordinated, from expensive sweater to handmade loafers:

"We're so glad to see you," she exclaimed, as Rob shook Donovan's hand and the two men slapped each other around in masculine camaraderie. "Is this Lucas? My, he's gotten big. Such a cutie!"

"Naturally," Thea said, carrying her offspring into the apartment. "When you think of his parents, it's no wonder."

Angela danced up to get her share of the attention, and for a few minutes the living room was a hubbub of different conversations going on at once. Lucas needed changing, and Pam escorted Thea to the changing table in Angela's room. "Angela big girl," the young person in question told Thea. "No diapers."

"Only at night," Pam agreed. Angela climbed up to watch the process, chattering about the "tiny baby" and pointing out the major differences between Lucas and herself, until Pam set her down and told her to let her father in on her recent discoveries.

When they were alone, Pam edged herself onto the white-painted dresser and contemplated Thea. "So Donovan found you all right."

Thea stared at her. "What do you know about it?"

"Tell me first," Pam said, twisting one curl uneasily around her finger. "How do you feel about it? You're glad, aren't you?"

"I'm—overwhelmed," Thea said at last, honestly. "I haven't sorted it all out yet." She narrowed her eyes at Pam. "You told him where I was, didn't you?"

"He didn't fink on me, did he?" Pam drew herself up. "And no, Miss Suspicious, I didn't tell him where you were. He guessed."

"You hinted, then. You must have."

Pam's shoulders slumped. "You are angry. I thought you'd be so happy to see him you'd forgive me. And I didn't even come down and stick my nose into it, though I was dying to know how things went between you."

Thea chewed her lip. "I'm not mad," she said, smiling tentatively. "You were right all along, you know. You told me I was just making trouble for myself, and, boy, was that true."

"He was upset about the baby." It was a statement, not a question.

"Not so much about Lucas," Thea said slowly, ordering her thoughts as she spoke. "He seems to have taken that in stride."

"Amazing!" Pam shook her head. "I would have sworn that man had a lifelong allergy to babies."

"Not all babies," Thea protested. "He had bad experiences as a kid, you know. All those foster homes."

"Rob told me." Pam considered it for a minute, then shrugged. "So he likes the baby. What's the problem?"

"It's me he wanted to take apart," Thea admitted. "Because I didn't tell him in the first place. So you can say 'I told you so' with a clear conscience."

"I wouldn't say it," Pam declared, patting Thea's shoulder. "Well, at least you're still alive." She slid off the dresser. "We should get back to the party. Did I tell you I've got a sitter to come in, so we can go out to eat?" She smiled. "Somewhere besides Burger Bob's, which is the only place we ever go with Angela these days."

"I didn't know." Thea picked up Lucas, cuddling him protectively. "Lucas has never been with a strange babysitter before. It's always me or R.J."

"That R.J.'s pretty strange, if you ask me," Pam said, sniffing. "Don't worry, Noemi is perfectly reliable, and dotes on babies. Angela will be going to bed soon, and Lucas can have her whole attention."

Thea stuffed supplies back into the diaper bag. "I don't suppose we'll be gone that long," she said, reassuring herself.

"Well, long enough," Pam said plaintively. "I'm looking forward to getting away from the domestic scene for a while, remember." She held out her arms for Lucas, and Thea let her have him while she finished tidying the table. "He's a darling little man," Pam cooed. "Too bad he isn't old enough to be ring bearer at your wedding."

"What wedding?" Thea slung the diaper bag over her shoulder. "I'm not getting married."

"You're not?" Pam shook her head, tsking. "That Donovan. He told me he was going to marry you. That's the only reason I hinted where you might be found. He should do right by you and the baby."

"He is," Thea said. "He's offered child support. And he's mentioned marriage." She smiled apologetically. "I'm the one who's holding out, Pam. Donovan would get married like a shot."

"And you don't want to?" Pam wrinkled her forehead. "I don't get it. Why not?"

Put on the spot, Thea couldn't summon up any glib arguments to defend her position. "Well," she said lamely. "There doesn't seem to be much point. Marriage just means sharing responsibilities I don't know if I want to share."

Pam turned out the light. "You're crazy," she said flatly. "You don't want to share dirty diapers? Getting up in the night? Laundry? Trust me, girl. Put the man out of his misery. Why be a single mom when you can be a family?"

She led the way down the hall. Donovan had brought up the porta-crib and the sack of bakery products Thea had selected for Pam. The men were finding a lot to talk about, and Pam chattered on, but Thea kept going over her friend's words and could only give absent responses.

Was it selfishness that kept her from marrying Donovan? Or hurt feelings that he hadn't wanted to get married when she'd first suggested it? Or the need to punish him for not being there when she needed him, even though she had kept him away herself? Those weren't particularly elevating reasons to refuse marriage, she admitted. In fact, it shamed her to find such pettiness inside herself.

It's more than that, she argued silently. But watching Donovan as he laughed and replied to Rob's sallies, she had to wonder. Maybe she was crazy, after all.

THE RESTAURANT WAS ELEGANT but unpretentious, with a neighborhood feeling and excellent food. After the waiter had taken their orders, Pam spread her arms along the back of the banquette and smiled hugely. "A whole dinner," she gloated, "that I didn't have to cook while Angela 'helps' by tossing the salad—all over the floor."

"So that's why the salads have been so crunchy lately." Rob chuckled. "It is good to get away from the little darlings."

"I don't know," Donovan drawled. "Babies can be pretty addictive. They make you frazzled, they drive you nuts, but you can't stand it when you think someone else is getting all those cute little smiles."

His eyes met Thea's across the table, and she felt embraced by the tenderness she saw there. Sharply she longed to go back to the time when they had felt secure in each other's affections, before Donovan's job and her pregnancy had come between them.

No. She wouldn't dream of a life without Lucas now. It would be unfinished, incomplete. Much as her life without Donovan was.

Confused, she toyed with a bread stick and glanced around the restaurant. The tables were starting to turn over as early diners left. Nearby was a couple just finishing their desserts. Thea smiled as she saw the woman offer a bite of her chocolate cheesecake to her companion. He savored it and presented a bit of raspberry mousse to her. They seemed very content with each other's company, although the woman must have been several years older than her companion. She was a queenly blonde, built on the lines of Betty.

Narrowing her eyes, Thea gazed at the man seated opposite the blonde. He was small, dapper, with dark hair slicked back and a hot, passionate gaze. He looked just like the picture Betty was circulating of Raymund Neves.

Thea grabbed her purse and scrabbled in it, looking for that flyer Betty had given her, which she had casually thrust into the depths of her purse. Had she cleaned it out since then?

"What's the matter, Thea?" Pam's voice cut into her thoughts. "You look pale."

"I'm fine," Thea replied automatically. Her fingers closed around the flyer and, keeping it inside her purse, she unfolded it. The features were blurred, but the bearing was similar. She looked at the man again. He was getting to his feet, signaling the waiter. They were going to leave, and she would never know if he was the man who had bilked Helen.

The blonde got up and headed toward the bathroom. The man still waited for the check. "I—I'll just go splash some water on my face," Thea mumbled, clutching her purse and standing up. "I'll be okay."

"Let me come with you," Pam said, concern in her eyes.

"No, no." Thea backed away. "Really. I'll be fine."

She hurried after the blond woman, entering the rest room close on her heels and going to the sink to wait for the woman to emerge from her stall. She didn't have the slightest idea what she hoped to accomplish, but somehow she must find out who the man was and how to get hold of him again.

The blonde came out and washed her hands. Thea combed her hair, watching out of the corner of her eye as the blonde unfastened a elegant crocodile handbag to get out a makeup kit.

"That's a gorgeous handbag," Thea blurted.

"Thanks." The woman smiled proudly. "It was a gift from my man friend."

"He must have good taste." Thea put her comb away and openly admired the purse. "I think I saw you in the dining room. Is he the dark, handsome man?"

"Yes," the older woman said, outlining her lips. "Rafael is very good-looking." Her eyes, reflected in the mirror, grew misty. "I always feel fortunate that he came into my life."

"Love is the motivating force, isn't it?" Thea felt ridiculous, babbling to a stranger, but perhaps there would be an opening for the information she sought.

"It is very powerful," the other woman agreed. She put her lipstick back into the makeup case and selected a compact. "Rafael has shown me so much more than my late husband ever could, rest his soul."

"Oh, husbands." Thea managed a light laugh. "My husband is hopeless with money, and I'm not much better. Really, we need someone to take us in hand."

The blonde glanced at her sharply. "Why, Rafael is a financial planner. He has totally reorganized my financial picture. I'm sure he could do the same for you."

"Really?" Thea tried not to show her exultation. "Perhaps we could give him a call Monday. What's his number?"

"I have his business card here," the blonde said, fishing in her crocodile bag. "No, really, you can keep it. I can always get another one." She laughed gaily. "Amazing that one can make contacts even in the ladies' room, isn't it?"

"Amazing." Thea gripped the card as if it were gold. She wanted to shout with triumph, but she forced herself to wait until the blonde had left the rest room before she grinned broadly at the mirror and examined the card. "Rafael Cruz, CPA" was printed on it in florid script. She felt certain that the man was Raymund, but that would be for the IRS to find out. At least she had found a lead for them.

She managed to eat her dinner and join in the conversation, but she was on fire to get back to Santa Cruz and talk to Patrick Lasswell about her clue. Several times she noticed Donovan's eyes fixed on her in concern, but she didn't want to go into it all in front of Rob and Pam. Later, when they were alone, she would tell Donovan about it.

Lucas hadn't suffered from being with a stranger. He was asleep when they got back to Rob and Pam's apartment. The adults sat for a while in the living room, talking, but Donovan reminded their hosts that they had a long drive back.

"We've hardly seen you," Pam lamented as Thea got together the baby equipment and picked up Lucas out of the crib. He was limp with sleep, draped warmly across her shoulder.

"I know. You'll have to come down for a day. Bring Angela and we'll do the beach."

"That sounds like fun." Pam brightened. "And of course, Angela is the right age."

"Right for what?" Thea asked absently, feeling Lucas's diaper. He was dry, so she didn't have to change him for the ride back.

"For a flower girl." Pam nudged her in the ribs. "There'll be a wedding before long, I can feel it."

Thea had to smile. "Maybe," she said, when Donovan came in to fold up the porta-crib. "And maybe not."

"You'll come to your senses," Pam said blithely. "I could tell you were thinking about it all during dinner. Just don't run off and deprive us of the fun."

"What fun is that?" Donovan followed them into the living room, carrying the porta-crib. "What are you two hatching up?"

"Nothing more complicated than a beach picnic," Thea told him, giving Pam a warning glance. "Thanks, guys. It was fun."

They drove in companionable silence for most of the ride back. Thea was reluctant to tell Donovan of her Nancy

Drew routine in the restaurant, not knowing how he would take it. After all, if it was Raymund and the IRS prosecuted him, Donovan wouldn't be investing in Babycakes.

"So what's the matter?" Donovan broke the silence, making Thea jump. "You've been acting strange since we went out to dinner."

"Have I?" Thea laughed uneasily. "I guess I have." She chewed her lip, trying to think of a good way to put it. "There was a guy in the restaurant who looked a lot like that picture of Raymund that Betty has been flashing around."

Donovan laughed. "There must be thousands of short, swarthy Lotharios in the Bay Area."

"This guy really looked a lot like him," Thea insisted. "He was even with a woman who resembled Betty. Maybe he goes for that statuesque older type. Anyway, in the ladies' room she started talking about how he'd reorganized her finances. I'll just bet." Thea snorted. "Right into his own pocket."

Donovan frowned. "You think you found out enough about this man from talking to his companion for five minutes in the ladies' room to be sure he's Raymund?" He shook his head. "That doesn't sound very likely."

"It's a hunch," Thea said, trying not to sound defensive, "like what stock's going to split two-for-one. I'll just give the guy's business card to Patrick and let him take it from there. No harm done if he's not Raymund."

"Yeah," Dononvan said, "except for siccing the IRS on him. I wouldn't wish that fate on anyone."

"And what if he is Raymund?" Thea demanded. "Aside from Helen's money, if he is Raymund and I don't turn him in, that woman he was with tonight is going to wake up much poorer one of these days."

"True," Donovan agreed grudgingly. "Well, it's your call, Thea. Do what you think best."

"I will." Thea regarded his profile thoughtfully. They were driving south on Highway 1, with the ocean pounding on the left and sloping hills on the right. Donovan's face was silvered by moonlight sifting into the car windows. He glanced at her, catching her eyes for a moment before he turned back to the road.

"It's beautiful tonight, isn't it?" she whispered, staring at the road uncoiling before them in a long silver ribbon, the ocean rolling and surging, the hills that harbored dark shadows of folds and trees.

"Yes." She felt his eyes on her face again, and warmth curled through her. *I want him,* she thought, and then, *I love him.*

But she was somehow shy of saying it, there in the car. Perhaps later, when they went dancing—

"I'm not really dressed for dancing," she said as they approached the outskirts of Santa Cruz.

"You look lovely," he told her simply. "But if you want to change, you can. Or we could put on some tunes in my room and dance there."

The promise of more than dancing in his voice made her shiver. She tried to keep her voice level as she answered. "That would be nice."

Donovan turned into the driveway, parking next to her car. He followed with the porta-crib as Thea carried Lucas to the cottage.

R.J. was waiting for them. Lucas roused briefly, and Thea nursed him before tucking him into the crib. "Get some rest," she told R.J. before she left. "I'll probably be back late."

"I figured." R.J.'s eyes were shrewd. "Take your time. I'll rack up on the sofa."

Outside, the darkness was like velvet, soft to the touch. Stars glittered overhead, and roses spilled their scent into the air. Donovan's arm around her waist should have anchored Thea, but she felt that she floated down the path. Just that warm touch sent an electric message to the rest of her body.

Donovan led her around to the front of the big house. Miss Sophie's windows were still lighted, to Thea's surprise, and inside she glimpsed Miss Sophie playing cards with Mr. Castigliano. "Decadent," she murmured to Donovan.

"I think it's nice," he whispered back. "They're getting a kick out of each other's company."

Thea felt decadent herself, creeping up the stairs to Donovan's room, trying to avoid the squeaking boards. He opened his door and escorted her in, but didn't turn on the lights. There was moonlight spilling in from the big windows, and he could see well enough to turn on the stereo. Music floated into the room. He held out his arms to Thea, and she moved into them.

At first she held herself a little away from him, not wanting to melt entirely at his touch. But her breasts brushing his chest created galloping sensations. His pelvis meeting hers, hardness into softness, made her catch her breath. At last she molded herself against him. The heat generated by their two bodies was nearly unbearable, but it was constant, at least, not taking her by surprise with every movement.

He gasped and his lips found her ear. "You feel wonderful in my arms," he said, his voice a husky whisper. "You feel like you belong here."

"I do," she murmured, so low that he might not have heard her. But she could tell by the way his arms tightened around her that he'd caught her words.

"You know," he said, breathing raggedly, "I don't believe you've seen how comfortable my new bed is."

"I don't believe I have." Thea smiled up at him, reaching one hand to trace the planes of his face. He was so familiar, the man she had loved for years. And yet there was a new dimension to him, an openness and vulnerability that moved her deeply. She brought his head down and kissed him softly on the lips.

He buried his face in her hair. "Oh, Thea. I've needed you, wanted you so much." He held her a little away, looking deeply into her eyes. "I love you. You know that, don't you? Nothing that changes in your life or mine can change that. I love you."

"Oh, Donovan." Thea pulled him closer, rubbing the tears away from her eyes on the smooth cotton of his shirt. "I love you, too," she vowed. "I couldn't stop. There's more love, now, than ever before. I love you, and Lucas, because he is both of us, together."

His lips stirred the hair at her temple, moving down her face until she lifted her own mouth for his kiss. It was light at first, the warm softness a tingling, comforting pressure on her lips. But the flames inside her were only banked down. In another moment fire seized the kiss, escalating it, deepening it.

She barely heard Donovan's hungry moan as she parted his lips with her tongue, driving into his mouth, seeking the heat and flame she knew were there. Her hands clenched in his fine, dark hair, holding him there, keeping his mouth on hers until there was no breath left in them.

They broke at the same time, chests heaving, hot gazes locked together. "Thea," Donovan said, his voice heavy and labored. "Let me undress you, love."

"Do we still have clothes on?" It took an effort to move her hands to his jacket. "Take it off, Donovan."

"I will." He found the zipper on her dress, sliding it down with hands that trembled. "So beautiful..."

Suddenly Thea was aware that in the year and a half since they'd last made love, a lot had changed in her body. She made an involuntary motion when he released the front catch on her bra and stroked that away, too.

"I'll be gentle," he promised, recognizing the onset of anxiety, but not realizing where it came from. "You must be extratender here, from nursing Lucas." His hands fanned across her breasts, cupping them, his thumbs lightly teasing the nipples. She watched his dark head, the fascinated gaze that followed his stroking fingers. "Your breasts are bigger," he breathed. "Nipples...darker." Bending his head, he took first one, then the other, gently between his lips. "Sweet," he murmured, nestling his head between her breasts. "You taste sweeter than ever...."

"I'm leaking milk," Thea whispered. "Do you mind?"

"It's wonderful." His eyes lifted to meet hers. "I'm envious that you can feed our son." He put one hand on either side of her head and pressed a gentle kiss on her lips. "Maybe I'm even jealous of him, for having such a divine lunch counter."

Thea surprised herself by laughing, a thready sound that made her breasts bounce against his still-clad chest. "You've got too many clothes on," she said. Her fingers fumbled with button after button. "Whose idea was it to make men's clothes so hard to get out of, anyway?"

"What about panty hose?" He had disposed of her bra and was pushing her dress down her hips. "They're no piece of cake, I can tell you."

At last his chest was bare. Thea slung his undershirt into the corner and rubbed herself against him with abandon. Simultaneous "Ahh's" of pleasure broke from both of them. But his belt was still in the way, digging into the soft flesh he'd exposed. She unfastened it, hampered by his attempts to get her panty hose off before she'd kicked off her shoes.

By the time they could tumble, naked, onto the bed, they were helplessly smothering their laughter. Donovan bounded up once again to lock the door. "Just in case," he told her, coming back, "there's an earthquake or something, and someone misguidedly tries to save us."

She stared up at him, the hard masculine lines of him bold and exciting in the streetlight-spattered darkness. "I think I need saving right now," she said, her voice a throaty purr. "I'm cold, Donovan. What are you going to do about it?"

"I'll warm you." He flipped back the covers and arranged her on the sheets. "I've dreamed of having you here." His hand brushed the hair away from her face and traveled down her neck. "I missed you so much, Thea. I need you with me."

"I know." The words had a hard time making their way out of her throat for the big lump that had formed there.

He ran his hand over her breast, tracing something—one of the stretch marks that was the legacy of her pregnancy. "I have more," she told him dryly.

"I know." He found them on her belly, his touch setting up a clamor inside her. "They're beautiful, too."

"You must be in love." She choked the words out. "Only an idiot or a man in love would think stretch marks are beautiful."

"Everything about you is beautiful," he said simply. "Here, and here—" His hands explored her hips, her thighs, brushing up the insides. "The skin here is softer even than Lucas's." His voice lowered to a husky croon. "And here..." His lips followed the path his fingers had woven. "So womanly, so hot and damp..."

She twisted beneath his hands and lips, her own hands finding déjà vu in the familiar territory of his back, his arms, the lean flanks and tightly muscled buttocks. He had changed very little in his absence from her bed. She remembered the little hollows at the base of his spine, the strength in his shoulders, the heavy, virile weight of him. "Donovan," she gasped. "Please..."

He moved up her body, his hair-roughened chest sliding against her in a teasing caress. His fingers slipped slowly into her slick warmth, sliding out again to spread that slickness onto the tiny bud of sensation that quivered beneath his touch. She sank her fingernails into his back and then moved her hands to find and touch the long, hard length of masculine desire that brushed impatiently against her thigh.

"Dangerous," he muttered into her ear, flicking his tongue out to send hot shafts of pleasure through her. "You're playing with fire...."

"Burn me." She tugged gently, and he brought himself over her, hesitating.

"It's been so long, babe." He rubbed against her, moistening himself with her dampness. "I don't want to hurt you."

"You won't." She arched upward, trying to capture what she needed so much, wanting the length of him inside her, merging them.

With agonizing slowness he slid into her, testing her readiness, filling her gradually. She cried out at the beauty of it, and he stopped. "Okay?"

There were no words to answer. She grabbed his hips and pulled him farther in. This time, his cries mingled with hers.

He was still for a moment, allowing her to stretch and clasp him with the folds of her womanhood. At the feel of that delicate pressure, he moved, thrusting gently farther until she sheathed him fully. They gazed into each other's eyes, passion hazing and enflaming their vision.

He brought his lips to hers and her eyes drifted closed, leaving only sensation: the velvet feeling of him within her, the rocketing pleasure that blazed through her, the quivering tension of his shoulders betraying the firm control he kept.

That, at least, she could do something about. Her fingers crept between their bodies, where they were joined, finding and circling what they sought. With a moan, he moved, plunging into her and withdrawing, at first deliberately and then with increasing abandon. She moved with him, her body possessed by wildness, giving free rein to the needs so unbearable, so intense. The sound of her breathless cries was buried in his shoulder, her hands were urging him closer, closer.

He brought one hand up to touch her breast, rolling the nipple gently, bringing a new dimension of need to her. Then his lips were on her breasts, suckling first one and then the other. "Sweet," he whispered again, licking, his tongue sweeping over her nipples. "Thea . . . love . . ."

Thea wound her legs around him, demanding, wanting—until he took her over the top, and she fell down, trailing magnificent flames from the explosion and finding the dark peace on the other side.

Afterward he cradled her in his arms, smoothing back her hair and murmuring to her of how it had been for him, telling her what she did to him, until she moved her languid hands over his body to see for herself if the things he said were true or not.

They were.

Hours later, she woke beside Donovan, her breasts heavy with unclaimed milk. She slid noiselessly from the bed, pulling the covers gently up over his shoulders, slipping on her dress and gathering up her underwear.

The big house was quiet as she stole down the hallway. She hadn't gotten to the bottom of the stairs when a shadow loomed up beside her. "I'll see you home," Donovan whispered. He wore only jeans, zipped but not snapped, and carried a sweater.

"Don't be silly," she whispered back. "You don't have to get up now."

"I'm not." He grinned at her as they reached the back door, his teeth a slash of white in the moonlight. "I'll see you home, and then I'll go back to bed. With you."

"At least put on that sweater," she scolded. "What will R.J. think?"

"She'll think we've been having a night of it," he said softly, stopping her in the path. "And she'll be right." His lips found hers, lingering. "No regrets?"

"None," she told him. "It was perfect."

His face grew sober. "Thea, what about birth control? I totally lost track of it."

She had to smile at his solemn face. "I didn't," she confessed. "I, ah, used a device. After I put Lucas to bed."

He swung her in his arms. "Conniving wench," he growled. "You planned all along to work your wiles on me."

"Exactly." Her voice was a husky purr. "Lucky for you that you gave satisfaction, mister. I might have had to beat it out of you otherwise."

"Very kinky." He kissed her once more just as R.J. opened the door.

"So you're back, finally." She glanced at Donovan's jeans. "Had a good time?"

"Wonderful." Thea smiled at her dreamily. "How's Lucas?"

"Sleeping." R.J. motioned them in and paused on the step. "But he wasn't interested in the bottle when he woke up a couple of hours ago, so if you want to feed him—"

"Right." They watched her walk down the path, and Thea pulled Donovan inside. "If you're staying with me tonight," she told him, "you'll have to share the bed with a baby. That okay with you?"

"I look forward to it," he said, following her down the hall.

CHAPTER FOURTEEN

"YOU'VE BEEN SINGING off-key for the past five days," Helen said irritably. "Do you mind putting a sock in it, just for a little while?"

"Sorry," Thea said meekly, stirring her tea. "I didn't realize I was doing it."

"Unconscious singing," Helen grumbled. "That's the worst kind. And what a choice of songs! 'Smoke Gets in Your Eyes,' for heaven's sake. 'Some Enchanted Evening.'" Her lips twitched, and then a wistful smile broke through. "Nice week?"

"Very nice." Thea thought about waking up next to Donovan every morning, with Lucas tucked in on her other side. No matter how decorously Lucas went to bed in his crib, he always seemed to wind up in the big bed by morning. It made mornings a family experience, so cozy she had a hard time pulling herself away to go to work.

Helen did not have the appearance of someone who'd been enjoying the past few days. It made Thea feel guilty.

"You don't look as if you've been getting enough rest." She offered the plate of muffins to Helen again.

"Rest? What's that?" Helen picked up a muffin and broke it open, staring moodily at its inside. "Tunnels," she pointed out.

"Yeah, I know." Thea inspected her own muffin. Its center showed small holes, as if tiny moles had been at work there. "We're all under a lot of stress until Patrick gets this Raymund thing straightened out."

Helen groaned and took a bite of muffin. "The suspense is killing me," she agreed. "How long does it take, anyway? The government won't have it figured out until we're old and gray and poor."

Thea patted her hand. "I know," she said sympathetically. While she'd been spending her off time the past few days with Donovan and her baby, enjoying everything from shopping for a new car to picnicking in the park, Helen had been suffering through the agony of waiting to find out if the man Thea had spotted was really Raymund, and if so what the IRS would do about it. "I thought Jack was taking your mind off things."

"He's no help," Helen snorted. "The guy spends half his time dragging me around to look at vacant office buildings that might be suitable for a Mothers' Milk Bank or some such thing, and the other half, mooning around like a lovesick teenager."

"I think it's cute," Thea said, smothering a smile. "Probably when he was a teenager he was too cool to have a crush on anyone."

"It would be cute if it was anyone but me." Helen dug a gob of butter out of the dish and slathered her muffin with it.

"You're eating butter!" Thea leaned across the table, noticing for the first time that it wasn't cluttered with all the bottles of vitamins and bags of herbs she'd grown accustomed to. "You really must be feeling bad."

"It's nothing." Helen waved vaguely around. "I decided I was going overboard on the health-food thing."

"But what about your cholesterol? What about the new you?"

"Guess the old me is breaking through." Helen looked up, and Thea was aghast at the misery in her eyes. "I know I should be glad that we're near the end of this IRS thing, and that Donovan is ready to invest if we need it. But for some reason I just can't get my enthusiasm up."

Thea opened her mouth to speak, then bit her tongue and was silent. If Helen truly didn't know the reason she was so low, it was not for her partner to point it out, especially when it might be just imagination.

But she couldn't resist a casual remark as she took her cup to the sink. "So I guess Patrick will be by today to fill us in on what's happening."

Helen abandoned her apathetic droop. "If he doesn't deign to keep us informed," she vowed, "it really will be the last straw. Maybe he'd like another cake in the face, delivered right to his office! Or how about a tart—one of those plum-custard tarts! That would fix him!"

Thea hid a smile. "I don't know," she said, heading for the door. "I think he's kind of cute, too."

"Cute!" Helen followed her out, charging down the stairs as if she'd heard the call to battle. "He's about as cute as a great white shark! Domineering, dictatorial—you can tell he's had his own way too long in his family. Somebody ought to wise him up."

"Somebody will, one of these days, I'm sure." Thea opened the back door. "Looks like we're having a busy morning out there."

The cheerful clatter of plates and cups, the buzz of brisk conversation, came from the store. "I'll help out in the front," Helen said. "Can you finish off the cakes? Then we can manage without you for the rest of the morning."

Thea settled down with the tubs of icing and an array of cakes. She wasn't working as fast as she could have. Her mind persisted in harking back to the past few days, and she would suddenly realize that she'd stood for several minutes, spreader in hand, smiling fatuously at a partially frosted cake.

It was a relief when the back door banged and Donovan breezed in, carrying Lucas on his hip as naturally as if he'd always done it. He set down the diaper bag by the playpen and came over to slide his free arm around her waist. "Busy?"

"Uh-huh." She lifted her face, accepting his kiss, and then had to find a kiss for Lucas, who pulled demandingly on the front of her shirt. "Did you bring him for take-out food?"

"He wouldn't accept a bottle from me, and R.J. was busy helping to install the new dryer in the big house," Donovan explained. "So I just brought him to the source."

Thea wrinkled her nose at him and settled into her desk chair with Lucas on her lap. "Wash your hands and frost those cakes for me while I do this," she ordered. It was gratifying to see Donovan obey so promptly. He picked up the spreader, a wide, flexible piece of plastic with no handle.

"How do I use this thing?" Dubiously he dipped into the tub of chocolate-fudge frosting. "Uh-oh. Got too much on." He popped a finger loaded with frosting into his mouth. "Hey, this is good stuff. Why bother with the cake?"

"The cake is good, too," Thea told him. "And you'd better not eat up our profits."

She talked him through one cake, but his efforts were less than satisfactory, and when he offered to spread cream-cheese frosting on a carrot cake she forestalled him.

"No, no. I'll be finished in a minute. When Helen sees the mess you made of that cake she'll fire you."

"She never hired me," Donovan said loftily, "so she can't do that. Can I have one of these muffins?"

"Help yourself."

Helen barreled through from the store. "I thought I heard a man back here," she said, glancing at Donovan. "It's just you."

"Only me," he agreed, smearing some of the cream-cheese frosting onto his muffin. "Hey, I think I like the idea of getting into the bakery business. I see what the attraction is." He looked soulfully at Thea, who laughed, switching Lucas to the other side.

"Through his stomach," she said to Helen. "That's the way to a man's heart. All this time I thought the modern man didn't fit that profile."

Helen watched Donovan eat his doctored muffin, a considering expression on her face. "It looks horrible to me, but it might have appeal in the high-sugar crowd. Sort of a cross between a muffin and a cupcake. I'll have to remember that."

"See how useful I am?" Donovan dared to put on another gob of frosting. "Product development. I see that as my niche."

Helen snorted. "Next thing you'll be putting chocolate frosting on a bran muffin or something." She glanced at the unfinished cakes. "Really, Thea. What were you thinking of? This cake isn't fit to feed pigs."

"I know," Thea said meekly. "Sorry."

"Wait a minute." Donovan ate the last bite of his muffin and spoke up bravely. "I did it, Helen. With my little spreader." He used his best smile. "I'll do better next time, I promise."

Helen's lips twitched. "You should wear an apron next time," she said, pointing at the brown stains on Donovan's blue sweater. Her smile faded. "I thought you saw yourself as the board of directors, Donovan. Were you planning to work here, too?"

"Well, I might spoil a cake once in a while," Donovan said consideringly, "if I can get rid of it for you afterward."

"No, no," Helen said, slapping his hand away from the badly frosted cake. "I may have a use for that here." She cocked her ear, hearing a car stop in the alley behind the kitchen. In another moment, Patrick Lasswell stood in the back door.

He wore his customary sharp business suit, but he wasn't carrying his briefcase. In his eyes Helen saw an expression that was intent, almost anguished. It pulled at her somehow, some way that she didn't want. She tossed her head defiantly.

"So, we thought we'd have the pleasure of a visit from the government today," she greeted him, impelled to sarcasm. "Did you bring the thumbscrews, or are you saving them for Raymund?"

Patrick smiled, but it was obviously an effort. "No thumbscrews. Not today."

"Coffee, Patrick?" Thea looked at Helen reproachfully and motioned him to a seat.

Helen had to admit that the man looked haggard and unwell. "Need a croissant or a muffin?"

He shook his head. "Thank you kindly, but no thanks. I haven't the stomach for it today."

Helen refused to be taken in. It was a ploy for sympathy, and if there was anyone that didn't need sympathy, it was Patrick. She eyed him suspiciously. "What's wrong? Have you found out that this guy in the city is Raymund? Is that what makes you feel so bad, that you have to let me off the hook?"

Patrick's mouth twisted. "You have an interesting idea of what would cause me pain." He crossed the room until he stood in front of Helen. "As a matter of fact, there's good reason to believe that Mr. Rafael Cruz is also known as Raymund Neves, and also as Roberto Guitarez. Turns out there are several federal agencies looking for him. We may have to fight with the Justice Department over who gets to prosecute first."

Helen stared at him for a minute, disbelieving, and then turned to Thea. "Did you hear?" she whispered. "We're okay!"

Thea thought her grin might split her face. "It does mean we're off the hook, right?" She looked anxiously at Patrick. "Is there some hitch?"

"No hitch." He said the words firmly. "We'll try to recover the money from him. You don't owe us anything."

"Yippee!" Thea seized Donovan, and with Lucas they did a little dance. Helen, for lack of someone else, seized Patrick, but he stiffened.

"What's the matter? Don't want to see us celebrate?" Helen gave him a friendly grin, but he didn't reciprocate.

"I'm turning your case over to another agent." Patrick's voice was strained, breaking into the hilarity.

In the moment of silence that followed this announcement, Jack Guerneville poked his head in the back door. "Good morning, bakers," he said merrily. "How's my little sweatshop today?"

"Fine," Helen snapped, not taking her gaze off Patrick. There was some message in his eyes—a message that was too incredible to be true. "What do you mean? Why? Why are you doing this?"

Patrick's eyes narrowed. "I thought you'd be pleased," he said evenly. "Your antipathy to me is very obvious."

Helen dropped her gaze. "I don't . . . well, pleased is not exactly how I feel right now."

"How do you feel?" Patrick's voice lowered. Helen had to turn away.

Jack interrupted, his voice hostile. "Oh, this is the IRS man," he said, coming to stand by Helen. "Don't worry, honey. If they make you pay, I'll be glad to help you foot the bill."

Helen shrugged away from the arm he laid across her shoulders. "Thanks, Jack, but it's not your problem."

"It is," he insisted. "Everything about you is important to me!"

Helen glanced at Thea, who misread the entreaty in the look. "Really, Jack," she said, jumping into the argument. "We just found out that the IRS will prosecute Helen's former bookkeeper, and we won't be liable for the money at all." She looked at Patrick. "Thanks to your hard work, in good measure," she said, smiling hesitantly.

Patrick retreated into impassiveness. "Just doing my job, Ms. Willits. Your new agent will be calling on you soon with more information."

Helen pounded a fist into her palm in frustration. "This isn't fair! Why should we have to break in some other IRS agent? You can't do this to us!"

Patrick's expression tightened. "Under the circumstances, it's all I can do."

"What are the circumstances?" Thea asked gently.

Patrick shook his head. "I'm not at liberty to say."

Helen tore off her apron and tossed it to the floor. "I can't believe it! Just when we'd gotten used to you."

The ghost of a smile crossed Patrick's face, and he bowed in her direction. "I'm flattered, I think."

"You shouldn't be." Helen scowled back at him. "I'm going to write a letter to the president! I'm writing one to

Fresno, too. You won't get away with this.'' The mutilated cake caught her eye, and she couldn't keep her fingers from toying with its cardboard base.

Donovan cleared his throat. ''You really don't have to worry, Helen,'' he said, glancing from her to the cake. ''Remember, I'm still interested in investing, even though you don't need the money now. You could really go places, open up new markets, start seeing some real profits.''

''Wait a minute,'' Jack said hotly. ''I've already told Helen I'll give her any money she wants. She doesn't have to diversify and market and all that stuff. She could just sprinkle gold dust on her cakes, if she wanted. No strings attached.''

Patrick looked from Jack to Helen. ''Very convenient,'' he said, spitting out the words. ''If I were you, I'd take the other offer. The strings are more obvious, but probably less binding.''

Helen rounded on him, the cake clutched in her hands. ''Who did ask you? What gives you the right to just butt in here, telling me what to do?''

Patrick took one stride toward her and wrenched the cake away. ''I don't have to keep my tongue between my teeth anymore,'' he said, his jaw clenched. ''I've removed myself from your case, and any conflict of interest it might cause.''

Thea cleared her throat. ''Jack,'' she said carefully. ''Donovan. Can I see you in the store?''

''What for?'' Jack moved reluctantly toward the door. ''I can't leave Helen here to face the sharks alone.''

''He's not a shark,'' Helen snapped, rounding on Jack. ''And please, leave. Everybody clear out! This is between Patrick and me.''

Thea herded them into the store, and Helen turned back to Patrick. He rubbed his jaw, looking a little bemused. ''Do you always get instant obedience when you order people around?'' He moved a little closer. ''For such a little thing, that's hard to believe.''

''Just leave my size out of this!'' Unfamiliar emotions were swamping her. She yanked the cake away from him and set it down, hearing Patrick's sigh of relief. ''Now what are you talking about? What is this conflict-of-interest stuff?'' She was nose to nose with him now, her head thrust up toward Patrick, his bent down to confront her.

''Feeling the way I do about you, I can't be impartial about your case.''

''Because you dislike me so much,'' Helen said dully. She could have sworn it was a different message she read in his eyes, but then she'd never been good at deciphering men.

''Dislike!'' His hands gripped her shoulders. ''I only wish it was that simple,'' Patrick shouted. ''A man's got a right to give the woman he loves a piece of advice now and then. But go ahead! Throw it away! I knew I was a fool as soon as I realized what was the matter with me. I should have my head examined for falling in love with you.''

Helen backed away a little, blinking. ''You—you're—'' She shook her head. His words stepped up that amazing turmoil inside her. She'd never felt anything like it, the yeasty, seething rise of some uncontainable force. She tried to retreat into bluster. ''You can't just walk in here and yell at me like that! Why should I believe you? This is just another ploy!''

''Ploy, is it?'' Patrick seized her in his arms and kissed her, fast and hard.

Helen was enveloped in heat—his heat, unfamiliar and totally masculine. It threatened to overwhelm her. Her arms flailed, and she scrabbled her feet for purchase on the floor. He held her with a wiry strength she hadn't dreamed was in him.

Then his lips softened, and all the conflict within her exploded. His tongue enticed hers into a sensuous battle. Her hands stole up to wrap around his neck, and her body turned to liquid in his arms. She realized that her arms had twined around him, her hands clutching his curly red hair.

"Wait!" she gasped, tearing her mouth away from his. "What's going on here?"

His chest heaved against hers as he struggled for breath. "We're kissing," he said thickly. "Let's do it some more."

She stared at him, losing herself in those bright blue eyes. "It's all wrong," she said faintly. "We hate each other."

His eyebrows quirked. "If this is your definition of hate," he said, glancing down at the way their bodies moved together, "I'd be interested in your notion of the warmer emotions."

When he pressed her even closer, she could feel the effect of their propinquity. Heat stabbed through her loins, hotter, stronger, than anything she'd ever felt. "You just want a new way to humiliate me," she protested.

He pulled away, his smile dying. "You've got it wrong. I'm the helpless one here. I can't work, can't sleep. I've been driving my family crazy. All for a hard-hearted woman."

He let her slide down him until her feet touched the floor again, and his hands fell away. The intensity of her longing to have them back startled her. "No! Just a minute!"

He stood in front of her, drawing deep breaths, his eyes fixed on her as if he had no power to tear them away. And indeed, she realized she couldn't stop gazing at the electricity that snapped in those blue depths. "You say you turned us over to someone else because you're in love with me?"

He nodded, still staring. "Is it so hard to believe? You seem to have that effect on a number of men."

"I don't know where you get that idea." With an effort, she turned away, fidgeting once more with the cake. "My love life has been a disaster, both times."

He moved to stand behind her. She could feel his warmth and his energy and power reaching out to her. It would be so seductive to take one step back and have him cradle her in his arms. "Only two times? Well, that's more than me. I don't think I've ever felt like this before."

She turned at that, impulsively. "You've never been in love before?" She searched his eyes. "Garbage! The way you kiss, you must have been practicing for the past thirty years."

A slow smile moved across his mouth, mesmerising her. "You like that? Good." He moved a step closer, crowding her against the table. She felt the thrill of his pursuit—not a threat, but a challenge that excited her. "I'll admit to kissing my share of the girls, and perhaps more than kissing a few times. But not for love. Not like this."

"So you don't really know what you feel," Helen said breathlessly. "Let's wash out all this love stuff. It doesn't work."

"It works." He moved another step toward her, his thighs imprisoning hers, his hands braced against the table on either side of her. "This time, fair Helen, it's right." He lowered his head and their lips fused instantly. She quivered and was glad when his hands wrapped around her arms, holding her, keeping her against him. They were gasping again when he broke the kiss. "There's no denying this," he panted into her ear.

Almost unconsciously she fitted herself against him, her hips rotating gently against that hard, masculine length. Her breasts were aching, heavy with passion, like the dreams she sometimes had, when a lover held her, murmured to her, only to vanish as she woke, awash with frustration.

But this lover was solid—very solid. Helen allowed a faint smile to lift her lips. She pulled one of his hands away from her back and brought it to her breast.

He froze for a moment, and then his fingers moved in tiny, enflaming circles. "Helen—" There was strain in his voice.

"We hardly know each other," she managed to get out. "But, Patrick . . . oh, that feels—"

"If you touch me," he said fiercely when her hand stole down his chest, "I won't answer for the sight that will greet your friends when they come back in."

"I have to touch you," she murmured into his chest. "I want to very much." She lifted her face to his, wishing she could be bold and confident, but only sounding shy. "Let's go upstairs."

He held her face in his hands, staring into her eyes, his own so bright she could hardly bear what she saw there. "I thought you'd never ask."

THEA, PUTTING HER HEAD through the swinging door, heard their footsteps trotting up the outside stairs and grinned in satisfaction. "All clear," she told Donovan over her shoulder. "They've gone."

Donovan followed her into the bakery. He was still carrying Lucas, who had acquired a bread stick and was busy strewing pieces of it around. "Upstairs?" He raised his eyebrows. "Guy's a fast worker."

Jack loomed behind Donovan, his face a careful blank. "So, I guess this is really the brush-off. I mean, when the woman you're wooing takes some other guy upstairs, it has to mean something, right?"

"I'd say so." Donovan gave Jack a commiserating look. "There's no accounting for taste."

"Well—" Jack hunched his shoulders forlornly. "I don't want to stick around. Tell Helen that if she decides to expand, I'll be glad to put the money up for her." He held up a hand when Donovan would have spoken. "I know you plan to invest, but Helen—well, it was her bakery first. I don't think she'd like having to share it with so many others."

"You're right," Thea admitted. "We probably will just go on with our previous plans, now that we're in the clear from the IRS."

"Great." Jack opened the back door, unable to resist a glance up the stairs. "See you around." He turned to Donovan. "We still have to go over plans for that clinic."

"Clinic?" Thea was puzzled. "You're going into the medical business?"

"For your midwife," Jack said, a little more animated.

"Faith?" Thea looked from Jack to Donovan. "What's this about?"

Donovan seemed reluctant to explain, so Jack took it upon himself. "I have a couple of vacant buildings," he told her. "The real estate people raised everyone's rent a while back—something I didn't know about—and a couple of tenants couldn't make the cut." He shrugged. "It's too late to cry over that spilt milk. They've found new places, and I've got empty buildings. No matter what they say, I'm not putting in expensive boutiques and fancy jewelry stores. One of the buildings would be great for Faith's clinic. The last tenant even left a hot tub and beefed-up electric service. Just needs a little remodeling."

"It's a great idea," Thea said, grinning. "That clinic is always being pushed around because of rent increases. I know they won't have that problem with you."

"Hey," Jack said, a little embarassed by her enthusiasm. "It wasn't my idea. Donovan thought it up. And I'm not just in it for the strokes, you know. I'll get tax credits and depreciation for renting to a nonprofit group." He turned to Donovan. "That's the beauty of this whole venture fund. The money does good stuff, and the investors get great write-offs. Win-win, as they say in the boardroom."

"What venture fund?" Thea poked Donovan. "You haven't said anything to me about a venture fund."

"We had other things to talk about," Donovan said, his eyes meeting hers. "I just didn't get around to telling you what Jack and I have been planning while you're mixing up the muffins."

Jack looked from one to the other of them. "Don't mind me," he said forlornly. "I'm the only one that's off the ark today. You're all going two by two, and poor old Jack Guerneville is the odd man out." He slipped out the screen door and called back through it, "I'll be in touch, Donovan."

They listened to his car drive away, and then Thea regarded Donovan thoughtfully. "So," she said. "About this venture fund. And the clinic for Faith. What else is there you're not telling me about?"

Donovan's smile vanished. He looked steadily at you. "I've told you everything important. Like, I love you. I love Lucas and our little family. I want to make it official."

"You've made it official with those words," she whispered. "That's enough for me. What more can some piece of paper add to our lives?"

His jaw clenched and he stood up, holding Lucas easily. "Let's talk about it at home."

THE MESSAGE LIGHT was blinking on Thea's telephone when they walked into the cottage. Thea rewound the tape and a stranger's voice came into the living room. "Uh, I'm looking for Donovan." The man's confident tones were over-

laid with uncertainty. "Please ask him to call Bob Metlock."
A phone number with a New York area code followed.

Thea switched off the answering machine and stared at
Donovan. "Your past life is calling," she said, attempting
a chuckle. It came out hollow. "Help yourself to the
phone." She carried Lucas down the hall for a diaper
change.

Donovan dialed the number for Gaskell Associates,
cursing under his breath at the bad timing of Bob Metlock's call. He made his voice sound cordial, though, when
he returned the secretary's greeting and waited for Bob to
come on the line.

"Donovan! Got you off the beach, I see." Bob sounded
his usual driven self.

"Yeah, the surf's up all right," Donovan said. "What's
happening with you?"

There was a pause. "Guess you've had a nice vacation,"
Bob offered. "All rested up and ready for action by now."

"Not really." Donovan stalled for a moment until he
could find out what was behind the call. "Can never have
too much vacation."

"Really? I get bored." The words were perfunctory at
best. Bob cleared his throat. "Thing is, Donovan, there's a
company in Scotts Valley we're looking into. And since
you're on the spot, so to speak, I wondered if you could go
over and check them out. No need to identify yourself. We'd
rather they didn't know we're interested."

"Takeover stuff, you mean," Donovan muttered. He had
never liked the secret scouting around for companies with
undervalued stock or big cash reserves, which could be
snatched and plundered by savvy investors.

"Maybe, maybe." Bob sounded jovial. "What say,
buddy? Want to take a look-see for us?"

"No." Donovan didn't even have to think about it. He could glimpse a corner of the bedroom from where he stood. Thea brought Lucas over to the rocking chair there and settled down with him in her arms. He would be changed and drowsy, a compact weight that felt so good. Donovan knew how his son would smell, clean and fresh with that sweet baby odor. More than anything right then, he wanted to put his arms around his family and hold them close, secure.

"This must not be a good connection," Bob gabbled. "I could have sworn you said no, Donovan."

"That's right." Donovan turned back to finish breaking off his former life. "I sent you a letter of resignation over a week ago, Bob. It should have arrived by now."

There was another silence, and Donovan knew his letter had gotten there, was probably on Bob's desk at this moment. "We don't like to lose someone of your caliber," Bob said finally. "Tell me, son. What can we do to get you back on the rolls?"

"Nothing." Donovan tried to make his voice polite but firm. "I've decided to go into a different line of work, Bob. No conflict with Gaskell Associates. And no offense, but I feel that my usefulness to you peaked a few months ago. I'm just burned out."

"I understand," Bob said, but it was clear he didn't. "Listen, take a few more weeks. Hell, take a couple of months. Think it over. We could offer you a very advantageous posting in Japan. There's lots of action there, son. You'd be in the thick of things."

"No thanks, Bob," Donovan said wearily. "My resignation really is firm. It's been good working with you, but I have to move on now. Thanks anyway."

Bob argued for a few more minutes, but Donovan barely listened. From the bedroom he could faintly catch the sound of Thea humming a lullaby. It seemed more important than what Bob was saying.

"Sorry," he said at last. "You know, Brice is pretty good at scouting takeovers. Why don't you give him the opportunity?"

"I'm not sure he's ready to go solo yet," Bob grumbled. "But thanks for the tip." His heavy sigh echoed through the receiver. "Let me know if you change your mind in the next few weeks. It'll take us a while to line up that Tokyo connection."

Donovan thanked him and hung up. He rubbed the back of his neck and then straightened. Though his life in New York had been over several weeks ago, it felt like years since he'd had to go looking for takeover targets or figuring out ways to get the biggest share of a new company or any of the other aspects of his job he'd found distasteful.

Thea came out of the bedroom. "Business call?" Her eyes, he saw, were wary.

"Old business." He followed her into the kitchen and leaned against the counter while she put the kettle on. She wouldn't look at him. Instead she opened up the dishwasher and began aimlessly to unload it, stacking plates and glasses on the counter. He opened cupboard doors, finding the right places to put things away. They worked silently together for a few minutes. When the kettle whistled, both of them jumped.

Thea turned off the heat. "Want some tea?" He didn't want any, really, but if they had tea, they would sit at the table to drink it, and then maybe she would look at him. She was nervous, obviously. He knew, because he also was wound tight. He was afraid to disturb the tenuous balance they'd managed to find over the past few days.

You're after forever, he reminded himself. Forever was worth a few risks.

"They want me to take back my resignation at Gaskell," he said abruptly. "I told them no dice."

She glanced at him and turned back to the teacups. "I heard."

He carried his cup to the table and concentrated on dunking the tea bag up and down. "Aren't you going to ask me why?"

She shook her head, working on her own tea bag. "You'll tell me if you want me to know."

"Thea," he burst out. "We used to talk about our jobs, our goals. We used to tell each other everything. I want that again, but you—you aren't letting me in."

"I could say the same." Her voice was soft. "You have a lot going on that you haven't told me about."

He acknowledged the truth of that with a curt nod. "I guess I'm afraid," he said slowly, "that you won't approve, that you'll think it's foolish or unworkable." He took a deep breath. "I want financial security for you and Lucas, Thea. For all of us."

She smiled, then. "Lucas has financial security," she said stoutly. "He's better off than I am right now. But, Donovan, I don't worry about money. As long as there's a stock market, I can survive. I expect to have my investment fund built back up after all this IRS stuff blows over."

He found her calm certainty comforting. "You do have a leg up on the rest of us," he admitted wryly. "I have to follow the trends and juggle a lot of figures, and you just arrive there by some mysterious art. It's not really fair to the mortals around you, you know."

"I do all the work, too," she argued. "I read up on the market and follow my choices before I plunge. But it's true that I can't explain how I know what to buy. I mean, I could say it's the price/earnings ratio, or a new product announcement, but the truth is, I just know which one will go up."

"No need to apologize." He reached across the table and took her hand, turning it over in his, studying the fine lines on her palm. "I'm glad you'll always be able to take care of yourself." He glanced up. "I shouldn't have railed at you like that when I first got back. I didn't mean to imply that the bakery was a poor investment." He shrugged, releasing her hand. "The shock of it all, I guess. Anyway, I'm sorry. Please feel free to tell me anything. I won't be judgmental."

"Same here," she said, watching him across the rim of her cup. "Why don't you tell me about this thing you're involved in with Jack Guerneville?"

He pushed back his chair and prowled restlessly around the small spotless kitchen. "I know you didn't like parts of my job," he said abruptly. "Well, during that year in New York, I got to dislike them, too."

She made a vague, assenting noise to encourage him to keep talking, and he found it reassuring somehow. "Everything was different without you there to keep it in perspective," he said, fiddling with the dish towel that hung over the refrigerator handle. "Before, it was easy to think it was a job—important, but not my whole life. In New York, it got bigger and bigger, like a nightmare balloon. I couldn't escape, and I couldn't face it, either." He turned to her. "I needed you to keep me sane," he said simply. "Without you, I realized what part of my life was really important."

She looked away, uncomfortable. "I can't be responsible for making you happy," she protested. "That's too much to lay on anyone."

He swallowed. "You don't have to make my happiness," he said thickly. "Just be with me. That's all I ask."

There was silence for a minute. Then Thea asked, "What are you going to do now?"

Marry you, he wanted to say. But he'd said it already, and she hadn't accepted yet. He mangled the dish towel a little more. "Jack and I were talking," he said with an attempt at lightness. "He has money, and he knows other people with money. Maybe not the most advanced social consciences in the world, but people who would like knowing that their money benefited someone besides themselves." He tried a smile. "As long as it doesn't affect their profits much, you understand."

"Of course." She smiled back. "You're going to invest in nonprofit projects? Is there any return there?"

"Some," he said. "And in times of inflation and high taxation, the write-off you get offsets the modest nature of the profit. Low-income housing, for instance. You can't take big bucks off the top of the development, but over the long term your money is sheltered from taxes and earning a respectable return."

"Sounds good," she said judiciously. "So Jack is going to organize the money, and you're going to run the fund?"

"That's the size of it." He walked over to the back door, looking out through the screen of trees to the street a hundred feet away. "You know, you could make your own driveway out to that street and not have to use the big house driveway."

"I know." She blinked a little at the change of subject. "Donovan, what's in it for you? What are you going to get out of running such a low-key fund? It won't pay nearly as much as you've made in the past."

"It won't take my whole life, either." He didn't turn around to endure the doubt in her eyes. "I want time to spend with you and Lucas. I don't want to work twelve hours a day. It'll be enough to live on, if you'll handle my investments for me." He did turn then, giving her a strained smile. "What kind of foundation do you have under here? Strong enough to build on a second floor?"

She waved his words away impatiently. "You're changing the subject, Donovan. We need to talk about the future."

"Okay," he said equably. "Talk."

She blinked, disconcerted. "Well," she said lamely, and then took a deep breath. "You've been mentioning marriage pretty often lately."

He watched her, his hands in his pockets so the tight fists wouldn't give him away. "That's right," he agreed cautiously.

"But you didn't want to before you left for New York." She looked down at her hands. "Before you found out about Lucas."

"Listen," he began, and passed a hand through his hair. "Anything I said or did then should be excused. I was not fully informed. And I didn't realize just how important you are to me."

"I know." She raised her eyes, and he could have groaned aloud at the love and pain he saw mixed there. "I told myself all the time you were gone that I didn't need you, that it wasn't important for you to be here with Lucas and me." She swallowed. "But it was—it is. I'm glad you've decided to stay here, Donovan. I—I guess you might as well move in with us, since you pretty much are living here already."

Her last words faltered. He was staring at her, wondering why her reluctant invitation should hurt so much. "Thea," he said, closing his eyes. "Why—"

She came to him then, wrapping her arms around him. "It's what you want, isn't it, Donovan? What's the matter? Why do you look like that?"

He broke away from her and strode blindly toward the front door. "I'm sorry," he said, and realized that he'd said it over and over. "I'm sorry. I'm sorry."

Thea stood in the kitchen, wondering what she'd said that was wrong. Somehow she'd wounded him, sent him away, when she'd been trying to achieve the opposite.

He didn't want to live with her. That much was obvious. She let her injured pride have full sway for a moment before she pulled it in.

"He's been very cleverly bringing over a little of his stuff every day," she told herself, carrying the cups over to the sink. "A man who does that is a man who wants to move in lock, stock and barrel."

So what was the problem? She hadn't exactly phrased her request in a flattering way, she supposed, perhaps because she wasn't sure how far into her life, and Lucas's, she was willing to let him.

She slipped into the bedroom where Lucas slept, his lips slightly open, his eyelids looking too translucent to keep the afternoon sun at bay. He was precious, and since his birth she'd thought of him as only hers. Didn't Donovan understand how hard it was for her to think about relinquishing any of her sweet responsibilities?

But there were other responsibilities. She left the bedroom and looked out the front window, half hoping to see Donovan coming back again. But she knew he wouldn't come back, not after she'd made such heavy weather of inviting him in.

"What about your responsibility to him?" she scolded herself. "How much love can there truly be, when you're still so selfish about sharing what you have—what you stole from him?"

She dashed to the telephone and dialed the big house. R.J. didn't have her own phone, and it took Miss Sophie a while to answer. Miss Sophie always held the telephone away from her mouth for fear of being too loud, and as a result it was difficult to hear her.

"Theadora, my dear!" Miss Sophie twittered faintly. "How nice to hear from you! Are you away?"

"No," Thea said, trying not to sound impatient. "I'm in the cottage. I need R.J. to come down. Is she there?"

"Well, she's just giving Joseph—Mr. Castigliano—a hand. I'll go see if they're done. We decided to put a clothes dryer in, too, you know," Miss Sophie confided. "It's so exciting. I've been handing them wrenches and things all morning."

"That's great," Thea said, grinding her teeth.

"So I'll just go check on Rosalie Jane for you," Miss Sophie said. There was a clattering from the receiver, the sound of diminishing "oh, dears" and "now wheres?" Finally R.J. picked up the receiver and agreed to come down right away.

Thea paced back and forth in the living room. She didn't know yet what she'd say to Donovan, but she would have to make up her churlishness in some way.

R.J. stumped in. "We turned on the gas," she annouced. "No bad smells, nobody keeled over. Guess there's no leaks."

"Great," Thea said absently. "Lucas is sleeping. I just need you to listen for him while I go out for a little while."

R.J. nodded. "This doesn't have anything to do with Donovan, does it?" She inspected her stubby fingernails as if she expected to find them suddenly painted fuschia. "He went up to his room a little while ago looking like he'd lost his last friend."

"He thought so, I guess," Thea muttered, heading for the big house. Couldn't he see how much she loved him?

Couldn't he tell from what she'd said that she really needed him?

She flung open the back door of the big house. Miss Sophie and Mr. Castigliano were standing there, hand in hand, listening to the dryer toss clothes. They turned to her, their faces wearing big grins.

"Works like a charm!" Mr. Castigliano's voice boomed over the noise the dryer made. "And everything tight as a drum. Isn't that something, missy?"

"It's great, Mr. C." Thea tried to escape, but Mr. Castigliano wasn't finished with her.

"We put a gas line through right here," he explained, pointing it out to her. "Maybe next we'll move out the water heater, and get a little more room in Miss Sophie's kitchen."

"That's a pretty big undertaking," Thea said, glancing at Miss Sophie for signs of panic. But Miss Sophie beamed fondly at her in-house plumber.

"Joseph is so very clever with these things," she said to Thea. "He's quite a man, you know." She clasped her hands around Mr. Catigliano's arm, and his skinny chest swelled.

"It's nothing," he said, gazing adoringly at his landlady.

Thea had to smile, looking at the two of them. "Congratulations on the laundry," she said, and left them alone with it.

Faith was coming down the stairs. "I wanted to look at our new facilities," she told Thea. "It'll be nice not to have to hit the Laundromat."

"It does make life easier," Thea agreed.

"That fellow of yours," Faith said abruptly. "He's really something, you know? I've been seeing clients in my room for a couple of weeks because the clinic is out of a home, and a few days ago Donovan brought some guy around who owns a building that's vacant and is willing to give us a below-market, long-term rate.'' She smiled, but looked searchingly at Thea. ''Do you think it's really for real? I'd hate to get everyone's hopes up and have it fall through.''

''If Donovan says it will happen,'' Thea said firmly, ''you can bank on it. I'm so pleased, Faith!'' She hugged the other woman.

''I wondered why he was putting himself out, but he said he's Lucas's father,'' Faith said, putting a hand on Thea's shoulder. ''That's true, too, I suppose.''

''Yes.'' Thea glanced up the stairs. ''He didn't know anything about it until recently.''

''I guessed that, after talking with him,'' Faith murmured. ''He said something about wanting to make sure the clinic was around for the next time.''

''Next time?'' Thea assimilated that. ''Thanks, Faith. I'll talk to you later.''

She took the stairs two at a time. Donovan's door was closed, but when she tried the knob, it wasn't locked. She burst in and stared at him.

He was lying on the low, wide bed, his hands behind his head. ''I heard you coming up the stairs,'' he said dispassionately. ''You sounded like you were in a hurry.''

''I am in a hurry.'' Thea put her hands on her hips. ''You can't just walk out when I've asked you to move in with me! You could at least have the courtesy to say yes or no!''

''No,'' he said, still staring at her. ''I won't move in with you, Thea.''

She should have been discouraged, but there was something, deep in his eyes, a spark that gave her hope.

She kicked off her shoes and launched herself at the bed, landing on top of him with a pained ''oof!''

''What was that for?'' He rubbed his shoulder, where her head had made a landing. ''You could have knocked us both out!''

She paid no attention. Straddling him, she put one hand on each side of his head. "You'll have to move in with me," she said, emphasizing her words by bouncing gently on him. "Married couples do traditionally live in the same house, you know. And I intend to live the most traditional of lives."

That flicker in his eyes grew stronger. "You do?" His mouth began to smile. "It isn't that traditional for the woman to propose, you know."

"When the man doesn't come up to scratch," Thea informed him, "we women have to take matters into our own hands." She bounced again, this time finding the exact spot on his torso to make the maximum impact. "We'll have a lovely house, after we remodel the cottage," she said, rubbing her hands on his chest and sliding a little lower. "We'll have the traditional 2.5 children."

"Maybe we should round it up to three." He shifted slightly on the bed. "Thea—"

"We'll make love exactly twice a week," Thea decided. "I believe that's average."

Donovan arched himself under her, making his arousal obvious. "I intend to be above average in that respect."

"So you accept, then." Thea captured his head between her hands, staring urgently at him. "You'll marry me."

"You'll marry *me*," he corrected, the smile growing on his face. "You really want to?"

"Of course." She closed her eyes in relief and collapsed on his chest. "Oh, Donovan, I couldn't bear it when I thought you didn't want to live with me anymore. I thought it must be because of Lucas, and yet I know you love him."

"You're darned tootin'," he growled, holding her close. "I'm not spending another minute away from either of you. I didn't know how important it was for me to have a family until you presented me with one."

Thea raised herself on one elbow, peering anxiously into his face. "You won't feel trapped or coerced, will you? I know how difficult that business with Cecily was. I don't want you to feel that way again. I couldn't bear it."

"Cecily? What's she got to do with any of this? Don't talk foolish, woman." He gave her a little shake and kissed her chin. "Maybe, in my self-centered youth, I thought it would be a mistake to become a parent." He looked at her, his face serious. "I still don't know what kind of job I'll make of it. I didn't have any too good an example, you know."

"I know," Thea said softly, smoothing the hair back from his forehead. "But you certainly know what kinds of things are not good in a parent. I bet that's worth a lot."

"Right." He closed his eyes and the tension drained from his expression. "I was kind of hoping," he mumbled, "that maybe in a little while—after some above-average nights together—we could get a little more practice in parenting."

"Faith told me what you said." Thea increased the pressure delicately on the central portion of Donovan's anatomy. "It sounds good to me. Lucas doesn't want to be an only child."

"Wonderful." He gazed up at her, his eyes luminous with desire and satisfaction. "You're giving me everything I want in life, Thea. I'll do my best to reciprocate. Starting with giving you my love."

Thea's happiness spilled over in a laugh of contentment. "It just goes to show," she whispered, lowering her lips to his, "that you can have your cake and eat it, too, if you're lucky."

Harlequin Supperromance.

COMING NEXT MONTH

You'll flip . . . your pages won't!
Read paperbacks *hands-free* with

Book Mate • I

The perfect "mate" for all your romance paperbacks

Traveling • Vacationing • At Work • In Bed • Studying • Cooking • Eating

Perfect size for all standard paperbacks, this wonderful invention makes reading a pure pleasure! Ingenious design holds paperback books OPEN and FLAT so even wind can't ruffle pages – leaves your hands free to do other things. Reinforced, wipe-clean vinyl-covered holder flexes to let you turn pages without undoing the strap . . . supports paperbacks so well, they have the strength of hardcovers!

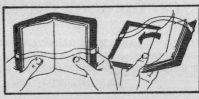

Pages turn WITHOUT opening the strap

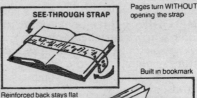

SEE-THROUGH STRAP

Reinforced back stays flat

Built in bookmark

BOOK MARK

BACK COVER HOLDING STRIP

10" x 7¼" opened.
Snaps closed for easy carrying, too

Harlequin Superromance®

LET THE GOOD TIMES ROLL...

Add some Cajun spice to liven up your New Year's celebrations and join Superromance for a romantic tour of the rich Acadian marshlands and the legendary Louisiana bayous.

Starting in January 1990, we're launching CAJUN MELODIES, a three-book tribute to the fun-loving people who've enriched America by introducing us to crawfish étouffé and gumbo, zydeco music and the Saturday night party, the *fais-dodo*. And learn about loving, Cajun-style, as you meet the tall, dark, handsome men who win their ladies' hearts with a beautiful, haunting melody....

Book One: *Julianne's Song*, January 1990
Book Two: *Catherine's Song*, February 1990
Book Three: *Jessica's Song*, March 1990